Paul Geddes, whose six
of Corruption and Goli
for many years in Londo
the Army and has also pr
in East Sussex.

By the same author

The High Game
A November Wind
The Ottawa Allegation
Hangman
Goliath
A State of Corruption

PAUL GEDDES

A Special Kind
of Nightmare

GRAFTON BOOKS

A Division of the Collins Publishing Group

LONDON GLASGOW
TORONTO SYDNEY AUCKLAND

Grafton Books
A Division of the Collins Publishing Group
8 Grafton Street, London W1X 3LA

Published by Grafton Books 1989

First published in Great Britain by
The Bodley Head Ltd 1988

ISBN 0-586-20409-1

Printed and bound in Great Britain by
Collins, Glasgow

Set in Times

'Che Fece . . . Il Gran Rifiuto' by C. P. Cavafy from *The
Poems of C. P. Cavafy* translated by John Mavrogordato is
reproduced by kind permission of the author's estate, the
translator, The Hogarth Press and Harcourt Brace Jovanovich,
Publishers.

At any given moment, a man may, by the sudden decision of his will, introduce into the course of events, a new, unexpected and changeable force . . .

Sainte-Beuve

1

The Cahill story was the lead in all the tabloids, consigning to minor columns the sexual odysseys of starlets and snooker players. The headline writers had enjoyed twisting the knife. Cahill, after all, was fair game. IRISH CABINET'S AIDS SCANDAL; GUILTY SECRET OF IRISH GOVERNMENT'S PERFECT FAMILY MAN; TERRORISTS' DUBLIN ALLY WAS AIDS VICTIM.

Mansell's eye, travelling to the end of the rack that displayed the Sunday newspapers, finally reached the *Clarion*, supreme for offal on all occasions. GAY DISEASE KILLED BRITAIN-HATER CAHILL: HOSPITAL COVER-UP EXPOSED.

When he had first heard a whisper of it, over lunch at his club the previous Friday, he had suspected it to be one of those sick jokes lobbed across the divide between the communities. But the earlier references to pneumonia as the cause of Cahill's illness had been abruptly dropped. Someone in the know had talked. From the Dublin hospital where he had died a week ago had come the brusque acknowledgement: it had been AIDS.

The soft whistle that had gone round the Irish capital became something more shrill in the North. The most implacable opponent in the Dublin Cabinet of any further deal with the British that failed to preserve the dream of sovereignty over Ulster, the jaunty champion of the boyos, the man who always found weasel words to avoid condemning the IRA, had been swept from the scene by a fate that made the carefully cultivated image of uxorious domesticity something for the birds.

From the group in the ruling party that Cahill had built

around himself, attempts at damage limitation were half-heartedly under way. It was said that during one of his visits to the United States as Minister for Commerce and Industry he had suffered an illness; he must on that occasion have been given a transfusion of blood that had been infected with the AIDS virus. But no one could recall previous mention of an illness during his travels. From the press spokesman in the Ministry came silence.

For Mansell, once the ambitious fast-lane Private Secretary to Ministers in Whitehall, now, on the crumbling side of fifty, no further on than Head of Personnel in the Central Crimes Bureau, Ireland and its agonies had long ceased to hold any fascination. Ireland was a compound of television images of destruction, of voices harsh with unforgiveness or hushed in misery; a place where all the answers had been tried and found wanting and the best policy for both governments was surely the covert avoidance of any such thing.

Shifting his gaze from the tabloids, he reached for his customary choices elsewhere. But the beginning of another item in the *Clarion*, relegated by the Cahill story to the bottom of the front page, had caught his eye. He looked back. Unease began to seed his bowels.

At last he straightened from the rack, to stare at July rain breaking aginst the shop window. He was conscious of a desire to turn back the clock, to return to the condition of not having seen the item. To pretend he hadn't became seductive. The story was claimed to be a *Clarion* exclusive: it might not be picked up elsewhere. And, even if it was, there were few capable of making the connection he had made; certainly none in Whitehall. He could walk out of the shop and do nothing more.

Instinct, a neurotic itch, warned against. Waiting in the wings for just that decision would be some further event, its shape as yet unseen, that would expose him as having chosen inertia. The nettle had been presented: it had to be grasped. Taking the *Clarion*, he added it to his other papers and left the shop.

Outside, the façades of this genteel segment of Twickenham no longer offered their assurance of Sabbath calm. The day, like the weather, had turned sour. Bald patch growing colder under the rain, stooped now with more than the disenchantments of the years, he made for home.

Placing the *Clarion* under the bundle of files in his study he had brought home to work on provided a postponement of decision. When he began to tackle the files in the afternoon, he still left it undisturbed, telling himself that later it might read less ominously.

But Hilda Mansell, bearing him tea, saw the newspaper's edge and pulled it out.

He lifted his head reluctantly. She had been washing her hair and tinting it differently in pursuit of some desire he preferred not to analyse.

'Whatever made you buy this?'

'There's something I needed to read.'

He looked down again but she was not to be fobbed off. Sighing he pointed to the news item and waited grimly while she read it.

BONDAGE GIRL IN HARLEY STREET DEATH MYSTERY
Clarion Exclusive by Rob Gates

Mystery surrounds the last hours of beautiful Sylvia Keysing, 29, of Overdean Mansions, Fulham who crashed her car early on Wednesday and died soon after arrival in hospital. According to sources at the hospital, there were clear signs on Sylvia's body that she had taken part in bondage sex shortly before she died and that the sex game may have gone too far. Now friends are speculating that Sylvia was in a state of fear and shock when she jumped into her smart red sports car outside a plush Harley Street apartment block soon after midnight.

Frank Wilde, a caretaker in a nearby block, saw Sylvia crash. He told me he was walking his Alsatian dog when Sylvia hurried out of a building opposite Princess Street. 'She might have been in a panic, running away from somebody or something. The car hit a streetlamp seconds later. I was the first to reach her but there wasn't much that could be done.'

Sylvia was well known at several London nightspots. She is believed to have acted in films in Italy at one time and spoke of expecting to make a commercial for a famous perfume company shortly.

Last night a close friend in clubland said, 'Sylvia was a first-class driver. It's difficult to imagine her crashing like that unless something was wrong. She hardly drank and was very level-headed.'

Hilda Mansell looked up from the paper. 'I don't – '

'There's only one apartment block opposite Princess Street.'

'Well?'

'Antrim has his flat in that block.'

She shook her head. 'You aren't suggesting she was with Antrim before she crashed the car?'

'I think it's very likely.'

'Why jump to that conclusion? There are plenty of other flats in the block.'

'When he came into the office on Wednesday morning, he looked terrible. I was waiting for him, we had a meeting arranged. When I asked him if he was all right he mumbled something about a rather unpleasant shock. We finally got down to the business but I noticed he hardly listened while I was talking.'

'Tell me something new,' she said.

She was out to needle him, because he hadn't mentioned any of this before. He straightened the pile of files. 'Thursday and Friday were the same. Some experience had definitely thrown him.'

'Even supposing that wasn't just coincidence, what if

10

he *did* have a girl visit his flat for sex games? There's no law against it!'

'*Not* just a girl – '

'All right, she was a tart. Isn't that *his* business? After all, he's not married to that horsey woman any longer. The bit about the girl being in a panic and having marks on her body was probably invented to spice the story up anyway.'

He ran his fingers over his scalp, let them linger on the bald patch to check its current boundaries, then shook his head. 'I can't shrug it off. I've always had a feeling Antrim could become a problem in this way. He was a menace with the secretaries at one time. I hoped he'd pull his horns in when he became Director of the Bureau. If he's now using prostitutes, having them come to his flat, sooner or later it's going to make a news story. Somebody will find out what his position is and talk to one of the scandal sheets. Or he'll be found in some knocking-shop when the police walk in. I can see the headlines – HEAD OF CENTRAL CRIMES BUREAU WAS BROTHEL CLIENT; SAYS HE WAS MAKING OFFICIAL ENQUIRY.'

He raised his eyes to the ceiling. 'There's not a chance the police would hide his identity. Anything likely to get the Bureau's wings clipped they'd see as manna from heaven.'

'Are you sure you haven't convinced yourself Antrim is involved because you loathe him?'

When he ignored the taunt she said, 'You're hoping you've discovered something that will result in him having to resign from the Bureau.'

Her skirt – a favourite, he recalled – had acquired a smear of oil from somewhere. He toyed with the thought of pointing the fact out, as a means of bringing to a close their discussion of Antrim. But she had become too interested for it to work.

11

'The fact is this item fits with an incident while he was in the Army.'

'Which must be at least twenty years ago.'

'. . . All the same.'

She was scoffing. 'You know you can't be certain she was with him. Forget what happened in the Army. Ignore the whole story. Why not pretend you didn't see it?'

She understood nothing. 'Because I'm the bloody Establishments Officer, it's my *business*! The reason I was moved from Transport to take the job was because as an outsider I'm expected to stop unpleasant little facts like this being hushed up. I *have* to do something.'

'But what? You've no proof. If you tackled Antrim he'd probably say that you were talking rubbish and boot you out of his office. And if the girl had really been with some randy Arab in that mansion block, who could blame him?'

Her expression was triumphant. She began turning the pages of the *Clarion* and glancing rapidly at its other treats. 'Anyway, that wasn't why you were transferred from Transport. You know they moved you to Somerset Square because you irritated the roads lobby by always plugging railways. If you hadn't you could have stayed there. You might even have been a Deputy Secretary by now. Then you wouldn't have to be dealing with these Bureau people.'

She was tuning up for a well-worn theme. 'Let's not go into that,' he said.

She sighed and held up before his eyes the centre pages of the *Clarion*. The obligatory naked girl with pursed lips and gigantic mammary development gazed out.

'I suppose this doesn't do anything for you.'

He gave her a blank stare.

'Perhaps *you* want a little bondage friend.'

She was getting under his skin but he didn't intend to

let her know it. He reached past her to the drawer in his desk that held last year's diary. 'I have to discover if my guess is right.'

'You mean you're actually going to tackle him?'

'No,' His finger paused at the telephone number he needed. 'I intend to take counsel.'

'Whose?'

'Ludo Fender's.'

She raised her eyebrows. 'I thought he'd retired from the Bureau.'

'He has. But he knew Antrim better than most. He's also extremely shrewd, not to say wily. The fact that he's no longer in the office makes it easier to talk to him about this. After I've finished work tomorrow, I'll drive down to his cottage.'

His sudden decisiveness had surprised her. She watched him impassively as he moved to the telephone, dialled and listened.

Finally he replaced the receiver. 'Out confessing his sins or hunting butterflies, I suppose. I don't remember his having any other hobbies. I'll try him again after dinner.'

'Is he still disgustingly fat?'

'He'd taken some weight off when I last saw him. He had to do it, after the heart attacks.'

She started assessing in the wall mirror the effects of her hair-tinting session. 'I never felt easy with him at office parties. That terribly over-polite manner . . . I used to wonder what he was really thinking. Do you trust him?'

'He can be devious. But he used to end up doing the right thing most of the time. Anyway I want his views on this.'

She turned back to the front page of the *Clarion*. 'If he's sensible, he'll tell you that you're making a fuss about nothing. I'd leave Antrim to carry on with whatever it is

13

he gets up to. He may be objectionable to you in the office but I find him attractive. If he propositioned me for sex games I might be tempted.'

He could get one home at last. 'You're pretty safe,' he said.

She was reading about Cahill now and apparently hadn't heard. 'You should be thankful Antrim's normal – fairly normal anyway. Imagine if he'd dropped dead with AIDS.'

True enough, he told himself, things could be worse. At least, with Antrim, there's not much likelihood of running into anything like the Cahill story.

But there he was wrong.

2

'Bondage,' said Fender. 'What would you say is now the public *perception* of it?'

His expression conveyed a mock-innocent concern to be instructed. He waved his glass in Mansell's direction. 'No doubt you keep abreast of all this. As an Establishments Officer.'

'Not especially.'

'Isn't that rather remiss? An aspect of inter-personal relationships!' He pronounced the phrase with elaborate emphasis. 'I'd supposed that by now the Civil Service College would be including that sort of thing in its courses.'

Looking pleased with himself, Fender put down the cutting from the *Clarion* and reached again for the whisky. They were drinking Chivas Regal, Mansell had noted with interest; evidently retirement had not occasioned economies on the lubrication front.

'Sade,' Fender went on. 'He would have made a stimulating lecturer on the subject, don't you think? The argument that inflicting pain is fundamentally pleasurable to man has its attractions. Consider the amount of organized cruelty in the world. Did the Marquis know something all those humanists have missed? No doubt he saw himself as a dry confronting the wets. One can feel a certain sympathy, unspeakable though his habits were.'

Mansell watched Fender rest scuffed suede shoes against the pile of logs in the inglenook. There was no way of knowing how long this would go on. Nor was there any safe means of cutting it short. It was consistent with past experience that apart from a brief mournful shaking of the head, Fender's reaction so far to the news item and the suspicion of Antrim's involvement had been a vaguely philosophical discourse, laced with elephantine humour.

Not that his remarks about the Marquis and the current social status of bondage were irrelevant. But they constituted for the most part a sort of overture while thoughts of more precise application assembled behind a curtain of enigmatic smiles and nods. For Fender to have tackled the point at issue at once would have been as remarkable as a cat devouring its prey as soon as it was trapped.

In a corner of the room in which they sat, the tick of a grandfather clock marked off the seconds of this waiting game. Still to come at the end was a fifty mile drive back to Twickenham. With an effort Mansell mustered patience and let his eye wander round the room. The furniture was pleasant oak, except for a faded divan and the vast armchair used by Fender himself. A bowl of flowers, arranged by a steadier hand than Fender's, glowed on a side table. On one wall there hung a painting of a woman of some beauty, possibly the wife who had died in childbirth in Calcutta.

Fender had let his head fall back to survey the ceiling beams above them. The enormous mound of the stomach rose and sank. Diminished somewhat since the time of the heart attacks, it remained a notable sight. A vision came into Mansell's mind of Fender's internal organs laboriously pumping and cleansing, in a relentless battle to maintain this great edifice of flesh.

'So what,' Fender said at last, 'was the incident that echoed so uncomfortably when you read the news item?'

'It goes back to his service in the Army.' Mansell took out his diary to consult the note he had made. 'I checked my recollection as soon as I got into the office today. When he joined us from the intelligence people, they sent

16

over their own papers. As far as they went they were satisfactory but they didn't include any of his Army records. When I enquired at the time, they explained they hadn't taken copies although they'd been satisfactory. To be on the safe side I called for them and took copies for the file I'd started.

'The papers were mostly complimentary. A great deal was said about drive and initiative. However on character there'd been a brief period of doubt while Antrim was serving in Germany. A young German girl had made a complaint to his commanding officer. She said that Antrim, then a lieutenant, had raped her. The story was that she had met him at a club some weeks before. He had behaved perfectly well until one night when they went back to his flat after attending a party. Antrim produced some cord and leather equipment and pretending it was all a great joke persuaded the girl to let him tie her up. After a while she decided it wasn't a joke at all so far as she was concerned. She asked him to set her free. He refused. Then he raped her. She handed over a doctor's report that was certainly consistent with rough handling.

'The allegation was taken very seriously. When Antrim was questioned, he emphatically denied the rape and said nothing had happened between them to which the girl hadn't consented quite freely. She enjoyed that sort of sex game, he claimed. It was decided he should stand trial at a court martial. Three days before it was due to sit, the girl announced she was withdrawing her charges. There'd been no rape. She'd accused Antrim of it and of tying her up against her will because she was angry with him. She'd invented it because he'd said he wasn't going to keep a promise to marry her.

'The officer who wrote up the whole business ended his report with these words. "I have naturally considered whether Fraulein Bornemann's withdrawal of her original story, which was extremely circumstantial and persuasive, may be explained by her having been bought off, either by Lieutenant Antrim himself or someone acting on his behalf. The contrast between her attitude at the beginning and now is certainly very striking. I can only say I have seen nothing to substantiate the possibility. Given Lieutenant Antrim's previous unblemished character and consistent denial of the allegations it may therefore be thought wrong to leave any suspicion attaching to his name."'

'Not the most ringing of exonerations,' Fender said. 'However one must assume it was based on a dispassionate assessment of the facts. Presumably no similar incident was ever reported?'

'There was none in the papers.'

'So what are you left with?'

Mansell paused, striving to be just. 'Nothing specific. I keep reminding myself of that. Of course I needn't tell you he hasn't behaved like a monk over the years. A fair number of the more attractive females on the staff must have been bedded by him before he rose to his present dizzy heights. But none of them complained of their treatment.'

He hesitated again. 'There *is* one thing which could be relevant however. You may not know that when Antrim's marriage was breaking up he was having an affair with Antonia Strachan. No doubt they thought it was a secret but it got back to my staff management people. While this was happening, we had a railway strike. Hazel, my secretary, who commutes from Byfleet, needed a bed in London for the duration and Antonia offered to put her up in her flat in Little Venice. On the first morning Hazel walked into the bathroom not realizing Antonia was already there. Antonia was wearing just a slip.

18

'Across her shoulders and upper back Hazel noticed quite extensive bruising. There were also some marks on her wrists which suggested she had been handled very roughly. Hazel went out of the bathroom without Antonia knowing she'd been there. She subsequently told me what she'd seen because it worried her. We'd had two of the women staff, living in the same neighbourhood as Antonia, mugged during the previous month. Hazel wondered if the same thing had happened to Antonia and if for some reason – pride perhaps – she'd decided not to tell anybody. I thought it over for a while but felt I couldn't tackle her on the basis of what Hazel had seen.'

He looked into his whisky. 'I now suspect there may have been another explanation for those marks. But I can hardly invite her to tell me if she allowed Antrim to beat her up when they were in bed together.'

Mansell became aware that Fender's cheeks had darkened; they were now the colour of burgundy. He said icily, 'The idea of her taking part in that sort of thing is both absurd and offensive.' He levered himself out of his chair and went to pour another whisky. He hadn't even glanced in the direction of Mansell's glass. It was plain he was very discomfited.

Perhaps, Mansell thought, his streak of prudishness had surfaced. For all his heavy humour about bondage and the Marquis de Sade, he had always seemed queasy about sex. When he had been an Assistant Director, quite mild erotic jokes were liable to provoke from him a curious mixture of embarrassment and ill-temper. Subordinates had to learn quickly the sort of things he regarded as unsuitable for humour. He had been known to fix a visiting foreign panjandrum, embarked on some earthy anecdote, with an outraged glare before turning his back on him.

The remark about Antonia Strachan had hardly fallen

into the category of a joke. But there was perhaps another factor. Fender had championed her from early days in his Division at the Bureau. The way in which she had coped with sudden widowhood and later with Fender's illness in Canada when they had gone there together over the Stradbrook affair, had reinforced his admiration.

When Antrim had called Fender back from retirement to carry out some enquiry in Rome for the Prime Minister about which Mansell had never heard the details, it had been Antonia he had insisted on taking as his aide. In that lonely mind, she had perhaps occupied a pedestal fashioned from pure white marble. If so, the thought of her in a sado-masochistic relationship with Antrim would be quite a jolt.

Casting about to restore the situation, he said, 'I agree it's difficult to think of her in – in those terms.'

Fender turned round again. 'Quite impossible. It was a brief affair as I recall. Hardly serious. She's a very sensible person.' His composure was returning. Reaching down with a grunt, he took Mansell's glass and replenished it.

A door closed somewhere in the cottage. Moments later Mansell saw the outline of a figure moving, past the window, towards a gate at the end of the garden. It was the stout woman, dressed unwisely in light-coloured slacks and a shiny purple blouse, who had served their dinner; apparently a non-resident replacement for the house-keeper who had declined to follow Fender out of London on his retirement. Fender had introduced her with his customary ornateness. 'Mrs Bastin, my ministering angel. Existence without her would be a sorry thing.'

The encomium was presumably well-worn by now; her features had displayed no emotion when Fender uttered it. Mansell guessed from small signs that there was a chillier, unpublished appraisal. A curiously intrusive quality dominated Mrs Bastin's manner. As she moved about the table during their meal she seemed to be challenging them not to overlook the smallest particular of her contribution. Glancing occasionally at Fender's face, Mansell had concluded that the angelic music was proving less than heavenly.

Fender watched Mrs Bastin's progress down the garden. As the gate closed behind her he said with a hint of relief, 'That was The Woman going home. Before it gets dark, we might take a turn in the garden.'

His movements were ponderous but seemed to cost less effort than of old; moreover the walking stick collected from the hall was not now used for support but to indicate what Mansell was to note and admire. He was plainly much fitter. His mind remained as sharp as ever. He had been an infuriating colleague; yet it seemed a sad waste that he was no longer around to counter-balance soulless men like Antrim.

Beyond the garden gate an evening haze hung over a valley of fields and woodland. Unlike the front of the cottage on the village street, the scene this side was pastoral. In retirement Fender had chosen to live in a look-out between two worlds. Perhaps that had been because he knew that neither by itself would offer what he wanted.

But what *did* he want of life? He had sought and enjoyed power once. He had cracked the whip and others had jumped. Perhaps he still hankered for it, despite the cultivated appearance of being above such things. Power, after all, was something for which the taste lingered long after other appetites dulled and faded.

There must have been other desires, other tastes, once. But he had concealed them from prying eyes behind a mask of elaborate politeness and with gestures calculated to imply that his physical proportions and awkwardness left him only the role of a grotesque. If he had had a private life involving more than his religion and the pursuit of butterflies, it had remained a mystery. The death of his wife so early in their married life had obviously hit him hard. Perhaps it was because of that he had allowed himself to become gross. He should have re-married of course. But in the years Mansell had known him, Fender would never have been an appetizing prospect for any woman he invited to become the second Mrs Fender.

They had paused by the garden gate. Sweet William grew under a climbing rose, yellow and silken. Mansell pointed enquiringly at the rose. Fender said briefly, 'Céline Forestier.' He moved on. For some reason he didn't want Mansell lingering at that spot.

He stopped again by another flower bed. 'I think I would be right in saying you have never exactly *liked* Antrim. Is that fair?'

'I accept he's efficient. And the flourish with which he does things impresses politicians. All the same I wish you had still been around to succeed Harkness when he died.'

Fender gave a small shake of his head, apparently neither accepting nor quite rejecting the compliment. 'When he joined us, *I* was impressed like everyone else by his energy and determination. Later I came to see the weaknesses of course – that overwhelming ambition which led to so much risk-taking, the arrogance. Worst of all, the editing of facts to show himself in a favourable light.'

He had never spoken so frankly about Antrim before. His fingers were plucking leaves from a lavender bush. Crushing them, he held his palm for a moment under Mansell's nose.

'Antrim is unfortunate however. I feel a little sympathy.'

'How is he unfortunate?'

22

'He suffers from the same disability as the Tin Man. You remember the Tin Man of course?'

He enjoyed being surprising. Mansell frowned. 'Not very well.'

'He sang a sad little song about what he lacked. A heart. Antrim was born without a heart. It makes him incapable of both love and compassion although I suspect he would very much like to experience them. Unfortunate behaviour can often be explained as a desperate attempt to feel something of the emotions observed in others.'

They seemed to be in danger of drifting down another by-way where they would no doubt meet up again with the Marquis de Sade but still be skirting the problem in hand.

It was getting late. In the moment Mansell drew breath to put the question he had formulated on the drive down, Fender said, 'I see your difficulty. The newspaper story can't be ignored, you must pursue it. Although I still can't credit Antrim with being so mad as to have the girl visiting him in his flat.'

'You spoke of risk-taking.'

'I did.' Fender's eye travelled morosely along the flower beds. 'I did indeed. How can I help you?'

They were making progress at last. 'My immediate problem is to decide *how* to pursue it.'

'I noticed the newspaper gave the girl's address somewhere in Fulham. She probably shares a flat with another girl in the same line of business. If so, enquiry there might establish whether or not it was Antrim she visited that night.'

'I looked into the possibility before coming here. At lunchtime I went to the apartment block and talked to the porter. I told him I was a journalist following up the *Clarion* story. It was very unproductive. He said that Sylvia Keysing had lived alone since the man who had shared the flat with her moved out six months ago. He'd disappeared in a hurry because the police were making enquiries into a mail order business he'd been running. She had no friends in the block and never told people what she did, although the porter had guessed she was a call-girl. None of her clients ever seemed to go there and he had no ideas about them.'

Fender sighed. 'That leaves the anonymous close friend who provided the final paragraph of the story – assuming he or she isn't the journalist's invention. The only way to pursue that would be through the *Clarion*. A course on which you no doubt hesitate to embark.'

It was twilight. Fender paused by a bush at the end of the path they had been following. Without change of tone he said, 'You grow buddleia of course in Twickenham . . .? There is a silly fashion for despising it because it will thrive anywhere. But it is the most perfect host to butterflies.' With surprising delicacy he touched and stroked a flower head.

It seemed they were off on another excursion; but he turned with sudden briskness. 'A nightcap, I think. Perhaps we can work out a suitable way for you to tackle Antrim direct.'

Mansell followed him into the cottage. If he was to be home at a reasonable hour he couldn't delay floating his proposition any longer.

'Before we consider that, there *is* one other possibility. When I got back from Fulham I decided to ring round the hospitals to discover which she'd been taken to. I eventually managed to find out the identity of the next of kin who'd claimed the body. It was her mother, a Mrs Iris Keysing. She's some sort of curator living in Oxford. I have the address.'

'Curator of what?'

'That wasn't clear. It occurs to me that while she may

not have had much to do with her daughter, she should at least be able to name one or two of her friends in London. That way I might ultimately get to somebody who can say who the Harley Street client was.

'I'd thought of going up to Oxford and tackling the mother. But I realized, talking to the porter today, how inadequately service in the Department of Transport had equipped me for this sort of thing. You have had a lifetime making sure that enquiries don't blow up in your face. I *had* wondered whether you would consider – '

'You want me to go . . .?'

'Would you be willing . . .?'

Fender's pause was barely perceptible. He smiled. 'If you really think I can help . . .'

Not the smallest amount of persuasion had been necessary: he was already relishing the prospect. He had taken out his diary. 'Tomorrow, unfortunately, I am off to visit my sister. From her, I go to Chipping Camden – a rather important expedition. Some Large Blues were sighted a while back. You may not appreciate the significance but everyone thought they had disappeared from the British Isles. They proved elusive on my last visit but I've had a message that this week I should be lucky. However, you would presumably be willing for the interview with Mrs Keysing to wait a few days. I would be happy to go on to Oxford.'

It was irritating to have butterfly-sighting take priority over finding out whether he had to cope with the implications of having a Director who invited whores to his flat for bondage games or worse. But a small delay was perhaps tolerable. And he didn't want to lose the benefit of Fender's advice.

'That would be very helpful, Ludo.'

He had hoped to get away without another session in

the sitting room but Fender had already uncapped the Chivas Regal again. 'And how is your charming wife?'

'Well, thank you.'

'Vivacious as ever, no doubt.'

He suspected irony but couldn't be sure. When he nodded, smiling, Fender said loudly,

'Splendid!' He made it sound as though his admiration knew no bounds. 'And now tell me – what is the other news from the Great Wen?'

He dredged up what Whitehall gossip he could remember.

Fender sat, with hands clasped across the sliver of belly where a shirt button had given up the unequal struggle, listening intently, occasionally pontificating. The air of rural detachment with which he had greeted Mansell at the cottage door had vanished. His mind was reaching out to the old challenges, the midnight crises, the sound of the alarums along the corridors of Westminster.

'The idea of you in retirement makes no sense,' Mansell said, as he finally made his escape. 'A commercial company with corruption problems would jump at your experience. Why not become a sort of consultant? Would you like me to make some enquiries?'

Fender spread his hands wide, an affecting picture of regret. 'I'm well past that sort of thing, I fear.'

He was as big a liar as ever.

3

It was a narrow crooked house, built in the more sombre of the Cotswold stones. Its age was hard to judge. Presumably some conservationist campaign had saved it from the development that had turned the area into a warren of shops and offices; but if architectural merit had played a part in winning reprieve, it was hard now to identify. A board by the street door displayed an announcement: The house of Betsy Frogg.

A stifling heat filled the street. Fender wiped sweat from his forehead, wondering if Mansell could have got Iris Keysing's address wrong. Moving on, he found another announcement in a glass-fronted box, on the side wall leading to a yard. This was longer, a typed sheet, discoloured by sun and condensation. He took out his reading glasses and studied it.

Betsy Frogg, it seemed, had been the maker of Oxford's finest cakes in the eighteenth century. Her trade had been ruined by a competitor who put it about that the flour in her cakes caused madness. On a January afternoon, a few months later, the rival's two small children had disappeared and were never seen again. Betsy, according to rumour, had enticed them into her kitchen. In the oven in which she had baked the cakes, she had cooked the children. Then she had eaten them.

Nearly two centuries later, the owner of the house, excavating the floor of the cellar, had discovered a quantity of bones, pronounced by expert examination to belong to the skeletons of two young children.

The concluding words on the typed sheet struck a

27

brisker, more contemporary note. 'Admission to The House of Betsy Frogg, including the kitchen, 70 pence (children up to 16 half-price).' Some initials followed: 'I.K.'

Mansell had got the address right after all. Iris Keysing, curator, was guarding the shade of Betsy Frogg.

Fender returned to the street door and found a bell push. Above him a window opened. A woman said, 'You wanted to visit the house of Betsy Frogg?' The tone of the voice was sing-song; she might have been addressing a child.

He judged her to be in her fifties. She had been pretty once and still recalled the experience with erratic industry. The blonde dye in the hair badly needed renewing and her lipstick had wandered too far beyond the margin of the upper lip.

'I *was* hoping – '

'She closes at four o'clock I'm afraid.'

'Ah.' He glanced at his watch, mildly pondering the use of the third person singular. The time was a quarter past four. 'In fact, it was – '

She was speaking again. 'But she won't like you to be disappointed after a long journey.' Her bright hazel eyes were taking in every detail of his appearance. 'It's a hot day for journeys.'

He frowned.

'Wait there,' she said and shut the window.

He considered her words while he waited. He had left his overnight bag at the railway station. Nothing in his appearance could have told her how long his journey had been.

When she opened the door, he saw that she was small, bird-like. Her clothes were a curious mixture of utility and the exotic. Bangles clattered on her wrists. The skirt looked well cut, if rather short. Its effect was spoiled by the red slippers edged with rabbit fur that encased her feet.

'Mrs Keysing?'

Her answering smile suggested complicity. She showed no surprise that he knew her name.

From a table behind her she had picked up a roll of tickets. 'The cellar is extra. But you'll want to see it. A pound in all.'

He hesitated then decided in favour of a waiting game. 'It sounds most interesting.'

As he fumbled for the coin, he said, 'How did you know I'd made a long journey?'

Her eyes slid across his gaze, the manner arch, a little teasing. She didn't answer his question. Instead she handed him a ticket and turned towards the stairs. 'She likes us to start on the upper floors.'

The early part of the tour was perfunctory. Fingers impatient on door latches, she hovered behind him while he entered Betsy's bedroom, her sewing room and her parlour, all sparsely but more or less appropriately furnished. Whenever he glanced back at her, she was examining him carefully but not unfavourably.

In the kitchen her presentation became livelier. She asked him to look inside the baking oven when he seemed in danger of neglecting it.

'She had to cut them up quite small. Even then they were cooking for days.' Her eyes rested on his face, willing a response. Then she laughed, again with the message of complicity, a sharing of something private to themselves.

The room was chill. Fender buttoned his jacket. 'Strangely, I don't remember the house from my days as an undergraduate here. Yet I must have passed the notice outside quite often. I had a room nearby.'

'It's not strange. There wouldn't have been a notice.

Nobody knew it was Betsy Frogg's house before I came. The man who sold to me had found the bones but he'd done nothing with them. Even now the stupid people who write the tourist guides haven't mentioned it.' She looked contemptuous. 'Why should visitors just be sent to the colleges? They want to see something more than *buildings*!'

When they reached the steps leading to the cellar, she propelled him down with insistent prodding but remained at their head. There was remarkably little to see. What seemed to be old cooking and agricultural implements hung on the walls. On a couple of trestle tables a miscellany of antique bric-a-brac had been spread. Alongside was a glass case with several bones inside.

He put on his glasses again to inspect them. After a while she called sharply, 'Are you a doctor?'

'No.'

'What are you thinking?'

'One or two of the bones seemed a little odd.'

She gave a derisive laugh. 'Of course they're odd. It was *all* very odd! How did Betsy persuade them into the kitchen? They would have known who she was! That was the *really* odd part!' Her fingers reached forward to the light switch on the wall as a signal that his time was up. 'She was so *clever*!'

On the ground floor again, he said, 'Thank you, that was fascinating. I have a small confession to make. I actually came here to see you, not the house.'

'To see me?'

'Yes.' He had decided on boldness. 'I knew your daughter, Sylvia. She'd spoken of you once or twice and told me where you lived. After I read of her death I wanted to meet you. I felt you must be very alike.'

She seemed to take it in her stride. 'What's your name?'

'Frobisher, Leonard Frobisher.'

30

'In business?'

'No, I'm retired.'

'I don't remember Sylvia mentioning you.'

'Unfortunately I didn't know her for long – I'm not surprised.'

She nodded. 'So you wanted to meet *me*?' She liked the idea. Her expression became encouraging and also a little sly. Their intimacy, until now confined to a secret understanding about the house, had become a more special thing. 'Would you care for a cup of tea?'

She led the way to a sitting room next to Betsy's parlour and left Fender for a minute or two. It was fussily overfurnished, the mixture, like her clothing, occasionally bizarre. Ornaments from the thirties or earlier were on every flat surface. A pierrot lifted the skirt of a dancer to look beneath, a clown stood ready to deliver cigarettes from his mouth at the touch of a button. It was a haven of junk frivolity.

When she returned, she said, 'I knew about most of Sylvia's clients. We were good friends – more like sisters than mother and daughter, people used to say.'

From a sideboard she picked up a photograph in a silver frame and handed it to him. It was a theatrical publicity portrait of a girl with pale blonde hair held by a broad bandeau. 'Nineteen forty-eight,' she said, 'I was in rep.'

He inclined his head in suitable awe.

'You didn't recognize me, did you?'

'On the contrary. You've hardly changed.'

With a brusque movement she snatched the frame from his grasp and turned away. For a moment he thought he had overdone it. But she had taken the photograph only to substitute another, more modern one, presumably of Sylvia.

'We used to meet in London. I'd close early for the

day. We'd have tea at Fortnum's then go to the cinema or do some shopping. She always had the best of everything, as I expect you noticed. She was like me in that.'

She returned the photograph to its position a few inches from her own. 'I hope she was good to you.'

'Yes.'

'Did you like something special?'

It seemed best to agree. 'Yes.'

She shot him a glance that was meant to be flirtatious. 'I taught her of course. You're not much use if you can't do the specials. We're all different, aren't we?'

The whistle of a kettle sounded and she disappeared again. When she came back she was carrying a tray. Beside the teapot was half a fruit cake still in a supermarket wrapping. He became conscious that the heat and his walk through the streets from the station had made him very thirsty. But as she handed him his cup he saw below the rim a halfmoon of lipstick.

He was about to embark on his probing when, reaching forward to take a piece of cake, she said, 'Your wife – was she very young?'

'I'm sorry . . .?'

She repeated it. He stared bewildered.

'Losing the baby at the same time . . . that was hard.' She screwed up her mouth as though in pain.

The shock was like a physical blow. He sat, appalled, wondering how much more there was to come. But she was silent now, resting her head against the back of her chair, eyes fixed, witnessing something at a distance.

He found words at last. 'You have a remarkable gift.'

She sat forward again to pick up her cup. 'A lot of whiteness – like a tent – what was that?' The tone was matter of fact.

He shook his head.

'There was no tent.'

32

'In the *room*.' She was a little impatient. 'All around.'

He was being compelled to go back, to open a door he had shut and hoped never to see through again. His situation was humiliating, a little ridiculous. But for the moment she had achieved a curious dominion over him.

Then unwillingly he saw. 'Above the bed there was mosquito netting. It was raised – like a canopy. Do you mean that?'

She made a satisfied sound. 'Yes.'

With an effort he became calm again. His thoughts remained confused. If she had insight of this kind, he could have no confidence she would not sense that he had lied about knowing Sylvia. But her expression remained unsuspicious. He decided to press on. 'I'd hoped to see Sylvia myself the night she died. But she had an appointment with another man. A civil servant who lives in Harley Street.'

She gave a laugh. 'Civil servant? Sylvia didn't bother with *civil servants*! She liked interesting men, real men. Men with ink in their pencils.' She winked. 'I expect that's why she liked you.'

'Are you sure about that? I thought she mentioned that he was a civil servant.'

'No, the man in Harley Street was a journalist. Alistair something – I don't remember the other name. She met him ages ago when she was staying with Carl Lissack.' She paused to observe his reaction to the news. 'Did she tell you she was a friend of *his*?'

'I don't think so. Do you mean the City man, the financier?'

'He was mad about her. She lived in his house near Guildford for a while. He wanted her to stay longer but she didn't like being away from London. He told her she could order whatever she wanted when she was there. He gave her a car once. It was because Alistair came to the house to do an interview with Carl Lissack that he met Sylvia. He wanted specials too although they didn't become friends until later, after she'd moved back to London. He took her to Paris once.'

Her eyes were studying him carefully. 'This civil servant you mention – is he a high-up? What's his name? I could look in Sylvia's diary to see if it's there.'

He shook his head. 'Don't worry. If the person she was visiting that night was this journalist, I obviously misunderstood something she said.'

She looked mildly disappointed. 'Another cup of tea?'

'Thank you, no.'

She crossed her legs, allowing the skirt to ride high above the knee. She was hoping to make him look at her thighs. Despite the signs of wear and tear elsewhere, they had remained in excellent shape. But the rabbit fur slippers were no encouragement to licentious thoughts.

'I can tell you're very lonely,' she said. 'What will you do now Sylvia's dead?'

'I'm not sure.'

'We all need spoiling occasionally.' Her smile was wheedling. 'How far away do you live?'

'Sussex.'

'But you go up to London quite often I suppose.'

'Not very often.'

She wasn't yet discouraged. 'We might meet somewhere. Perhaps where you used to go with Sylvia. Would you like that? I'd better give you my telephone number. I'm always here.'

He wrote it down conscientiously then looked at his watch and sighed. 'Reluctantly I must be on my way.'

At the street door she squeezed his arm, still hopeful. 'Don't forget. Call me any morning. Most afternoons too.'

34

He raised his hat but she still held him. 'I can tell you something interesting.'

He waited.

'A man – a very important man with a big desk – is going to offer you something. I don't know what it is or whether you'll accept it. But it'll happen quite soon.'

He felt the same chill he had known inside the house. 'I'll remember your words.'

As he turned a corner of the street he saw the house's grim reflection in the plate glass front of a shop. Iris Keysing had stayed on the step to watch his progress. She was rubbing the side of a slipper against the other ankle, clutching the door frame as she did so. She had guessed that he would be looking at the reflection because she waved.

It was past eight o'clock when his train delivered him at Paddington. There was plenty of time to cross London and catch another train home. But melancholy had taken possession of his soul. That terrible clairvoyant moment when Iris Keysing had drawn back the curtain had undone him.

Watching from the train window as the sun lengthened across racing fields he had felt the memories rise like snakes to coil about his mind. He was back in Calcutta waiting for that moment when the sun disappeared and a vivid landscape abruptly became monochrome, a body drained of every drop of blood. In the space of time it had taken him, summoned by the doctor's call, to drive from his house to the nursing home the transformation had happened. From now on, he had thought, it will always be like this in the evening.

In the station concourse he bought a newspaper in search of escape. But there was nothing there of comfort. A passenger jet had blown up over the Pacific Ocean. Famine was reported from the Sudan again. Only from

Northern Ireland was there mildly hopeful news: a Loyalist demonstration, organized to bring pressure against a further deal with Dublin, had attracted only half the numbers expected.

Standing irresolute beside the bookstall, he thought of the silence of the cottage in Mayfield, of twilight taking over the garden, and the ghosts of what-might-have-been waiting for him in the shadows. The otherness of London, for all its crowds and fumes, was suddenly desirable.

There was a case on practical grounds for staying overnight. Instead of some gnomic telephone conversation on an open line, Mansell could be reassured in person about the identity of Sylvia Keysing's Harley Street client. Summoning a taxi, he gave the name of his club.

At the porter's desk he encountered a reverse: no bedroom remained vacant. Irritation pricked through the melancholy. He made the porter go over his accommodation chart again but his manner made it plain it was a polite formality. 'Unfortunately, Mr Fender, what with Wimbledon and the Test Match . . . I could try the United Planters for you. As you know we have an arrangement – '

He made extravagant noises of repulsion, recalled the previous occasion he had gone there, when tepid food and torn sheets and the incontinence of the club cat had made his stay intolerable, and finally turned away. 'I shall telephone a friend.'

Dialling the number, he acknowledged to himself the truth, that it had been all pretence from the moment when the porter had confirmed there was no room. He had welcomed that moment because it had suddenly made possible something inhibition had until then excluded.

He heard the receiver being lifted at the other end and stiffened against the possibility that the voice would be a visitor's. But it was hers.

'It's Ludo,' he said.

She made welcoming noises, asked how he was.

'I find myself unexpectedly in London for the night. But my club is full up. Before I try the hotels I wondered – '

'You'd like to stay?'

'Is it at all possible?'

'Of course, do come.'

'You're sure I won't be interrupting a party or anything?'

'Not even anything. It'll be lovely to see you.'

He couldn't bring himself quite to believe she meant it. But she was there and he would soon be with her again. That was everything.

4

He was still labouring up the stairs as Antonia opened her door. At first glance, it seemed he was once more putting on weight. But the tissue wrapping of the large bouquet clasped in one hand had added a misleading volume to his outline. He wore one of the grey flannel suits that did duty throughout the year. On his head a panama had replaced the homburg normal on visits to London. At a guess, he had spent the day at the Oval Test match.

Presenting the bouquet, he bent forward. For a moment it seemed he might be embarked on planting a kiss on her cheek, a gesture of unprecedented audacity. But he was merely putting his overnight bag down in order to squeeze her forearm.

His features looked tired, even drawn. She pushed him into a seat with a large whisky and water while she went to put the flowers in a vase.

'Where have you been today?' she called from the kitchen. 'Test Match or Wimbledon?'

'Unfortunately neither. Oxford.'

'In this weather that must have been nicer than London. Were you visiting friends?'

'No, I was paying a call on a rather disconcerting woman.'

She smiled as she plucked leaves from stems. 'I don't think of you being disconcerted often. She must have been formidable.'

She heard him grunt. '*Was* she?'

'She was odd. Have you ever heard of Betsy Frogg?'

She laughed. 'No.'

'Betsy Frogg lived in the house of which this woman is the self-styled curator. She killed and ate two small children in her kitchen one January day. Or perhaps over several days. That is, if she ever existed. Of which I'm not at all convinced.'

His voice became louder. He had left his chair to come and stand in the doorway of the kitchen. 'I suspect she may have been invented for the benefit of credulous tourists.'

'Why were you interested in Betsy Frogg?'

'I wasn't. Only the woman. I was undertaking a small enquiry.' He ran his finger over the door frame. 'I think you have painted in here since my last visit.'

He was being secretive as usual. If she asked more questions he would turn them aside with enigmatic responses. But she remained curious. If, as seemed possible, the Bureau had called him in to help over an investigation, it would be interesting to learn why.

She placed under the grill the chops providentially laid in at lunchtime and turned to preparing a salad. She felt him touch her hair quickly with the back of his hand in a gesture known to her.

'And how are you, Mrs Strachan?'

'Fine.'

'You've acquired no tan so far this summer. Why?'

'No gardening in Shropshire at the weekends – too busy here.'

'You've taken no leave yet . . .'

'No.'

'You're not overworking I hope.'

He was adopting his inquisitorial tone, affectionately meant but trying.

'No, Ludo, I'm not overworking.'

'And why are you still not remarried?'

She gritted her teeth. This tack, like the gesture with

39

the hair, was also familiar. 'Because there is nobody I want to marry.'

'Perhaps you are becoming over-critical.'

'Perhaps.'

'You should have gone to Canada with the man from the RCMP, Muir.'

She moved him to one side with a push in order to open the refrigerator. 'We were really very different people. I've told you all this before. I'm irredeemably urban, I shall always live in a town. He's the opposite. He couldn't wait to get away from headquarters in Ottawa. The wide open spaces of Alberta were what he wanted – where he was brought up. That's why he resigned from the police. We'd never have agreed on where to live.'

'You could have tamed him.'

'Where marriage is concerned I'm not interested in taming. Or in being tamed.'

She wanted to add: now leave me to run my own life.

Fender remained hovering uncertainly near a counter top. Away from intellectual challenge and bureaucratic manoeuvring, he could appear disarmingly vulnerable. She found it impossible to stay annoyed with him for long.

He had picked up a tomato and the ancient knife she used for exploring any lack of enthusiasm in the waste disposal unit. 'Can I assist perhaps?' He held them before him, eager incompetence awaiting the summons to glory.

She removed them from his fingers. 'I'd rather you didn't. Perhaps you'd like to go and watch the box. I shan't be more than a few minutes.'

He was obediently seated in front of the television set when she returned to lay the table for their meal. A panel of talking heads was being questioned on current affairs by a studio audience. One of the heads she recognized as belonging to Plowright, the Secretary of State for Northern Ireland. Someone was putting to him a query about where he considered the main blame lay for the fact that peace in Ulster still showed no signs of breaking out.

Plowright sat forward, gazing into the camera with suitable gravity. He had good features and fine blonde hair, kept winningly thick at the temples. In his middle-forties he retained an athletic air. More than any politician she knew, he conveyed the impression of successfully holding cynicism at bay, of keeping at least some of the idealism of youth.

'It would be easy,' Plowright began, 'to reply that the blame lies with the terrorists, the men of violence. That would be a half-truth and neither you nor I nor anyone else here tonight wants to deal in half-truths. Because, if one goes to the heart of it, the blame for what we see in Ulster today really lies with politicians, by which I mean all politicians of every party on both sides of the Irish Sea. I plead guilty along with the rest – I know very well how little thought I gave to the subject when I was setting out in politics. And I had less excuse than most, having during my Army career served in Ulster and seen the problems at first hand.

'It was Edmund Burke who nearly two centuries ago characterized the posture of British governments towards Ireland, except in times when actual crisis made it impossible, as ". . . total neglect . . . utter oblivion . . .". What Burke was railing against was the lack of real will to tackle the profound mistrust dividing the communities. Mistrust is a cancer alongside which no healthy tissue can grow anywhere. There is no point in arguing how much or how little of that mistrust is rooted in reality. We must simply accept that one community is gripped with deep fear of the political power of the other while the other is possessed of a no less haunting fear of the religious pretensions of the first. As Secretary of State I have had to recognize that whatever successes we might score in

41

the war with the terrorists on both sides, there will be no peace worthy of the name under the shadow of these fears.'

Plowright's gaze went slowly round the audience. He seemed entirely confident that not even the competitive instincts of other panel members were going to break into the silence he had chosen to impose.

'Those are the realities. Leave blame aside. Is there now hope of changing those realities? The answer is – yes. The scene itself is changing very rapidly. The politicians themselves are changing. I want to say nothing tonight about what the evil men are anxious to avert – the possibility of a new agreement between the British and Irish governments aimed at breaking down the mistrust I've talked about. But for reasons that reflect a remarkable sense of responsibility on the part of political leaders in Ireland, Catholic and Protestant alike, we do have our steps on a ladder that could take us out of the abyss. I don't deny that events over which we have no control could kick the ladder away. But believe this – all of us who are involved accept we have an unremitting task. Don't let the cynics tell you it's mere shadow play. If the ladder *is* kicked away, we will create another and another until that beautiful province has the peace it deserves.'

Someone in the audience asked Plowright if he felt Cahill's death had made it easier to reach an agreement with the Irish government which would be acceptable in the North. Plowright shook his head in rebuke. 'We must get away from seeing these problems in terms of personalities. I have nothing to say about Mr Cahill's death except that the circumstances must surely induce in us all compassion for his family and friends.' He sat back to seemly applause.

Antonia heard Fender groan.

'You're not impressed . . .?'

'By what?'

'Leaving aside the rhetoric and the playing to the gallery, isn't it rather refreshing when a politician says the blame for a situation actually rests with politicians, himself included?'

'A politician fondling his conscience in public is the ultimate indecency.'

'Don't you think there is something different about Plowright, that he may succeed in getting the sort of deal with Dublin that will really have an effect?'

'Plowright is no different from other politicians except in minor points of style. When he was sent to Stormont, because the Prime Minister found his ambitions troublesome, he knew it was the equivalent of the salt mines, offering no hope of a political triumph. His purpose there has been to achieve a high profile and to ensure that when his present initiative fails – as it will, since it's far too ambitious – others will be blamed while he will attract admiration for his sterling endeavours, thereby turning to advantage the British public's mania for gallant losers.'

'You're not feeling very Christian today.'

'The practice of Christianity and the acceptance of reality are not mutually exclusive.' He bounced his palms on the sides of his chair and then stood up, satisfied he had obliterated Plowright for the evening.

When they began their meal he said, 'Tell me how things are in the Bureau.'

'Not a lot's been happening. The only excitement I know is that one of Twiss's officers has threatened to take himself off to No. 10.'

'Why?'

'He suspects a sinister cover-up and wants to protest to the Prime Minister.'

He laughed. 'Twiss, suspected of a cover-up? How unjust life can be!'

'His suspicions aren't directed against Twiss. His target's Antrim.'

It sobered him. 'Do I know this person?'

'No, he joined us after your retirement – at about the same time as Egerton in whom he's been confiding. That's how I know about it – from Egerton. His name is Loach, Bernard Loach. He came to us from a tobacco company which he'd left on grounds of conscience – he felt he was promoting disease. He's rather intense. I think he now sees fighting corruption as his personal mission.'

'He should be got rid of. People with missions are very dangerous.'

'He's not that extreme – just serious.'

He wasn't listening. 'Let Master Loach take himself back to commerce. No doubt there is room for still more dynamic entrepreneurs, more flexible marketing high-fliers. Did you know there was such an animal as *a flexible marketing high-flier*?' He articulated the words with venom.

'No.'

'One is being advertised for in the evening paper. There's a status to aspire to! The glorious cavalry of the private sector!'

He drained his wine glass, satisfied at having worked up a general diatribe. 'How is Egerton by the way?'

'He's still working in my section. Occasionally he asks if I've seen you lately. You excite in him an apprehensive fascination.'

She had guessed that would please him. He accepted the remaining chop with only token hesitation, then said, as she had known he would sooner or later, 'Tell me more about this creature Loach.'

'So you do want to hear?'

He shrugged, then smiled.

'The story is a bit complicated. A few weeks ago Twiss's

people received a tip that had originated with an ex-employee of a travel firm called Avarta Travel Services. She'd worked as secretary to the manager there and left when he refused to up her salary. The tip was that looking into the circumstances in which a man named P. R. Checkley and his wife had been able to take a three-thousand-pounds-plus holiday in Acapulco would yield some interesting facts. When Checkley turned out to be an Under Secretary in Defence Procurement with responsibility for supervising weapons contracts on behalf of the Army, Twiss gave the case to Loach with instructions to make urgent enquiries.

'Loach quickly established that Avarta Travel is a subsidiary of the same group that owns the Leverson Crouch Company in Belfast. And Leverson Crouch are manufacturing the Army's new anti-tank missile code-named Orange Tip. So the case began to look extremely important.'

Fender murmured: he was repeating the code-name. When she raised her eyebrows he said, 'You find them among the lady's smocks on a warm spring day – Orange Tips. Cannibals in their caterpillar state I fear. But wonderfully attractive. Someone in Defence Procurement has a soul.'

She nodded patiently. 'In this instance Checkley seems to have been feeding very comfortably off the Army's Orange Tip. Almost the first thing Loach discovered about work on the weapon was that the original specification had been jacked up no less than three times, each involving a large increase in the total cost. Abandoning development of some other weapon had left a certain amount of financial slack and Checkley seems to have arranged for the Leverson Crouch Company to take that up.

'Loach also discovered there was social contact between

Checkley and the chairman of the group of companies to which Avarta Travel and Leverson Crouch both belong. He was sure he was on to something big. Then Twiss was suddenly summoned to see the head of Defence Procurement. He's new since you left the Bureau, an ex-business tycoon named Jobell who made a fortune from waste disposal. Apparently Jobell had just been told by one of his minions that the Bureau was taking an interest in Checkley's conduct and was very irked that he hadn't been consulted before. He sent initially for Antrim but since he was on leave Twiss had to go.

'After Jobell heard Twiss's story he said he wasn't going to wait for the result of some interminable investigation by bureaucrats, he'd have Checkley in there and then – which he did, to Twiss's dismay. Jobell took charge of the questioning. Checkley was hotly indignant when asked how he'd paid for the Acapulco holiday. He acknowledged that it had been arranged through Avarta Travel and that the firm had been recommended to him in conversation in Leverson Crouch's office one day. But he had paid the full price out of his own pocket. He asked to be allowed to fetch the evidence for that from his home in Notting Hill. He came back with the travel company's receipt in his favour for £3100 and another from a Belgian dealer in porcelain for £2650 in respect of the sale, shortly before, of several pieces of Doctor Wall, which Checkley explained had been in his family for years. The balance had come out of his salary. The receipts seemed perfectly genuine. On the other hand there was nothing to show Checkley owned the Doctor Wall in the first place.

'As regards the working up of the cost of Orange Tip, Checkley demonstrated from letters on a file that the revised specifications had always been preceded by written requests from the Army. Not difficult to arrange of course. Jobell however said he was satisfied that everything was in order. In other words, he took Checkley's side.

'Twiss withdrew in disorder, undertaking to refer the facts to Antrim when he returned to the office. He found Loach waiting for him with some news that had just come in from enquiries into *Mrs* Checkley's circumstances. It seems she's having a very expensive house built in Porthcawl, a small seaside town in South Wales where she grew up. Her parents had been greengrocers there. The house is on a marvellous site overlooking the sea, with a private path to the golf course; five bedrooms, solarium, swimming pool with a sliding roof, lots of luxury throughout. Total cost, not less than £190,000.'

'Greengrocers have been known to make fortunes.'

'Mrs Checkley's parents had a very modest business, they couldn't have salted away so much. And Checkley himself has no private money. Twiss agreed with Loach that there really was a smell about Checkley. Antrim was due back in the office next day and Twiss had an appointment with him fixed for three in the afternoon. But within an hour of getting in during the morning Antrim called for all the papers. They were returned to Twiss with a minute saying that the investigation was to be discontinued forthwith. Twiss went to see him, supposing that when he heard about the house in Porthcawl he'd reverse that. But it apparently left Antrim unmoved. Twiss accepted defeat and returned to pass the instructions on to Loach who was staggered by the turn of events and asked for reasons. He was told Antrim hadn't given any, that this was not unusual for him and in any case as a junior officer Loach was expected to do as he was told without arguing. He didn't take it too well.'

'Doing as you're told is of course a mark of intolerable servility these days,' Fender said. He had taken against Loach.

'You're being unfair. Anyway he told the whole story to Egerton, saying it was a monstrous and obviously corrupt decision. Egerton tried to calm him down. Eventually he persuaded Loach to talk it over with me which he did yesterday. He was looking wild-eyed and ranting about the public being entitled to know what was going on. So I promised to make some enquiries.

'I knew that talking to Twiss would be a waste of time and went straight to Antrim. I said it wasn't my business but he ought to be aware he had a very disgruntled officer on his hands as a result of not giving any reasons for stopping the Checkley investigation. There was a danger Loach would form up to No. 10 or even talk to the press.'

Fender was looking more interested. 'What happened?'

'I got nowhere. He hardly listened.' She shook her head, remembering Antrim's abruptness, the beads of sweat at the hairline, the fingers never still on the desk. 'He seemed enormously preoccupied.'

'I'd heard he looked under the weather.'

She raised her eyebrows. 'How did you hear that?'

'Mansell happened to drop in for a chat the other day.'

He was dissembling of course. Mansell and he had never been so close that a call of that kind was likely. There had been business to transact, business of sufficient importance to warrant Mansell driving the fifty odd miles to Fender's cottage. This was possibly the explanation for the trip to Oxford and the interview with the woman who had proved so mysteriously disconcerting.

She said tartly, 'You must stop me if I'm telling you things you already know.'

'No, no.' He shook his head with great vigour. 'This is all quite new and fascinating, please go on.'

She began gathering together empty dishes. 'As I said, he simply would not listen, just threw out that there were perfectly good reasons why the investigation should not

48

go ahead. The public interest was involved but he wasn't free to disclose how. If Loach didn't like being left in the dark he could resign. When I asked if some intervention by Jobell had influenced him he said he was not likely to be bending his knee to an ex-dustman. So I gave up.'

'Do you think Loach will bite on the bullet?'

'I'm not at all sure. When I saw him the same evening and told him Antrim's reaction, he looked wild again and started to lecture me about Antrim belonging to a generation that always put expediency before principle. He also said he'd just received some new information – a few minutes before apparently – that confirmed his belief he wasn't just dealing with corruption on Checkley's part. In view of what had happened, he didn't intend to put it on a file, he'd find a better use for it. I said that was extremely silly of him and anyway I could do without being lectured. He then calmed down, said he was appreciative of what I'd done, promised to think things over carefully and disappeared.'

'He doesn't think Antrim is corrupt surely?'

She shrugged. 'He may.'

'I convict Antrim of a large number of weaknesses, but corruption is not one of them.'

'There *is* something wrong.'

Fender fiddled with the knife on his side plate, moving it from side to side. He had become uneasy, she was sure of that. But then he sat back as though suddenly reassured. 'I shall be interested to hear the outcome one day. It'll no doubt all be explained quite reasonably. What a delicious meal that was!'

Against all her refusals, polite and otherwise, he insisted he would help with the washing-up. Resigned at last, she gave him a towel and covertly observed the progress of each piece of china as she passed it to him to dry. But there were no disasters. He hung the towel up afterwards with a flourish as though they had been a team in this all their lives.

Later over coffee he was his usual self, by turns oracular and tentative, arrogant and sensitive, stimulating and impossible. But she sensed he was having to make a greater effort than usual. The happenings of the day, or perhaps just the heat, had taken a toll. Long before midnight, he announced uncharacteristically that she must be tired and took himself off to the bed she had made up for him in the spare room.

She had no sense of how long she had been sleeping when something awoke her. Below the door she saw there was light in the living room.

Going in she found Fender in an armchair, a dressing-gown over his pyjamas. His eyes were closed, his head tilted to one side. On his lap was a small book. It was the leatherbound copy of *The Imitation of Christ* she remembered noticing in his room when they made their trip to Ottawa.

She put her hand on his arm. He opened his eyes immediately. 'Ah,' he said, 'Antonia, I must have dropped off.' He was embarrassed that she had found him.

'Are you all right?'

'Just a little restless. I hope the light didn't disturb you.'

She glanced at the open book. The chapter heading read: *Of the Want of All Solace and Comfort.* 'So bad?' she asked.

'No, no.'

'What then?'

'It was simply that something this afternoon started a train of thought which prevented sleep. It became a grasping after the past. I should know better. Stupid.'

He closed the book with a flourish and placed it on the

50

table beside his chair. Doing so, he turned slightly. She saw with a shock that his cheek was wet.

Sitting beside him she reached for his hand. He let her take it but kept his eyes fixed on the wall opposite. She knew he was summoning up reserves to rebuild his defences. For a while she waited, listening to the silence with him.

'Come to bed,' she said at last.

He brought his eyes round to meet hers. She smiled to convince him of what she meant. He shook his head with sudden vehemence. 'I didn't intend you to find me like this.'

'I know.'

When she remained smiling, he said, 'It would be *wholly ridiculous* for you!'

'Why?'

'You know what I mean! Don't pretend out of pity that you don't.'

'I never pretend with you. I was happy that night in Rome. Can't you just accept . . . ?'

'Not what I find inconceivable.'

She shook her head. She was feeling sleepy and also a little irritated that he persisted in arguing. She stood up but continued to hold his hand so that he was forced to allow his arm to be straightened.

'Do you think God intended you should understand *everything*?'

Astonishingly, it seemed like a novel thought to him. 'No,' he said meekly.

All the same she had to pull him to his feet, like a reluctant child. But he came at last.

5

'Is it possible Iris Keysing didn't really *know*?' Mansell said. 'That she made up the story of the Harley Street client being a journalist her daughter had met at Carl Lissack's house on the spur of the moment?'

'Why should she make it up?'

'To impress.'

'Can there be anyone in the world who would expect the mention of a journalist to *impress*?' Fender said acidly.

'You did say she was rather odd.'

'Not that odd.'

Mansell sighed then frowned. 'I suppose I could try to find out if there *is* a journalist living in that block.'

Fender watched him swallowing the remains of his gin and tonic in a single gulp. Two predecessors had been despatched in a similar fashion. Once upon a time, Mansell would have viewed with a beady eye anyone at the Bureau who took medication before lunch with this urgency. Life as Antrim's Head of Personnel was exacting its price.

'I'm quite sure she wasn't making it up. Embroidering a little perhaps but no more. It *was* a journalist and she knew Sylvia had met him in Lissack's house. And the name in any case was Alistair. Stop worrying.'

Mansell's gaze wandered sombrely along the row of bottles behind the bar. His initial silence when Fender told him on the telephone earlier that he no longer had a problem had been revealing. He was disappointed. Unable because of some early afternoon meeting to accept Fender's invitation to lunch to hear the details, he had nevertheless elected to come hot-foot to the club for a drink, in the hope of discovering grounds for continuing to suspect Antrim.

'Am I right in thinking you're not wholly pleased?' Fender said.

Mansell applied vigour to his head-shaking. 'No, no, I'm very relieved of course.'

'You don't look it.'

'I suppose I'd convinced myself of the worst. Remembering the incident when Antrim was in the Army in Germany, I jumped to that conclusion. And Hazel's story about the marks she saw on Antonia Strachan's body rather added colour.'

Fender looked away. The story of the marks had settled into a sediment at the back of his mind. He had hoped he might in time forget it. Occasionally, without warning, an image would flash before him and he would wince. Mostly it happened when he saw love-making on his television set. The previous evening on his way to Antonia's flat he had steeled himself to reject the images before they took shape. He had found with relief that in the reality of her presence it had been relatively easy.

'Forget the whole thing,' he said. 'Be grateful there's no problem.'

'I daresay you're right. Thank you for your help anyway – I hope the trip wasn't too tiresome.' Mansell glanced at his watch. 'I ought to get back.'

As they left the bar he said, 'I wish you'd phoned me last night, Hilda would have been delighted to give you a bed. I suppose you stayed here.'

'Unfortunately all the rooms were taken.'

'So what did you do?'

Fender hesitated, reluctant to invite speculation by the truth. The situation was saved by a newcomer to the bar greeting Mansell. By the time their civilities had been exchanged and the other had moved on, Mansell had forgotten his question.

From the street door, Fender watched him hurry away across St James's Square. He had to decide between returning to the bar and going straight in to lunch. The first course would postpone departure from London a little longer. But there was no reason now not to catch the earliest train back to his cottage. The melancholy of the previous evening was no longer strong enough to subdue the loathing he felt for London in summer: the filthy pavements, the diesel stench of the buses, the hordes of back-packed tourists blocking each corner, asking the way to everywhere. He hated it. Yet he hesitated, regretful that nothing existed to detain him.

Across the other side of the hall, someone was trying to catch his eye, a familiar lanky figure, with hair that seemed composed of thin straw and round, pale-rimmed spectacles. Beneath the chin the ends of a blue-and-white spotted blue tie drooped.

Searching his memory for the name, he succeeded when he heard the voice, high-pitched and ironical: Roper-Hoare, once an Under Secretary in the Home Office. The principal tenor in the departmental choir, Roper-Hoare had found his voice coveted by the Treasury itself; to get him into their own choir, the songsters of Great George Street had been willing to overlook even his undoubted innumeracy. But the transfer had not happened. For some reason Roper-Hoare had been sent to the Northern Ireland Office at about the time Fender had retired.

'How good to see you,' Roper-Hoare was saying. 'Come and have lunch. Tell me what you're doing with your retirement.'

Livelier than Mansell, Fender reflected, but with much the same bloodlessness; hardly the ideal companion for lunch. But that was being uncharitable. Roper-Hoare was a decent creature, doing his best in a frustrating profession. And he would have gossip to offer.

He followed Roper-Hoare in his choice of curry, a foolhardy challenge to digestion in these days but, served as it was here, impossible to resist. 'Your master was displaying himself yesterday, I noticed.'

'You watched Plowright doing his stuff on *Questions Please*?'

'Briefly.'

'Were you impressed?'

'A fine head of hair, I thought.'

'Made more glamorous by a little artifice, I regret to reveal,' Roper-Hoare said. 'That is not a leak by the way. A journalist observed a bottle in his briefcase at the last Party Conference.'

'He gave an interesting reading of the part of a modest politician. The person I was with found him quite appealing. Is that the Department's view of Plowright?'

'Not entirely. He's too cold-blooded to inspire unqualified affection from officials. But it's the view of the populace if we're to believe the newspaper polls. When you consider how little chance a Secretary of State for Northern Ireland has for impressing the great British public his ratings are astonishingly high.'

'I found the self-abasement rather cloying.'

'Admitting to having been wrong about something, albeit when younger, is considered engaging by the image people these days. One or two of the younger Ministers have been trying it out.'

The curry had arrived. Fender lowered his head to allow the aroma of it to fill his nostrils. 'When he comes back from Ulster with nothing to show – '

'You can't assume that.'

'If you're thinking of the negotiations with Dublin he

talks about, another deal like the first agreement won't do anything for his reputation.'

'There had to be a curtain-raiser. That was all the first agreement aspired to. But Plowright is going for substance this time round.'

'In which case he's bound to fail.'

'Why are you so sure of that?'

'Because the problem is and always has been intractable.'

'Plowright would have anyone who even hinted that aloud inside the Department booted out within minutes. You mustn't underestimate him. He's a considerable operator. Neither of the communities really dislikes him too much which in itself is a major achievement. And he's handled the Prot leaders brilliantly. Most of them have been persuaded that the pork barrel which will be rolled out after a second stage deal with Dublin looks much too attractive to warrant more than ritual yelps of protest. Note the absence these days of pious fears – i.e. threats – of civil war looming if there's a new agreement. Of course some won't come into line. But they don't have the muscle to play the civil war card with real conviction.'

'Are you saying the paramilitaries won't stir?'

'The police believe they can handle anything on that front. Their intelligence nowadays is very good.'

'No general strike, no sewage in the streets?'

Roper-Hoare drew himself back from optimism just in time to avoid sounding too buoyant. 'I admit there can be no certainties where Ulster's concerned. But Plowright himself is extraordinarily confident. He believes that all we'll have to endure from the Prot leaders who've taken the place of Wedderburn and James Tull is a lot of hot air.'

He broke Bombay Duck onto his curry in meticulously judged pieces. 'And you mustn't forget the fact that the atmosphere in Dublin has also become very promising in the last month. The Taoiseach, who's clearly been persuaded the new deal would be advantageous, now seems to have a Cabinet that's united behind him. A joint industrial development agency and a joint police cross-border unit are already agreed. What we're waiting for is some assurance there'll be an amendment to the Irish constitution that waters down the claim to jurisdiction over the North sufficiently to spike the Prots' guns. Plowright's convinced we'll get it. He has his own sources in Dublin – very irritating to the Embassy there. Little notes have been coming out of his Private Office which begin, "I understand the Dublin Government intend . . ." I don't know whether he has a direct line into the Cabinet but he certainly seems to be abreast of its thinking. Perhaps the Taoiseach is feeding him encouragement on the quiet.'

'I see.' Fascinating stuff, Fender thought: how remote I am from it these days! 'The Taoiseach . . .' He repeated the word, let it roll seductively on his tongue. Other Gaelic words came back from schoolboy holidays spent in Cork, the cries of pedlars, even lines of verse. '*Roaig and Airig Fhuar . . . The Grianan and Davaar . . .*' He shook his head. 'What a magical language. The passion of the Irish for preserving their culture is so easy to understand.'

'No one is trying to stop them preserving their *culture*. I don't even mind them calling an airport an *aerphort*. As long as they don't insist on being prisoners of the past. They've everything to gain if they'll just accept the realities over the border and negotiate accordingly. As Plowright believes they will.'

'I'll believe it all when it happens.'

Roper-Hoare smiled indulgently, enjoying the sensation of tossing out facts as the whim took him, like a man feeding ducks from a paper bag. 'Let me tell you something else, Ludo. Plowright has the luckiest *touch* of any politician I've ever known. Think back to the position early last year before he took over as Secretary of State at Stormont. No new settlement was then remotely in prospect because of the influence in the North of two men.'

'Wedderburn and James Tull?'

'Precisely. They could and would have wrecked the smallest move towards another deal. But within a day of Plowright getting to Stormont, Wedderburn, the worst problem of all, was diagnosed to have cancer of the throat. He's still alive but only just and no one even consults him now. That left Tull as the principal problem. Plowright tries talking him round – without success. Everyone decides we face stalemate again. But then Tull writes himself off by driving his car into a river, presumably drunk as usual. Suddenly there's an opening again. Plowright's predecessors as Secretary of State in Northern Ireland all had those two to contend with. God however is gracious enough to remove them for *Plowright*. That's *real* politician's luck. Vital if you're as ambitious as Plowright.'

'And you believe there's nobody likely to organize major opposition with Wedderburn and Tull out of the way?'

'Nobody.'

Fender smiled sceptically. 'It sounds altogether too good.'

'I confess to wondering now and then if we're seeing a mirage. Anyway, we shall soon discover.'

'The American, Cleveland, who keeps telling television cameras that he is over here offering the good offices of the United States to the two governments – what exactly is *he* up to?'

Roper-Hoare rolled his eyes upwards. 'You may well

ask. Cleveland is the White House's contribution to solving the problem of Northern Ireland, the Middle East having proved altogether too difficult. The State Department are said to be spitting mad with the President – not that that's anything new. Cleveland has a suite in the US Embassy here with Office of the President's Special Envoy on the door. I'm told he has similar arrangements in the American Embassy in Dublin. He commutes between the two and is always around whenever we're negotiating with Dublin. He has an absurdly inflated entourage – two State Department people, a Trade specialist and somebody we're fairly sure is CIA, plus the usual secretarial and security back-up.'

'To what end?'

'Cleveland's main contribution, if you disregard his passion for inviting everybody to breakfasts at which he can pontificate, is in the area of investment and industrial development where some hefty American injections are on the cards once there's a deal. Occasionally but not often enough he disappears back to Washington to tell the President how he's getting on.

'The whole idea – a sort of cut-price Kissinger shuttle – was loony from the start. I know the Irish think the same. According to our Ambassador in Washington it was a personal whim of the President's resulting from some nostalgic reflection on his ancestry which is supposed to be traceable on both sides of the Border. He also wanted to keep Cleveland out of mischief back home in the States for a while. As if there weren't enough wild cards in the Ireland pack already . . .' Roper-Hoare rolled his eyes in the other direction.

'Plowright can't stand the sight of Cleveland, chiefly because at one time he was far too close for comfort to the Irish Commerce Minister who died of AIDS the other day and had been until then the main opposition in the Dublin Cabinet to another deal with London.'

'This was Cahill . . . ?'

'Yes. The word from Washington was that Cleveland had decided Cahill was the up and coming man in Irish politics and should be indulged accordingly. Thank God we don't have that problem to contend with any more, unless Cahill's widow who is quite a firebrand decided to step into his shoes. Gossip has it that Cleveland sleeps with her – was doing so even when Cahill was alive. By agreement. Very cosy.'

'Perhaps you should be arranging a comparable diversion for Cleveland here in London?'

Roper-Hoare said grimly, 'Don't imagine that thought had not already occurred to us. Unfortunately, he already has a comforter in the Embassy. A small, perfectly-formed Cultural Attaché, they tell me.'

Over the cheese they talked of other things. 'I suppose you still look in at the Bureau now and then,' Roper-Hoare said.

'Very rarely.'

'Antrim must surely like to pick your brains.' He was fishing in an idle way.

Fender shook his head. 'I'm very out of touch.' Listening to Roper-Hoare had at first intrigued him. But he had become depressed realizing the full extent to which the remark was true. He checked his watch. 'If you'll excuse me I shall skip coffee and catch my train.' The quicker he put all this behind him, the better.

Picking up his overnight bag in the cloakroom, he said, 'Good luck with the negotiations. If Plowright does bring off something of substance *and* can make it stick, it will be a good deed in a naughty world.'

'Reason has to win sometimes,' Roper-Hoare said. He was in danger of being optimistic again. 'The advantages

caught sight of Fender, she raised her eyebrows and smiled but said nothing.

'I'm sorry to bother you, Antonia,' Mansell said. 'You know Ludo of course. It was something we felt we ought to clear up tonight.'

She glanced back at Fender. The smile became faintly mocking. 'How's Betsy Frogg today?'

'Much the same I fancy.'

She was cool, wary, ready for any surprise they might be about to spring. He gazed into her eyes then quickly away. To pretend to himself he felt any objectivity about her was impossible. Only to others was he still able to put on a show of being neutral, the air of avuncular affection.

'What we wanted to check,' Mansell said, glancing at the paper on his blotter, 'is serial 146 on that file.'

She seated herself and opened it. 'It isn't a file I know. Who was Dyerson?'

'A *wunderkind* of the City,' Fender said. 'I seem to recall that after managing a pop group he progressed through pornographic videos to inventing some highly imaginative investment trusts. When imagination finally gave out, he went to Venezuela to avoid fraud charges. An exemplar of that mercantile enterprise to which we all owe so much.' He made noises in the stem of the pipe he had taken from his pocket.

Antonia was smiling at his words as she turned the pages of the file. Her smile faded when she began to read the serial Mansell had specified. At last she looked up.

'It should be an interview with the financier, Carl Lissack,' Mansell said, 'conducted by the Director some years ago.' He was trying not to appear embarrassed.

'It is.'

'I believe Lissack was one of the targets of the investigation by Loach which you mentioned to Ludo yesterday evening.'

'Yes.'

'When you went to the Director and queried his decision to stop the investigation – '

She interrupted him. 'I wasn't querying his decision, I was warning him that Loach was steamed up because he'd been given no reasons for it and that he might do something rash.'

'What I wondered is whether he mentioned to you that he'd personally known Lissack.'

'No, he didn't. In the context of the conversation we had there was no reason why he should have done.'

She looked mildly combative on Antrim's behalf. Fender felt Mansell's glance briefly upon him.

'What led you to check this serial?' she asked.

'We learned by accident that Lissack and the Director had a friend in common. It seemed best to get all the facts in case the wrong conclusions were drawn by others.'

She shrugged. Fender could see she was annoyed because Mansell wasn't being frank. Putting on his reading glasses, Fender reached out and took the file from her knees.

The serial was a two page note, signed by Antrim; there was an annex consisting of another page. He sat back to read.

'On the 14th of November, I telephoned Carl Lissack at the offices in Millbank and explained who I was. I said I was looking into some matters connected with the Dyerson Leisure Complex project. I knew he had once considered investing in it. If he could spare a little time, I would like to consult him.

'Lissack expressed reluctance at first. However he came round when I assured him I was not at all interested in his own activities. He agreed to talk if I would guarantee "no subpoenas". I said there was now no prospect of legal proceedings.

'Because Lissack was involved in meetings for the rest of the afternoon and was off to America early the next day, it was agreed I would go to his house at Rushers Lye, near Guildford, in the evening. Lissack said he would have guests about the place and he preferred they should not know he was talking to a member of the Bureau. I undertook to present myself as Alistair Cottrell, a freelance financial journalist interviewing him for a magazine profile.

'I arrived at seven o'clock. The house is an enormous Elizabethan pile with ornamental gardens and a thirty acre park. Round the back, I was told, there is a small zoo – Lissack likes wild animals.

'I was taken by a servant (black coat, striped trousers, stiff white collar) to a swimming pool decorated as a grotto which has been built into the cellars at one end of the house. Lissack was entertaining his guests there. About half of them were sharp-looking youngish men introduced as business associates. The remainder were girls, two of whom seemed to be permanent residents in the house. Larking about, largely in the nude, with Lissack acting as poolmaster, occupied the next three-quarters of an hour. Occasionally events occurred in and out of the water to general applause.

'Finally Lissack took me off to his dressing room in the main part of the house. While he was dressing for dinner he answered questions about Dyerson and his efforts to get his Complex project approved. I have incorporated what Lissack said in an annex to this note which I suggest can be passed to the Department of the Environment. It shows their Planning Appeals Inspector in a better light than previously, assuming Lissack was telling the truth. He seemed frank and was affable throughout. I should not care to have him as an enemy however.

'He invited me to stay on to dinner and I accepted. I was placed next to one of his two resident playmates, whose name was Sylvia. She made herself very agreeable and said she hoped any article I wrote would bring out the fact that, unlike most of his fellow-captains of industry, (on which she seemed very well-informed) Lissack had "real balls". I told her I would bear this in mind. She said I should telephone her if I needed any more pointers. She could in fact be very informative should we ever want to know more about Lissack's business activities.

'During the meal Lissack announced the wine was from a vineyard he had just bought in France. When I left he asked for my telephone number and said he looked forward to having lunch with me soon. He also presented me with a case of the wine. I am giving this to the canteen for use at the Christmas party.'

Fender passed the file to Mansell without comment. When they had both finished reading, Antonia stood up. She said, 'If that's all you want, perhaps I can go.' Her voice was a shade tart.

Mansell said heavily, 'I'd be grateful if you could stay a little longer. We need your help.'

She sat down again and glanced towards Fender. 'I suppose your visit to Oxford comes into this.'

'Yes, Mansell asked me to enquire about a certain individual.'

'A woman?'

'Yes.'

'A friend of both Lissack and Antrim?'

'Apparently.'

She showed impatience at the brevity of his replies. 'Are you going to tell me the relevance of that to a routine interview conducted years ago? Or isn't there one?'

'We have to make sure there isn't a time bomb ticking away here.'

'Any idea that Antrim stopped an investigation for corrupt reasons is ridiculous.'

'Loach doesn't seem to think so.'

'Loach doesn't know Antrim as well as we do.'

There was an uneasy silence between them. Mansell was getting restive, massaging the lapel of his jacket between finger and thumb; he was anxious to resume charge of the discussion. 'I understand Loach spoke of having more information which he was not intending to put on a file.'

'Yes.'

'We had wondered if in the interest of clearing this up you would talk to him again and get him to tell you what that information is.'

'I'm not sure he'd be willing to do that.'

'In view of the sympathy you've shown he's more likely to confide in you than one of us.'

'A better person to approach him would be Mark Egerton. It was Mark who persuaded him to talk to me in the first place.'

'I can't involve a junior officer in anything of this delicacy.'

She was reluctantly beginning to face up to the fact that she had no choice. 'Loach hasn't been seen in the office today. Mark told me he'd tried without success to contact him. Assuming he appears tomorrow I could tackle him first thing in the morning.'

'I would rather we got on with this tonight. Do you happen to know where he lives? If not, I'll ask my secretary to look it up.'

'His flat's in Formosa Street, Maida Vale – I dropped him off there one evening. I suppose I could call in on my way home. It's a few minutes' walk.'

'The ideal,' Fender said, 'would be for you to get Loach round to *your* flat and question him there. Explain it by saying you have to be back for a telephone call you're expecting. If we could be in an adjoining room while you're talking to him we could overhear what he has to say. In the event of there being some really grave revelation, Mansell might want to step out and take over.'

'He may not be home.'

'We must keep trying until he is.'

Clearly she felt no enthusiasm, was almost certainly against the whole thing; but she rose from her chair, resigned to doing what they asked.

Fender said, 'I suggest we accompany you back to your place now. You can then go on to his flat.'

She gazed at him flintily. 'Who *is* the friend in common, the woman?'

He felt a strong unwillingness to tell her.

'If I'm to help, I'd like to know all the facts.'

She looked very unyielding. Fender sighed. Out of the corner of his eye, he became aware with surprise that Mansell was unfolding the *Clarion* cutting from his note-case to hand it to Antonia.

He embarked on tamping his pipe, reluctant to see her face as she studied it. When finally he lifted his gaze, she was returning the cutting to Mansell again. A pulse was throbbing in her neck but her expression was inscrutable.

She picked up the file she had brought. 'I'll lock this away again and wait for you in the hall.' She was avoiding looking at them.

When she had gone, Mansell said, 'Interesting . . . I was watching her face as she read the cutting. She was shaken – but she wasn't surprised. She wasn't surprised at all.'

The ground floor at Loach's address was a liquor store. At the side a staircase led to two flats above. Antonia rang the bell opposite Loach's name and waited. There was no reply. Standing back she gazed up at the windows but they told her nothing: it was too early in the evening for any lights to be needed.

Since he hadn't been seen at the office all day, Loach could be anywhere, perhaps burrowing on his own account further into the Lissack/Checkley affair; or simply walking the streets in an effort to put it behind him. In the worst case he was now at No. 10, pouring it all out to one of the Private Secretaries there. In which event her mission was too late.

The manager of the liquor store was constructing a pyramid of lager four-packs as she went into the shop. She bought cigarettes. As she counted out her change she said, 'I wondered if you'd seen Mr Loach today. I believe he lives in the upper flat.'

He went back to his creation in the tin. 'I saw him going in at lunchtime or soon after.'

'He isn't answering his bell.'

'He's there all right.' The manager's expression was disenchanted. 'He had the radio raising the roof when I went up to my flat just now. Or maybe it's a record player. You'll have to beat on the door. Tell him to turn it down, my wife'll be back soon with the baby.'

She was sympathizing with him by the time she started on the second flight of stairs. The music enveloped her, defying all other distractions. It sounded like Mahler at his least optimistic. Now that she thought about it, the idea of Loach agonizing to Mahler over what he should do was about right.

There was no response even to knocking; but against the volume of competing sound that was hardly a surprise. She cursed in frustration, finally applied her attention to the lock. It was impossible for her to report failure back to Mansell and Fender on such pathetic grounds. Loach *had* to be rooted out.

The lock was a conventional Yale: a modest challenge to the skills dinned into her during the Mancini investigation, when getting through another such had produced the final damning piece of evidence. Taking out her bank card she went to work.

The bolt slid back with gratifying ease. She stepped into a small, dim hall. The radio or record player was playing in a room immediately on her left. Loach seemed an unlikely denizen of discos; yet it was difficult to imagine anyone tolerating quite such a wall of sound who wasn't. She knocked again before going into the room, visited by a momentary misgiving that she might find

73

Loach locked in the embrace of a fellow Mahler worshipper. But the room was empty.

She walked along the hall, past a bedroom and a bathroom, also unoccupied. At the end the hall narrowed and turned, to become a double-angled passage presumably leading to the kitchen of the flat. A chair lay overturned in her path. Bending to right it, she became aware she had received a caress, not quite the gentle searching of a hand but the delicate travel of knuckle down her cheek, affectionate and lingering. Astonished, she looked up.

Loach was above her, his body moving in a rhythm that matched the knuckle's greeting. For what seemed an endless moment her gaze locked with his eyes as they stared down. His expression conveyed a terrible unwinking anger that she had disturbed him.

Somehow she held the nausea back and retreated along the passage. It seemed as though her legs were fighting the currents of an enveloping sea. She made her way to the room where the radio was playing. Switching it off, she seated herself beside a telephone. From the pack she had bought earlier she took a cigarette and lit it, holding her wrists against her chest as she struck the match. Finally she dialled.

Mansell answered her call. 'Mrs Strachan's telephone – may I take a message? She's not at home at present.' He sounded rather like a butler.

'It's Antonia. I'm in Loach's flat.'

'I see.'

'I shan't be bringing him back.'

'No?' It was as though he was humouring her.

'He's dead. He's hanged himself in the doorway to his kitchen.'

Mansell uttered sounds of shock.

'I'm just going to call the police. Presumably you want me to do that?'

He was hesitating. 'I suppose they'll have to be brought in sooner or later. But if you'll remind me of the exact address I'll come round.'

'There's no point in your getting involved. I suggest you and Ludo hold on there. I'll be with you as soon as I can.'

He began speaking away from the mouthpiece to Fender. Then Fender came on the line. 'Are you quite sure you don't want us to come? A little moral support – '

'It would only complicate dealing with the police. I shall tell them I called here because of concern in the Bureau that Loach hadn't put in an appearance. Nothing more.'

'How did you get into the flat?'

'I fiddled the lock. I'll have to say the door was open.'

There was a pause while he thought about that. Finally he said, 'All right, I know you can handle it. I have a suggestion however. Delay your call to the police for a little longer. Enough to give yourself time to look round the flat. Loach may have kept some notes there that would be relevant to our particular interest. Don't forget to try his pockets.'

She gazed in front of her, remembering the eyes. Fender had sensed something because he went on, 'Perhaps after all – '

'Right,' she said. 'No problem.' It was nice he cared that much; but she wasn't accepting an invitation to be weak-kneed.

She stood up and looked about her purposefully, decided that the desk behind was a suitable place to start.

It was a simple melamine affair, with two drawers. The top drawer yielded blank paper and envelopes, the other was locked but clearly vulnerable. Bending to work on the lock with the small penknife she always carried, she became conscious that the cigarette had not done the trick, might even have made things worse. She stumbled to the basin in the bathroom. Bending over again, she thought of the only *good* thing: at least *they* weren't there to see.

7

As she turned the key in the door, she heard the mantel clock that had marked off time in the Shropshire house when she was a child. It was chiming midnight. Four hours had elapsed since she had left for Loach's flat.

Fender and Mansell rose to greet her. On the television screen a picture flickered. They must have tired of the sound because the set was silent. Their glances were solicitous but also expectant.

'How very unpleasant for you,' Mansell said.

She summoned up a smile. 'Finding him was. But it got better.'

She opened a window to let out the fug of tobacco. 'Sorry to be so long. I asked them to take a statement tonight to save my calling at the local station in the morning.'

Three-quarters of her whisky had been drunk. But on the drinks tray stood another, unopened bottle; one of them must have slipped out earlier for a replacement. They had presumably not eaten since no plates or crumbs were to be seen; in which case Fender in particular would be feeling sorry for himself.

She needed a large drink, preferably alone, before answering questions. She said brightly, 'You must be starving – it'll have to be omelettes I'm afraid. Why don't you have another drink while I'm organizing things in the kitchen? I shan't be long.' She went out, hoping for the best.

Before she was halfway through the glass of cooking brandy, they had loomed in the doorway. 'Perhaps we could be of assistance,' Mansell was saying, without conviction. They had not even poured themselves fresh drinks. She broke the eggs in the pan and resigned herself to working round them.

'What did the police say?' Fender asked.

'They thought it looked pretty straightforward. The position of a chair I found upended was consistent with Loach having kicked it away after fixing the cord round his neck. They asked me if he'd been showing signs of depression lately in the office. I said I didn't think so – just worry about his work. There were the usual questions about next of kin, friends and so on, which I couldn't answer. They'll be in touch with the Bureau for more details tomorrow.' She cocked an eye at the cooker clock. 'Meaning today.'

'And that's all?'

'They were slightly surprised they couldn't find a note for anyone. But suicide on the spur of the moment is apparently more common than I'd imagined.'

She managed to push them back into the living room by producing glasses and cutlery with a request for the table to be set for their meal. When she appeared with the omelettes, they were trying not to look impatient.

'What about the search you made?' Fender asked.

'It wasn't very rewarding. Loach seems to have kept very few papers of any kind. There was a locked drawer in his desk which raised my hopes. But the only things in it were a few press cuttings and a booklet produced by something called the Gay Medical Advisory Centre.'

Fender raised an eyebrow in Mansell's direction. 'Did you know Loach had interests of that kind?'

Mansell shook his head.

'He wasn't married . . . ?'

'No, I recall at the time we took him on he said he was

78

engaged. What happened to that I don't know. Perhaps he still is.'

Fender glanced back at Antonia. 'Any sign of a girl-friend having been living there?'

'None!'

'Letters?'

'The only correspondence was from his mother.'

'His mother,' said Fender on a rising note. In the absence of more constructive thoughts, he was about to twist Mansell's tail. 'Perhaps the engagement was for presentational purposes only. Afraid you wouldn't accept him in the Bureau if you thought he was homosexual, he decided to offer you a little reassurance.'

Mansell was beginning to look hunted. He was presumably imagining press stories after the inquest: they would describe how Loach, habitué of gay clubs and public lavatories, had despatched himself after a quarrel with a guardsman lover. He said stiffly, 'I don't think we need jump to conclusions of that sort yet. These press cuttings you saw – what were they about?'

She checked the notes she had made.

'Financial-page stories about Lissack and his business activities for the most part. An item dealing with a laboratory in East London where research into an AIDS vaccine is going on. Articles about Southern Irish politics – the longest was an analysis of the political balance in the Irish Cabinet. He seems to have been following the situation there quite closely.'

'What about his diary?' Fender said.

'Most of the entries were routine – dentist, barber, squash club – that sort of thing. There was one I thought it worth making a note of.' She read: '"7 P.M. Fay Gordon, 73b, Selmeston Court, West Finchley." That's for later today. It could be purely personal. On the other hand I have a feeling it isn't, that it might be connected with his investigation.'

'Which he'd been told to drop,' Mansell said.

'I think he may have found that hard to do.'

'Whatever Ms Gordon had to offer,' Fender said, 'Loach apparently didn't regard it as worth staying alive to hear.'

He was in a point-scoring mood, crumbling bread disdainfully between his fingers.

'I agree with what you said earlier,' Antonia said, looking at Mansell. 'We ought not to jump to conclusions. I don't think it's at all certain Loach committed suicide.'

She was pleased to see that Fender's eyes had risen sharply from the mess beside his plate.

'It's true it looked like suicide and that was obviously what the police thought. But I don't believe anyone of Loach's temperament, obsessed as he was by his investigation, would decide to end his life in the middle of it. Psychologically it doesn't make sense.'

'The police suggested it was a spur-of-the-moment suicide, didn't they?'

'I'm not convinced. Loach's investigation was a serious threat to at least two people, one of whom, Lissack, is rich and powerful. He could have decided that Loach had to be stopped at all costs. There was only one certain way of achieving that.'

'But he had been stopped already. Antrim had called off his investigation.'

'I think that Loach intended all along to disobey Antrim. He was determined to take his story to No. 10 and confront the Prime Minister with it. But he wanted more facts first, especially about what lay behind Antrim's decision. We don't know how he spent the last day or two. Was he interviewing somebody who then told Lissack? Or even seeing Lissack himself?

'I picked up two pieces of information tonight that make me think my theory is worth pursuing. After I'd finished giving my statement to the police I looked in again on the manager of the liquor store under Loach's flat. He told me that a day or two ago he saw Loach in the street about to get into his car. He asked him if he was going on a trip. Loach said, "Just down to Guildford." We know that Lissack's house is near Guildford.

'The other item he told me was that when he saw Loach going up to his flat at lunchtime or shortly afterwards there was a man with him.'

'Did he say what the man looked like?'

'He gave quite a good description: medium height, probably in his forties, light-coloured hair going thin on top, moustache. He thought he was wearing a hacking jacket.'

'Was there a diary entry for the lunch hour?'

'No.'

'So the meeting was unplanned.'

'Probably.'

They gazed at each other for want of something better to do. Eventually Fender said, 'We could be back to the homosexual angle of course.'

'He wasn't a homosexual,' she said. 'I would bet a lot of money on that.' She gathered together their plates. 'What *I* think is that this was someone employed to murder Loach and make it look like suicide.'

She left them brooding on it while she went to make coffee. When she returned they hadn't moved from the table. Mansell had a hand resting on his bald patch, possibly as an aid to thought.

'What do you think of my theory?' she asked.

He said reluctantly, 'We agree it can't be wholly ruled out.'

'So what are you going to do?'

81

'That is something we are having difficulty over.'

It was hard to believe that while she had been brewing coffee, Fender hadn't charted the course to be followed. By now she would have expected him to have written the play, given himself the starring role and talked Mansell into being a sort of stage manager. But his expression told her that he was temporarily at a loss. It seemed that on this occasion at least she was cast to play Inspiration.

She said, 'We still have a chance of discovering the facts Loach wouldn't risk putting on a file. When I first talked to him, he'd already taken Mark Egerton into his confidence. It's possible he subsequently told him what his new information was. Why don't I tackle Mark in the morning?'

Mansell's fingers were drumming the table. She supposed he was terrified she might give Egerton some hint of the suspicions they were dealing with. 'Don't worry, I'll be very careful.'

He shrugged finally. 'Very well, try to find out if Egerton knows anything. I've meetings set up for most of the morning. You and I had better meet somewhere privately at lunchtime.' He turned in his chair. 'Ludo, you'll be wanting to return to the country, I naturally don't expect you to stay on for this.'

She could have told him he was wasting his breath, there was not the smallest chance of getting Fender out of his hair at this stage. Already the jowls were being shaken. The expression was deeply supportive. 'No, no, I can't let you carry this alone. I suggest we foregather at my club for lunch when we can hear what Antonia has to tell us.'

He steamrollered on, before Mansell could get a word in. 'One suggestion. It would be useful to examine Loach's file for his investigation, there may be some clues of value there. Perhaps you could lay your hands on it and bring it along.'

Antonia sensed that Mansell's temper was wearing thin. 'You've forgotten I should have to go to Twiss for it. He would expect me to produce a convincing reason.'

'Can't you think of one?'

'Short of the truth which I do not feel free to reveal to him at this stage – no.'

She kept her eyes down. If she raised them, she would receive a look from Fender indicating a firm expectation that she would get round this trifling problem, employing if necessary a little sleight of hand.

Eventually he said grumpily, 'Very well, if you say so, we must do without it.' He embarked on the operation of rising to his feet. 'I must be off to claim the bed I reserved at my club.'

'If either of you would like to stay – ' she began.

'No, no,' Fender said, not looking towards Mansell. He buttoned his jacket with a good deal of emphasis. 'Mansell will be able to take my taxi on to Twickenham.' His cheeks had become a little pinker than usual.

Watching them descend the stairs, the one lean and nervous in movement, the other like an airship manoeuvring cautiously down to anchorage, for the first time that night she felt tension relax, and grinned.

She was conducted to their presence in the pastel world of the Ladies' Annex of Fender's club. Mansell looked as though he hadn't slept. Fender by contrast was plainly blooming. She guessed he was in a mood to take charge of events. She accepted a large gin and tonic and gazed about her. Other females, some in hats, all in sensible shoes, sat in moquette armchairs under the eye of their protectors.

'How considerate to allow Ladies to use an Annex,' she said.

Fender gave her a doubtful look. 'How did it go with Egerton?'

'Loach seems to have kept very little back from him. Apparently he had a source inside Lissack's house at Rushers Lye, a rather superior sort of maid, named Bridget Boyle. She told Loach that she disliked Lissack but took the job because she's allowed to keep her small daughter with her. Mark didn't know how Loach had managed to recruit her but she's obviously been very useful.

'It was through Bridget that Loach was able to confirm the existence of a close relationship between Lissack and Checkley. She took incoming calls quite often. Checkley gave his name freely at one time without volunteering any other details. Then, about three months ago, he switched to announcing himself as "James Francis". She cottoned on after a while to the fact that it was really Checkley's voice. Lissack always accepted the calls whatever he was doing. She said they appeared to be talking about contracts that Lissack's companies here and in Belfast might get or already had.

'Loach used to meet Bridget in a café in Guildford on her day off – Monday. There was also an arrangement under which she would telephone him if she had a special tidbit. She'd done so just before my second conversation with him on Friday last. Her news was that there had been a call from Checkley the previous night. She was able to hear Lissack's end of the conversation. It was obvious Checkley had rung up in a state of agitation and Lissack was engaged in calming him down. What made the deepest impression on Loach, according to Mark, was Lissack saying, "I tell you there's absolutely nothing for you to worry about. The man who matters knows that if he doesn't do what I say I can blow him out of the water."'

'That was the information Loach decided he wouldn't put on his file . . .' Fender said.

'Yes.'

'Did Loach tell Egerton what he thought it meant?'

'No. He said he had a very good idea who the person was and that Mark would be appalled if he told him the whole story. But he wasn't going to say more to anybody until he was ready with evidence that nobody could contradict.'

They were silent for a while. Fender sighed. 'We are all of course thinking of one disagreeable possibility. But there are several to whom those words might apply. The Head of Defence Procurement for example. We know what his attitude to the investigation was when Twiss went to see him.'

Mansell said grimly, 'The fact that continues to stare us in the face is that Antrim not only knew Lissack but made himself vulnerable by sharing a whore with him.'

'I don't see Antrim giving in to blackmail,' Antonia said. 'It's ridiculous.' But she was conscious of sounding less emphatic this time.

The waiter arrived with menus. When he had gone again, Fender said, 'Did Egerton have anything else to offer?'

'One other thing: Loach had said that at his regular meeting with Bridget on Monday, he was expecting her to come up with details of someone who might be able to add to his knowledge of Lissack's activities. A woman apparently. That might fit with the entry in Loach's diary for Fay Gordon, Loach could have telephoned her and made the appointment when he got back from Guildford.' She glanced at Mansell. 'I could follow it up, if you like.'

Fender intervened before Mansell could answer.

'Wouldn't it be best if I saw the Gordon woman? She'll be expecting a man anyway. I can pass myself off as Loach.'

He smiled modestly at Mansell. 'That is, if you think I can be of service. I see myself, of course, as very much under your direction.'

Mansell's gaze lifted from his menu card, moved on to the wall beyond. A few moments passed before he brought himself to speak. Then he said, 'Good of you to spell it out like that, Ludo.'

8

Fay Gordon was as tall as himself, slim and dark-eyed, and if a certain sharpness about the nose and cheekbones was disregarded, beautiful. The divide between her breasts was exposed by a white dress simple enough to seem like an overall. Her feet were bare. Fender raised his hat. 'Ms Gordon? My name is Loach. I think you're expecting me.'

Pushing back her hair with a forearm she gave a casual nod. 'Hi.'

He stepped inside the door of the apartment, avoiding with difficulty a pile of boxes and an animal cage. She seemed to be accepting him without hesitation or much interest, not even displaying that momentary surprise he saw in the eyes of others when confronted by his bulk. He guessed that very little surprised her.

She led the way down a corridor. 'You sounded different on the phone somehow.' A mild interest had stirred after all. 'Younger.'

'In the flesh I can be a disappointment.'

'Don't let it worry you. My father weighed twenty-three stones and died laughing.'

The legs were bare and elegant; she swung her hips with lazy confidence. It was evident she was wearing very little, if anything, under the white dress. He began to doubt the likelihood of Loach's appointment having anything to do with his investigation of Lissack and Checkley.

They were in a poorly-lit passage, its floor covered in floral-patterned vinyl. A poster of a girl's head had been roughly taped on one wall. A legend underneath seemed to have no relevance to the illustration: he supposed it related to some pop group. The features of the girl were close enough to Fay Gordon's to suggest she'd been the model. Through the perfume cloud she left behind her he was conscious of an animal odour. But this was rising from the floor.

At the end of the passage she opened a door. 'You can come and watch while I'm stripping.'

So he had undertaken a fool's mission. He was being paid back for the baiting of Mansell over Loach's possible homosexual tastes. He sighed under his breath while the tips of his fingers tingled. He was not indifferent to what lay beneath the white dress, even felt stirred by the thought of the spectacle Fate had arranged for him. Fay Gordon was no doubt capable of any demands he cared to make. Perhaps he should summon some up. But he knew that fear of humiliation would prevail.

He followed her, preparing the words that would negotiate his release, speculating on what the no-play charge might be. The room was as charmless as the hall. Here the animal odour was even stronger. He stared astonished. Apart from a single, hard-backed chair and a plastic-topped folding table set up in the middle of the room, there was no furniture. On a bean bag against the far wall a Sealyham terrier eyed him balefully.

Fay Gordon was indicating that he should take the chair. She turned to the dog. 'Jeffrey! Up again, darling.' Jeffrey rose reluctantly and allowed himself to be hoisted up on the table. He was keeping Fender in his sights.

She took a steel comb from a pocket of what was now clearly an overall. 'So what did you want to know about Carl Lissack?'

Fender sat down heavily. He felt a mixture of relief and regret. 'Anything you can tell me. I'm mostly interested in his friends.'

88

'What makes you think he has any?'

'Associates then – the people he does business with.'

She was hesitating. 'This Bureau you said you belong to. I don't know anything about it. It's not the police, is it?'

'No.'

'Because if you think you can persuade me into giving evidence in some case – '

'We don't prosecute people. We try to collect information about politicians and civil servants who accept bribes for favours – that sort of thing. The police are the people who prosecute.'

She gave a laugh. 'You'll have your work cut out to catch Carl giving bribes. He's far too clever. But when he whistles, they all come running. Don't they, darling?' She was addressing the dog now.

A compliment seemed called for. 'He's very handsome.'

'Do you know Sealyhams?'

'I was bitten by one once. Since then I'm glad to say our paths haven't crossed too closely.'

She glanced briefly at him for traces of residual injury. 'They have to understand you're the one on top.' She ran her fingers briskly under the dog's rear then stroked the tail up until it was rigid.

'He's doing a telly commercial job tomorrow. I have to get him right for that.' She went back to deftly stripping hair from the dog's coat. 'As far as bribes go, I can't say for certain I knew anybody who was definitely getting money from Carl. It wouldn't be done like that anyway. Of course he was always entertaining in that bloody great barn of a house, softening people up for some deal or other. Most of them I wouldn't recognize again if they walked into this room now. When you just know somebody for a night, he doesn't stick in your memory unless he's a real bastard.'

So she had been a resident playmate at Rushers Lye, like Sylvia Keysing. 'When were you last at the house?' he asked.

'Three months ago – that was when I walked out. Carl was *livid*.' She smiled relishing the memory. 'He had this enormously important party arranged, a Minister and somebody else coming for the weekend. He was relying on me and the other girl being around.'

'Which Minister was it?'

'The Irish one who died the other day, Cahill – wasn't that the name? The papers came out with the story that he had AIDS.' She grimaced. 'Another good reason for having walked out, I thought.'

He sat back, disappointed. 'Do you know why Lissack regarded the party as so important?'

'No, he just said he'd been trying to get Cahill to stay for some time. They'd had a lot of dealings over property in Ireland in the past.'

'Who was the other guest?'

'Somebody down from London. I don't think Carl ever mentioned the name.'

'Another politician? Or a businessman?'

'I've no idea. Carl had said he was going to introduce him to Cahill as an old friend. We were expected to back up the story. But apparently it wasn't true. Carl had all sorts of ploys like that.'

'So you don't even know his name?'

'No. The other girl told me when we met for a gossip a week or two later that he was a good-looking chap. He was also on the needle.'

When he raised his eyebrows she said, 'You know – drugging.'

'He told her?'

'No. The evening he arrived when they were swimming he made it plain he wanted some fun so she went upstairs with him. While he was in the bathroom having a shower, she glanced in his overnight bag and saw his hypodermic. When she told Carl about it afterwards, he wouldn't believe her at first. I don't know why – it was hardly the first time he'd had somebody who was either sniffing or injecting the stuff.'

It was moderately intriguing but not getting him closer to the interests that had brought him here. 'The other girl – was it Sylvia Keysing?'

She stopped work on the dog for a moment. 'You know about Sylvia then?'

'Only that she lived in the house for a time. I understand she died the other day.'

'Yes, she crashed her car.' She seemed inclined to pursue him on how he had known that Sylvia had been at Rushers Lye but then went back to her labours on Jeffrey. Curiosity was not her strong suit.

'The other girl wasn't Sylvia, it was Christine. She's still living there. She could tell you a lot more about Carl's business than I can. I don't see her talking to you though. She'd be afraid of Carl hearing about it. He can be very nasty!'

'What made you walk out?'

'Living in the sticks was getting me down. I can't think why Carl couldn't be satisfied with a decent house in town. I suppose he felt he was impressing people when he brought them in by helicopter and they saw the giraffes in the zoo running up to watch them land. It was comfortable enough of course. And he didn't mind how you spent your time as long as you were always around to entertain people when he needed it. He wasn't mean either, you could have pretty well anything you wanted.

'But I got to feel I was living in one of those open prisons. Although I went up to town quite a bit there was always the thought in the back of your mind that you had to check in at night – unless Carl was away in Ireland or one of his foreign trips. I got sick of that. Playing games with some of the slobs he expected you to sleep with wasn't a picnic either. He'd never agree to you saying no to anybody and one or two wanted really *weird* things. So when he kicked Jeffrey so hard I had to take him to the vet, just for piddling in his study, I thought, right, this is it, I'm going. If I hadn't, I probably wouldn't have had the chance to fix this deal for Jeffrey to do TV commercials. It's not a fortune but I'm meeting a lot of useful people at the same time.'

Fay Gordon paused to push her hair back again. There were pin-points of moisture on her forehead. Fender decided he had been harsh about the sharpness of her features. He admired the way she held herself. She had no doubt been a delectable sight romping in Lissack's grotto at Rushers Lye. But he felt no desire. Something about the way she handled Jeffrey was off-putting.

He took out his diary. 'I'd like to mention some names of people you might have met at the house.'

'All right. But as I told you, I don't have a good memory.'

'Someone called Checkley – he was a civil servant.'

'No.'

'He also used the name James Francis.'

'Doesn't ring a bell either.'

'What about Jobell. He's head of the government's Defence Procurement Agency.'

She shook her head. He closed the diary and watched her face. 'Cottrell – Alistair Cottrell?'

She frowned. 'Yes, I *do* remember him.' Her eyebrows lifted as though successful recollection had rather shaken her. 'I remember him quite well.'

'. . . Visiting the house?'

'Yes. It was when Sylvia and I were both living there.

He arrived one evening and stayed to dinner. He took a liking to Sylvia. She became a client of his after she left Carl. Maybe even before she left, I'm not sure.'

He felt satisfaction and apprehension in roughly equal proportions. 'Did you get to know anything about him?'

'Only from what Sylvia told me later. He wanted tricks, quite dangerous ones. And he liked to get rough.'

She went back to hunting mats of hair on Jeffrey's hindquarters. 'Carl was the same. He once hurt a girl so badly they had to get a doctor in. He paid her a thousand pounds to keep quiet.'

'Sylvia didn't mind that sort of thing?'

'She reckoned she could handle it, stop it before it went too far. If the money was good enough, Sylvia was game for anything. She liked danger. She was Carl's favourite on account of that. Even after she left him he would ask her to come back for special parties at the house.'

'Did Alistair Cottrell ever come back?'

'If he ever did, it wasn't in my time.'

'Did Sylvia tell you what he did for a living?'

'Only that he wasn't what he said he was when he first came to the house. He'd called himself a journalist. It was supposed to be connected with a sort of profile of Carl. But when she went to his flat she found out that he was something quite different, far more important. I tried to get her to tell me what but she never would.' She gave a crooked smile. 'She was quite fond of him, I think.'

'Do you suppose she ever told Lissack what she'd discovered about Cottrell?'

'She said Carl knew. He'd been amused that Cottrell was so keen on her and was getting her to go to his flat. The rest he knew already. Carl always knew things before anybody else.'

He guessed she still admired Carl a bit, notwithstanding the fact that he'd booted Jeffrey.

93

'Cottrell's one of the people you're interested in, then,' she said.

'Yes.'

'He's really something to do with the government, is he?'

'I'm afraid I can't tell you what he does.'

For once her curiosity had been aroused. 'Is he a politician?'

He shook his head. Her interest began to fade. She pulled Jeffrey round and stroked his tail erect again. 'He was quite attractive,' she said reminiscently. The anal ring quivered as she started scissoring the hair immediately about it. She planted a placatory kiss on the dog's head. 'But not like you, darling.'

As he had promised, he took a taxi direct to Mansell's house in Twickenham. Hilda Mansell opened the door. She looked as disastrous as ever, the blouse of vaguely ethnic character, the skirt wrinkling at the seams, the stockings an imitation of black lace. The hair had acquired a livid shade of chestnut since they had last met. He tried a few gallantries but without appreciably softening her expression of mistrustful reserve. There was no way he would ever please her; or she him.

Mansell seemed washed out; he complained of a sore throat. They settled in armchairs but Fender had barely embarked on describing what Fay Gordon had said when Hilda Mansell re-appeared to insist they eat. Over wafer-thin slices of lamb and *al dente* potatoes she said to Fender, 'I hope you agree with me that stupid story about the girl who crashed her car isn't worth pursuing any more.'

'Certainly one needs to keep a sense of proportion,' he said cautiously.

She glanced in Mansell's direction. 'I haven't seen much

94

of that lately. I'd hoped you'd tell him to forget it altogether. Everybody knows journalists invent most of what they write. If one took every story seriously – '

'I don't think we need go into it over dinner,' Mansell said.

It seemed touch and go whether she would yield but she did. For the rest of the meal her remarks were icily formal. Fender was still reaching for another cheese biscuit when she stood up. 'I suppose you won't want *me* here when you're talking about it. I'll put coffee in the study. Good night, Mr Fender, please don't keep him up late, I think he has a chill.'

Mansell played with the stem of his glass in an embarrassed way as she took herself off; he could hardly be blamed for preferring steam engines.

'I take it you haven't told her about more recent developments,' Fender said.

'No. She supposes it's just a matter of the story in the *Clarion*. She thinks I keep digging in order to *find* trouble.'

'I'm sorry.'

Mansell ran a hand wearily through his hair and rose to lead Fender from the room. In the study, when he had heard what Fay Gordon had said, he groaned. 'So we have to assume the worst. Lissack would have found the knowledge that Antrim was using Sylvia a useful card to keep up his sleeve for the future. When Checkley told him the Bureau were investigating their dealings over the Orange Tip contract, he decided to use it to get Antrim to close the investigation down.'

'That's still not certain.'

'But you agree I have to talk to him . . .?'

'There doesn't seem any alternative.'

Mansell closed his eyes. 'I'd like to discuss how it's to be done.'

'Whenever you like.'

But it seemed he was reluctant to tackle the subject straight away. Fender reached for his coffee. 'Suppose he convinces you that he *hasn't* been pressured by Lissack, that his reasons for closing the investigation down were *bone fide* – what then?'

'Wiping egg off my face I shall have to remind him we're still left with the affair with Sylvia Keysing. That since we can't be sure the press won't discover it was him she was with that night, no doubt he'll agree he must warn Finnessey of the possibility.'

'Who is Finnessey?'

'The new Permanent Under Secretary at the Home Office. He took over last year. Very sensible.'

When Fender pursed his lips, he said, 'I can't see any other course open to him. *I'll* have to tell somebody if he refuses to own up. Finnessey's the obvious person to confide in since it'll be the Home Secretary who will have to handle the political flak if anything comes out. On the other hand, it would be fatal for Antrim to go direct to *him*. I knew the Home Secretary when he was a Junior Minister in Transport. His immediate reaction would be to say Antrim had to resign and to tell Finnessey he wanted an investigation to discover if any more of us in the Bureau were being pleasured by the Sylvia Keysings of the world. Life wouldn't be worth living for months. Things like this need to be put to him very carefully, by someone who knows how to avoid setting off his panic button. If anyone can do that successfully, it's Finnessey. He'd make an announcement of imminent nuclear war sound like a mild deterioration in expected weather patterns. Finnessey is Antrim's best hope of survival.'

Mansell was better informed on the all-important facts of life in Whitehall than he had realized; and, considering his dislike of Antrim, he deserved marks for talking about his survival.

'Then it had better be Finnessey. When will you talk to Antrim?'

'He's off to France on holiday tomorrow. I'll have to tackle him when he gets back. By then we shall know if he said anything of interest to Antonia tonight.'

'Antonia . . . ?'

Mansell sat forward to pour more coffee. 'Sorry, I forgot I hadn't seen you since the latest development over Loach. I reported the facts to Antrim this morning. He didn't say much other than he hoped the media wouldn't make a meal of it. He was out at meetings this afternoon. As I was leaving to come home he telephoned to say he wasn't coming in again because he was going straight to a reception at the American Embassy. He said he wanted to hear the details about Loach from Antonia before his Brussels trip. She was to go round to his flat at eight-thirty, by which time he expected to be back.

'If I could have found an excuse for not sending her I would have done, of course. But I had no choice. So I had her in and discussed what she might say. She'll give as her reason for going to Loach's place the same one as she supplied to the police. She refused at first, saying that she wasn't going to start lying to Antrim. I persuaded her in the end that there was still too much doubt surrounding his position to allow her to be frank.' Mansell gazed into his cup. 'At least I *hope* I persuaded her.'

Fender frowned. 'Why do you say that?'

'After she'd left me, I thought of the affair they'd had. It must have been quite fierce while it lasted. Old feelings could revive when she's alone with him.' He glanced up at the clock behind Fender's head. 'I just wonder if by now she's still in our camp. Or if she's in his.'

9

Unable to find a cab, Antonia made her way wearily on
foot to Antrim's apartment. The streets were frowsty
from the leaden heat that had built up during the afternoon. In a mews off Portland Place, children were taking
it in turns to play a hose on each other.

She wondered how she would feel in the moment of
entering the flat. The last time there, she had been his
mistress, had even begun to suppose that when his divorce
was through they would marry. A time of madness: even
now remembering the self-delusion, the abdication from
rational thought, that total failure to see Antrim plain
brought the blood to her face.

Only on the Ottawa trip with Fender to investigate the
Stradbrook allegation, when she had met Muir, had sanity
started to creep back. Afterwards, in London again, she
had realized she had been living in a fantasy world; one
moreover where even the games had turned to nightmare
and she was no longer sure what sort of a person she was.
Muir had arrived to complete the cure so far as that was
possible. Muir with his laconic gestures and wry smiles
had been a catalyst. For a time it had seemed that he
would become something more. But it hadn't worked out.

Antrim's official car, delivering him back from the
reception at the American Embassy, went by and dropped
him outside his apartment block. He had seen her and
waited for her on the pavement. He was not quite as erect
as when they had first met but still good-looking, the
features smooth and regular, the bronze hair, like the
clothes, immaculate, the manner faintly but not unpleas-

antly arrogant. She knew, but without that disconcerting lift to the heart of a past era, why he had got under her skin.

He put out his arm to guide Antonia up the steps of the apartment block, that easy gesture employed with every woman of even remote bedability. '. . . Hope this didn't ruin your evening.' The tone lightly condescending: it carried the implication that there was surely nothing she would rather be doing. But she noticed his face was flushed and guessed he had drunk a good deal at the reception. That was something new.

As they ascended in the lift he said, 'Cold salmon and asparagus – assuming the caretaker's wife has done as I asked – all right?'

She looked surprised. He went on. 'Didn't Mansell tell you I was arranging supper?'

'No.'

He made an irritated noise. 'That man . . .' He pushed back the lift gate. 'Anyway, you haven't eaten, have you?'

He again put out his arm, this time upon her shoulders. His fingers searched the contours close to her neck, kneaded them briefly. Coupled with the announcement of a supper *à deux*, the gesture could be read as foreshadowing a proposition before the evening was out. On the other hand it had been mechanical, a kind of automatic writing on her flesh. What came over more vividly was the air of preoccupation, the nervous tension already displayed days before when she had gone to his office to warn him that by closing down Loach's investigation without giving reasons he was risking an explosion.

While he was getting drinks, she looked about the drawing room of the apartment. It seemed to be little changed, furniture and curtains and ornaments more or less as she remembered them. To that extent, being here was like stepping back in time. But she felt no melancholy, no regrets. Her breathing came easily. The room was dead for her.

One picture she recognized as new, a large Hockney. Since neither subject matter nor approach would have appealed to him, she supposed it had been acquired in the same campaign by which he had bullied the Property Services Agency to replace with modern paintings the nineteenth-century watercolours in his office. That had been a symbolic act on taking over as Director, a message to all that he was sweeping away the relics of discredited old fools like Lorimount and Harkness. Instead the visions of Eighties Man would prevail.

Returning with their drinks, Antrim removed his jacket and tie and sat down opposite her. 'Hot,' he said. He had opened the windows wide but the air remained stifling.

'Perhaps there'll be a storm.'

'It was murderous at the Embassy, I thought at one time the air-conditioning must have failed.'

'Was the reception for anyone interesting?'

'It was arranged for Cleveland, the President's envoy to the talks with Dublin. It was pretty pointless inviting me since I have less than nothing to do with them. God knows why I was there – I rather think Baxter accepted without consulting me.'

He wasn't being candid of course. He would never regard his presence at a function like that as pointless.

'Did you talk to Cleveland?'

'For a couple of minutes.'

'He looked very tough in his newspaper photographs.'

'I'd say he's tough but not particularly well informed. When I told him who I was, he asked me about the problems of smuggling arms into Northern Ireland from here. I suppose he has a hazy idea the Bureau must be the equivalent of the FBI.' He grimaced and lay back. 'It doesn't say much for the briefing the Embassy gave him.

However perhaps they decided not to bother too much. I have the strong impression they don't rate him among their more popular visitors from Washington.'

He had crossed his legs. As usual, one foot had begun to jig restlessly up and down. His energy seemed undiminished. But the skin along his jawbone was curiously shiny.

'I saw somebody I recognized limping about in Cleveland's shadow. A CIA man named Tom Busch I used to meet off and on when I was what Mansell chooses to call "a funny".' He grimaced again, this time with malevolence; she had not realized how warmly Mansell's distaste for Antrim was reciprocated. 'Busch acquired his limp in some exploit in Vietnam I could never get him to talk about. I bearded him and asked if he was ensuring Cleveland got the intelligence picture on The Troubles right. He said that would be too much to hope for. Cleveland, according to Busch, had asked for a profile of King Billy. He'd heard he was an influential troublemaker in the North.'

'A wit,' she said.

'He claimed his most important brief for Cleveland had been copies of reports by a Special Envoy of the Pope sent to Ireland in the eighteen eighties. Everyone apparently treated him as a stooge of the British government. He told Rome that no other mission he'd undertaken could compare with it for beastliness.'

Fender, with his appetite for all things papal, might appreciate the story. 'Is that what Busch is really supposed to be doing, briefing Cleveland on the facts? I wouldn't have thought there was anything left to discover about the Irish situation.'

'God knows. Perhaps he's keeping an eye on Cleveland. The State Department have their own men invigilating him as well. Very wise, I'd say.'

'Does Busch believe there's going to be a big new deal with prizes for everybody?'

'I didn't ask. With all the American money being waved about, there probably is. But the basic situation won't be changed. They've been reared on violence for generations, nothing's going to stop it.'

He said it comfortably, not just indifferent, at peace with the idea. Ireland could stew in its own juice.

Over the salmon, he said, 'About Loach: I wouldn't normally let this sort of thing bother me but I began to wonder this afternoon if his suicide could have had any connection with my decision last Friday to stop his investigation.'

She waited with a neutral expression.

'He seems to have supposed nothing else in the world could possibly matter as much as his bloody case. Mansell says he was immature and allowed himself to become obsessed. God knows why we recruited him with defects like that. I gather I was abroad when he came to an Appointments Board.'

'I thought he was just rather intense.'

'He must have been unbalanced. However since he'd confided in you, I thought you might have a view on exactly why he took his life. I had to talk to you tonight because I'm taking a holiday in France for a fortnight. I didn't want to leave it until I got back.'

She began cautiously, 'The whole situation's rather puzzling.'

'What made you go to his flat, by the way? He wasn't one of your own officers. Did you have any reason to think something had happened to him?'

'He'd been very upset on Friday when you wouldn't talk to him about your reasons for shutting down his investigation. I'd heard he hadn't been seen in the office on Monday or Tuesday. I decided to look in on him since his flat's nearby.'

Surprisingly he didn't ask exactly how she'd got in. 'I understand from Mansell that the police view it as pretty straightforward.'

'They did up to the time I left them.'

For a moment she suspected from his expression that he had caught a nuance she had not intended he should. But he nodded. 'Nothing in the flat in the way of notes, last letters and so on?'

'Nothing.'

'I gather the police asked you about his work.'

'They wanted to know if he'd been depressed. I said he'd allowed his work to get on top of him. They left it at that.'

'You didn't tell them anything about the actual case I hope?'

'No.'

'So do *you* think my decision had anything to do with his death?'

She shrugged.

'I suppose you believe I was wrong, that I ought to have talked to him on Friday evening?'

'I thought it a pity you didn't give him any reasons. He'd become very committed to bringing Checkley to book. Everybody else had encouraged him to think he was doing the right thing to press hard. Then you stopped him in his tracks.'

'As a junior officer he should have accepted what he was told to do without expecting explanations. In any case I wasn't free to give the reasons for my decision.'

'If you'd found the time to say even that to him it might have made him happier.'

He shook his head impatiently. 'It seems extraordinary to let the thing get to him to the extent of ending his life.

You don't suppose he'd persuaded himself there was something *wrong* with my decision?'

She felt a tingling in her hands. 'Wrong? How do you mean – wrong?'

'Perhaps he thought I was protecting Checkley or Lissack or both of them – that there was some hidden connection. Did he give any hint of thinking on those lines when you talked to him?'

'None.'

He fiddled with his fork. She noticed he had eaten very little of his salmon. 'It so happens, that if he *was* in the mood to think the worst, there's a note on a file that could have started him off. Do you remember the Dyerson case?'

'I remember the name. But I wasn't involved in it.'

'It must have been before you moved into the section with me. Ludo Fender was running the Division at the time. I went to see Carl Lissack because it seemed possible he could throw some light on what Dyerson had been up to. He provided a few snippets and gave me a rather good dinner at his house just outside Guildford. He invited me to lunch two or three times after that. I suppose he regarded me as a potentially useful contact.' She was conscious that Antrim was watching her as he talked. 'The file was closed long ago but would still be held in your section registry. If Loach had asked for it for any reason he would have been obliged to put his request through you. Has he asked for any files of yours lately?'

'No.'

'That's absolutely certain?'

'Absolutely.'

'How about when you've been on leave or away somewhere?'

'I haven't been away from the office for over two months.'

He grunted. 'I may have to do something about that file.'

Trying to make her voice casual she asked, 'When did you last see Lissack?'

'About two years ago at the Connaught. He tried pumping me for information on a business competitor he'd somehow discovered the Bureau was investigating. I had to fend him off. He didn't ring me again after that although I used to hear occasional snippets about him from a friend.'

To keep him talking without appearing over-interested was the trick that had to be turned.

'I've read somewhere that his private life is quite colourful. Does your friend know him well?'

'Pretty well.' He ate another scrap of the salmon, then pushed his plate away. 'At least she did. Unfortunately she died the other day.'

The ice was paper thin but she couldn't bring herself to back off.

'Was she a close friend?'

He looked up to gaze at her sharply, then shrugged. 'Not really.'

He was giving nothing away. But that was hardly surprising.

While she was finishing her meal he smoked a small cigar and drank more wine. He hadn't lost the tension in his features but, with Loach apparently no longer preoccupying him, his attention was beginning to focus on her. She was certain now that she wouldn't escape before he tried a pitch. She needed to make an effort to get him talking about the Checkley/Lissack business in what time remained. She said, 'I can't help being curious about your reasons for stopping Loach's investigation.'

He moved an ashtray to and fro beside his plate. 'It's extremely delicate.'

'I realize that.'

He hesitated. She knew he was trying to gauge if any advantage lay in pleasing her.

'Can't you say a little?'

'Well . . .' He shrugged. 'Don't ever let me down by repeating this. When I got back here from the West Country on Thursday evening, I was called to an urgent meeting. It was at a Minister's house. When I arrived I was asked about the stage we'd reached in the Lissack investigation. I explained. I was then told the government was in the middle of some crucial negotiations to which Lissack was making a vital contribution. Because of the importance of keeping his cooperation, it had been decided that action against him over his dealings with Checkley would have to stop. The balance of public interest lay in leaving him alone for the foreseeable future. I was given some of the background – I had to accept it made reasonable sense to back off for a while. Because of the delicacy surrounding the whole thing I agreed to keep the facts to myself and to present the decision to stop the investigation to staff in the Bureau as my own.' He tapped away ash from the cigar. 'That's why I couldn't say more to Loach. And it's up to you to forget what you've just heard.'

He had the ability to be a convincing liar. On the other hand she found it impossible to believe that over something like this he would deceive.

'So although we know he's a crook, he's to be allowed to get away with it.'

'Apparently.'

'And Checkley as well . . .'

'In his case through a piece of providential luck.' Antrim had risen. 'Now you know, let's forget about Lissack and Checkley. These days we never get the opportunity to see each other except across a desk. I often wonder about you.'

He moved behind her chair. 'Still living alone in that flat?'

'Yes.'

'No man around . . .'

'No.'

'Sounds bad.'

'Not really.'

'Someone told me you once seriously thought of marrying that Canadian, Muir. Is it true?'

'It was for a while.'

'You'd have found him hopelessly dull.'

Both his hands were on her shoulders, the thumbs gently pressing against the top of her spine. 'We had a good thing going.'

She kept her eyes ahead of her.

'Don't you agree it was rather special?'

'One changes.'

He was sliding his fingers under the shoulder seams of her dress. 'You couldn't change in that way. I know you too well.'

'You have to believe me.'

'I understand what *you* need. And you know what *I* need. Why don't we just get back to where we were?'

She jerked herself free from his grasp and rose. As she moved away, he swung her round to face him. '*Relax!*' His voice was quietly chiding as though she had been a little wilful.

She forced herself to look into his eyes. The expression there seemed to be a shifting mixture of desire, and threat and appeal. He no longer possessed quite the assurance she had once found compelling. Some draining away of confidence had happened; the search for an ultimate in his accounting with women had become soured by a suspicion that *feeling* would always escape him.

Gripping both her wrists, he twisted them up behind her. She experienced no fear but a certain apprehension. If she allowed him to continue forcing her backwards on to the sofa beside which she now stood, let his mouth cover hers while all the time the hurt from her wrists was growing, there could come a moment, once familiar, even intoxicating, when out of the blur of pain a fuse flame of pleasure would creep flickering and spreading until it and the pain were indistinguishable.

She forced her knee sharply into his groin and heard him gasp. His grip relaxed. By the time he had recovered, she had a chair between them.

He had not given up hope. He shook his head in mild reproof. Very slowly so as not to prompt an immediate reaction, he stretched out a hand and touched her upper arm.

'Don't,' she said.

'*Why not?*'

'I just don't want it any more. From you. From anybody.'

In defeat, his mouth went slack for a moment. She felt she was seeing how his face would crumble with age. Then he compressed his lips. 'All right, perhaps you'd better go. Do you want a taxi?'

She was being given an easier escape than she had thought possible. She shook her head. 'I can pick one up outside.'

At the door he said unexpectedly, 'Sorry about that, I rather let go. The fact is it's been a trying fortnight. I've been waiting to see if the press would pick up what could have been a rather inconvenient story. It doesn't look as though they will now. But it's left me feeling jagged.'

He smiled: assurance was returning. 'You won't be

talking about this, I hope. I wouldn't like Mansell to think I misled him about why I wanted to see you. He's easily shocked, I find.'

His expression boldly invited assent from her. He couldn't feel sure she would agree; but he was gambling on it. He would always live on the edge of danger, she thought; anything else would bore him. If he knew what had taken place between her and Mansell and Fender in the past few days, that would surely strike him as danger enough.

As she descended in the lift, she drew her first deep breath for what seemed an age. She could think of how she had dealt with him, not as a victory but as proof that she would never know defeat at his hands again. Yet, she had been aware of it being a near thing for a moment. Crossing the hall, she noticed her hands were shaking.

10

With Antrim safely on the wing, she had supposed another hole-in-the-corner conference could be ruled out; there would surely be a meeting in Mansell's room to talk over what she and Fender had gleaned.

She waited the following morning for a call. When by ten o'clock nothing had happened, she went to Mansell's office. She found him in the ante-room; an impassive Hazel was crushing tablets into a glass of water. He drank the result.

Over his shoulder as she followed him into his own room, he croaked, 'I seem to have something coming on.' He was certainly looking frayed.

'I was wondering when you planned to have a meeting.'

'We could talk now.'

'Won't Ludo be coming?'

'No.' He sat down heavily behind his desk. 'He had a call at his club early this morning. Apparently there was a storm in Mayfield last night which brought down a large part of his chimney. He's gone back to arrange for it to be repaired. He came to dinner with me last night so fortunately I already know what he learned from the Gordon woman.'

She waited: but it seemed he didn't propose to confide those details to her for the present. She sat down opposite him. A little satisfaction was managing to bubble up through his malaise. Having sensed in Fender the waxing of the old itch to take charge of events, he was relishing the prospect of being his own man again. Given that it was he who had ultimately to decide what, if anything, was to be done about Antrim and about the mystery of Loach's death, she could sympathize.

She began to tell him what Antrim had said about why he had had to call a halt to Loach's investigation. He adopted an elaborate frown; he was working up to be sceptical for some reason of his own. But before she had finished her account, the door behind her opened. Hazel placed a typed note on Mansell's pad and stood waiting.

He groaned. 'Can't Baxter put them off?'

'He's tried. The Treasury say somebody has to go through the justification with them this morning. He managed to speak to the Director on the telephone at Heathrow. It was decided you'd be the best person to do it in his absence.'

He cursed, letting his arms fall limply down the sides of his chair. He obviously wished he felt ill enough to announce he wasn't going anywhere except to bed. 'Why can't he stop his bloody Empire-building?'

Laboriously reading the note at an angle, she deduced the rest of the story. Antrim's annual campaign to extract more of everything from the Treasury had reached the moment of truth. Down in Great George Street the keepers of the purse were planning to suspend Mansell upside down and tell him the Bureau would have to make do with what fell from his pockets.

She left him stuffing files into a briefcase and went back to her own work. Within half an hour Fender was on the line. He had arrived at his cottage and had been trying to get through to Mansell. She told him what had happened. He grunted. 'So he's had no time to do anything?'

'I shouldn't think so.'

'Good. Tell him when he returns I've dealt with all that's necessary down here and am returning by the next train so that we can discuss the next move. If you'll both join me at my club again, at, say, one fifteen I shall be delighted to give you lunch. Will you tell him that?'

She tried picturing Mansell's face and was not encouraged.

'Are you sure you should come back so soon? What about your chimney?'

'The builder can get on with that without me.' He rang off.

She decided she was not going to be the Aunt Sally who delivered the message to Mansell. She left a note with Hazel and told her she'd be making her own way to Fender's club.

When she arrived, they were hunched over gins. The alacrity with which they rose to greet her suggested that the going had been sticky up to now. Mansell seemed more wan than ever. Fender by contrast looked ebullient; he had changed his suit and shirt and wore a small rose in his buttonhole. The calamity of the falling chimney had left no visible mark on his morale.

She told them what she had learned from Antrim, about the summons he had received to discuss the Lissack investigation, the order to discontinue the enquiries.

Mansell had drawn in the sides of his mouth while she talked but Fender was clearly enlivened. It was the sort of intrigue he relished. 'How very interesting – *fascinating*! Antrim was wrong to agree to withhold from staff the reason for the requirement. But I can sympathize – it was a difficult situation. What do you suppose is the role Lissack is playing which is so vital to the government at present? Something to do with the negotiations with Dublin perhaps?'

The speed with which he seemed to have accepted Antrim's explanation took Antonia aback. It was unlike him not to worry away for longer at unsupported pronouncements. She wondered if he was pretending to be convinced simply for Mansell's benefit.

He had turned to Mansell. 'I think we can now breathe more easily. I take it you feel reassured.'

'I'd like to think it over a little more, together with the Gordon woman's story.' Mansell's feelings were clearly mixed. But most of all, she suspected, he didn't want to agree with Fender.

'What *did* Fay Gordon have to say?' she asked.

When Fender had told her, she said, 'Did you ask her if Lissack used thugs against people who got in his way or were a threat to him?'

He shook his head impatiently. 'She wouldn't have known about that side of his affairs.' He hated any hint that he had overlooked a question.

She was disinclined to indulge his vanity. 'I wish you'd asked her, all the same. I'm absolutely convinced now that Loach was murdered. Lissack decided he was becoming too dangerous.'

She looked at Mansell. 'You do agree we have to go on digging – irrespective of what Lissack happens to be doing that the government regards as so important? Corruption is one thing. Letting him get away with murder is another.'

She was glad to see she had made him uncomfortable. 'I understand your feelings . . .'

'But . . .?'

He licked his lips. 'There is in fact another task I need you to take on before I can decide how to proceed. It's to do with Loach's source in Lissack's house.'

'The maid?'

'Yes, Bridget Boyle. She telephoned on Loach's extension this morning. I'd arranged for his calls to be diverted to my secretary for a few days thinking it would be as well to filter them. The call was to say that she wanted an

113

urgent meeting with Loach. She gave the address of a coffee bar in Guildford where she would be waiting at eleven-thirty tomorrow morning. Hazel avoided saying what had happened to Loach and simply promised to pass the message on. Obviously the woman must be seen – not in order to pursue Lissack's dealings with Checkley of course but in case she has any light to throw on – on other matters.'

She wasn't enthusiastic to oblige. He could after all ask Fender to go. If she hesitated long enough, Fender would jump in anyway, as he had over Fay Gordon. But she wouldn't then have the chance of discovering for herself if Bridget Boyle could make a contribution over Loach's death.

'All right, I'll see her.'

Fender was looking into the distance and blinking. If she interpreted the signs right, there was something being plotted. The explanation came after lunch when Mansell left them to take a call from Hazel. As his back receded across the room, Fender said, 'I have a favour to ask.'

She sipped coffee watchfully.

'I realize that returning from Guildford to London via my cottage would make your journey rather circuitous. But I should be immensely interested to hear what the maid has to say.'

She conjured a rough road map into her mind. At a guess the idea added at least another forty miles to the trip.

'I can telephone you as soon as I get back.'

'There could be difficulties on an open line. But I had another consideration in mind, I hoped to persuade you to stay to dinner. It's been a while since you came to the cottage.'

Nearly a year, in fact, she thought: Egerton had been

114

in the midst of his troubles over the Lauren Giordano affair and together they had gone to enlist Fender's help.

'Also,' he said, 'there is something I've just acquired I'd like you to see. I found it in a shop in Lewes. I think it will appeal to you.'

His cheeks had become pinker. From egocentric boldness he was beginning to slide into anxious entreaty. This was the way he always trapped her.

She smiled. 'I'll come.'

Mansell returned. With an elaborate gesture, Fender pushed back his chair from him, and shook his head sympathetically as Mansell suppressed a shiver. He clicked his fingers to catch the barman's eye. He was at his most benevolent. 'Medication for Mr Mansell, Victor. A large Remy Martin I think.'

Bridget Boyle was not as she had imagined her. Small and fragile-seeming, fastidiously dressed, one side of her face almost hidden by a curtain of glossy black hair, she sat reading an Irish newspaper in a corner of the coffee bar. The idea of so delicate a creature working in the hot-house atmosphere that must surely be the norm at Lissack's mansion seemed ridiculous.

The exterior proved deceptive. Beneath it was flinty determination that the world's opportunities to do her down would be limited to the minimum. She was tough and watchful. The news of Loach's death surprised but didn't rock her. Her response was calm. 'He always struck me as a worrying man.'

She lit a cigarette. 'So is it with you I shall be dealing now?'

'Yes.'

'You know when we had a meeting he used to pay me thirty pounds?'

'That'll continue as long as we need your reports.'

She eyed Antonia reflectively. 'You have the same sort of job?'

She nodded.

'Although you're a woman . . . ?'

'Just the same.'

'I doubt you'd manage that in Ireland.' She laughed. The sound was soft, with a lilt to it. She saw herself as on absolutely level terms.

'You lived there until recently, did you?'

'Yes.'

'What made you come to England?'

'To get work. And because of the child. Mr Loach told you about the child, I suppose.'

'I knew you had a small girl.'

'It's easier to get a decently paid job over here and keep a child with you. You don't see unmarried mothers much in the town I come from. It would make the priests uncomfortable.' She blew smoke and watched it rise. 'That would never do.'

If the meeting was to get on to the right footing, some authority had to be established over her. Antonia said, 'I haven't got too much time. Perhaps you'll tell me why you telephoned for a meeting.'

'I thought you would want to know someone else is taking an interest in Lissack. He says he's a writer, a journalist. I think that could be just a story.'

It seemed that about a week before, one of Lissack's gardeners had mentioned a man he'd met in a local pub. The man had said he was writing articles on the life styles of successful businessmen in different countries. He wanted some colourful stuff to work into his piece on the UK and had heard Lissack's domestic arrangements were in the right category. He said he would pay for inside information. The gardener, who hated journalists, told him to get lost.

Two days ago, a man, presumably the same, had got into conversation with Bridget on the bus into Guildford. After chatting her up for a few minutes he raised the same subject. After asking her if it was true there were orgies in the grotto under the house, the man made a reference to her Irish accent and mentioned he'd heard that an Irish Minister who'd died recently, Cahill, had been a guest in the house. Perhaps she'd like to earn a little by telling him what went on that weekend – who was there, was an orgy laid on and so forth. She replied she'd think the offer over and asked for a telephone number. The man said that would be difficult, he was moving around, he'd tell her more if she would meet him in Guildford the next day. She didn't go.

'Lissack receives a lot of attention from columnists,' Antonia said. 'What makes you think this wasn't a real journalist?'

'He had too much class. Also, he was an educated man.' She said it as though presenting the incontrovertible proof of a contrary. Irish journalists she'd encountered must have been a poor lot.

The coincidence of the Cahill visit having featured in Fay Gordon's story was faintly interesting; but none of this seemed likely to connect up with Loach and his enquiries. Only a grudging respect for Fender's omnivorous methods made her ask another question. 'Who else did Lissack have there for the weekend?'

'One of his usual girls was around the place. And a man who'd driven down from London.'

'Can you describe him?'

'About forty-five, average height, good-looking. Small moustache.'

Something stirred in her mind. 'Did he have fair hair?'

'Yes.'

'Was it receding?'

'Yes.'

'What was his name?'

'Ellis or Elliott, I think.'

She felt a sudden certainty it was the man the liquor store manager had seen going into Loach's flat. She leaned forward. 'It could be very important for me to discover this man's address.'

'I can't help on that.'

'Do you suppose any of the other servants would know?'

'I shouldn't think so. It seems he'd never been to the house before. I got the impression that Lissack didn't know him well.'

'Is there no way we can get a clue to who he was? *Think!*'

Bridget's eyes wandered over the table top. She was thinking all right but she was also enjoying the sense of dependence on her. Eventually she reached for the ash-tray to stub out her cigarette. 'There *is* one chance. His car, a brown Estate, was giving some trouble – I heard him talking about it to Lissack soon after he arrived. Lissack told me to get on to the local garage. A mechanic arrived the next morning and took the car away for a few hours. I don't know whether Lissack had the bill put on his own account. Probably he did. But if he didn't, the details you want could be at the garage.'

It was an outside chance, but worth exploring. She took down the name of the garage. 'Did you get the impression that Ellis or Elliott was treated as an equal by the others?'

It was the first question Bridget had found foxing. She put her hand under the curtain of hair and frowned a little. 'I think so. When I saw them together, it looked like that.'

'Did he talk to you at all?'

118

'Not much. He asked me where I came from in Ireland and mentioned he'd been in the North when he was serving in the Army. But that was all. Not like Cahill: he'd chat when I took him his morning tea. He discovered I was born near Killagaline where his wife comes from. We talked about local characters. On the Sunday morning he asked me to get him some aspirin because he felt unwell – they'd been up drinking until all hours. He told me he'd had a nightmare of being kidnapped by a gang of Prots from the North. One of them had had a hypodermic and said he was to be injected with a drug that would cause him to stand up in public and announce the Pope sent the Irish government its orders every Friday.' She gave the soft, lilting laugh.

Perhaps Cahill had laughed too, Antonia reflected. There weren't many more laughs left to him by then. He must already have known there was something seriously wrong with him.

'He hadn't long to live when he stayed with Lissack.'

'Dirty habits,' Bridget said. 'There's always a price.' She gazed sombrely at Antonia. Perhaps she was a good Catholic girl after all.

At the back of her mind she knew there was a question she had wanted to ask. She tried in vain to recall it. However there was something else she ought to explore, if only to discover whether Loach had ever raised it. 'Have you heard of anyone named Alistair Cottrell?'

'I don't think so.'

'He came to the house at least once.' She described Antrim's appearance. Bridget shook her head emphatically. 'I've never seen him. Maybe it was before my time.'

'Did Mr Loach ever mention the name?'

'No.'

A girl came to their table to clear away the empty cups. Bridget looked at her watch. 'I must catch my bus.'

'One more thing. Would you say Lissack is the sort of person who would employ strong-arm men to deal with people who became a nuisance?'

'Mr Loach asked me that once.'

'What did you say?'

'That he'd stop at nothing. Nothing at all.'

'Have you a special reason for believing that?'

'I know him,' she said simply. It was another of her pronouncements allowing no possibility of doubt. In her quiet, steely way she was very impressive.

'When do you want another meeting?' she asked.

'I'll let you know. What routine did you have with Mr Loach for him to contact you?'

'There would be a postcard signed Patrick. That was a signal for me to telephone. Perhaps we should have another name, as your handwriting will be different.'

They agreed on Teresa. When Antonia produced the thirty pounds, Bridget counted the notes as she placed them in her bag. She didn't say thanks.

'When you saw Mr Loach last Monday, did he seem different in any way?'

'Different?'

'I wondered if he was particularly excited or pleased – anything unusual.'

'He was very jumpy. I got the impression he'd been talking to somebody else during the weekend. He was pleased I'd been able to get him Fay Gordon's address but seemed to think that after all she wouldn't be able to help him much. He'd discovered something new and said he was having to face the fact that he wasn't dealing with corruption but murder as well. But proving it would be impossible.' She shrugged. 'I suppose you know all this.'

Outside the coffee bar, Bridget, waiting to cross the street, said, 'I remember he made a sort of joke when we parted. "If you don't see me again, you'll know I've ended up at the bottom of the Thames in a concrete suit."' She turned with a coolly questioning look. 'I suppose you're sure he did hang himself?'

11

Seated on the terrace of the cottage, she gazed above her while Fender fetched their drinks. A corner of the blue tarpaulin which covered the hole where half the chimney had collapsed was visible. The sky beyond displayed a sullen glare, harsh on the eyes. During the drive from Guildford the sun had begun its retreat into a gathering mass of high cloud. Here, at the cottage, its outline had finally vanished, leaving a legacy of shadeless heat.

In the garden beside her, roses were everywhere, oddly brilliant in this unblinking light. She saw that the Céline Forestier climber she had sent him for Christmas had been planted in a spot near the gate where a clump of nettles had once been preserved in the interests of butter-flies. There were signs of dead-heading in the main flowerbed. Although she knew a man came once a week to keep the garden in order, she guessed, observing the spent blooms grandly discarded on all sides, this had been Fender's work. His contribution to garden chores would be tailored to exclude all activity below the waist.

He came through the French windows with a tray on which, as well as their drinks there were dishes of savoury biscuits and olives, a rare act of pre-planning. He had taken unusual trouble over his appearance, the suit newish, the shoes freshly polished, his tie the impressive striped affair worn in Rome for his appointment with the Pope when he was pursuing the odd exploits of the *Vigiles*. The wayward spikes of hair usually visible at the point of his parting had been flattened too. He had decided that this was An Occasion.

His manner on her arrival, however, had signalled he was put out. She had been much later than expected. Any departure from a time scale on which he had settled in his mind always went down badly, regardless of the reasons. In the matter of expectation, he was rigid. Her explanation of having to go from the meeting with Bridget Boyle to the garage, in search of some record of the car repair that might identify Lissack's other weekend guest, of then returning to the police in Guildford to make further enquiries, he had listened to politely. But his expression said she had obviously dawdled on the way.

Now it seemed he had relaxed again. Subsiding into the other chair beside the terrace table he raised his glass to her. 'How very nice you look.' An odour of *eau de Cologne* drifted across. He had really pushed the boat out.

'Since it's her husband's birthday, I decided to give Mrs Bastin the evening off. I've arranged for us to dine at the restaurant across the street at seven-thirty. I hope you won't think that's too early.'

She smiled and shook her head.

Abruptly he levered himself up again and went off to the wall beside the garden gate. He came back with a bud from the Céline Forestier and placed it beside her with an awkward gesture. '*Your* rose,' he said. 'The perfume is very distinctive. Like yourself.'

He looked away quickly, quenching embarrassment. 'Loach's remark about having to deal not just with corruption but murder as well – what's to be made of that?'

'I find it totally baffling.'

'Yet he was clearly being serious.' He shook his head, frowning. 'Wanted – one corpse. But, *where to look*?'

He sighed and changed the subject. 'So the garage had kept a record of the car number.'

'Yes, it's registered to a company – Ellitt Personal Protection Services with an address in Crawshaw Street, Pimlico. The London telephone directory gives a Ronald Ellitt at the same address.'

'And you believe this could be the man the liquor store manager saw going with Loach into his flat . . .'

'. . . where he murdered him.'

'Don't you feel you're being a little premature in rejecting other possible explanations? Ellitt could simply have been a new source. He and Loach could have gone to the flat to talk.'

'Loach may have thought that was all they were going to do. In fact Ellitt went with a specific brief – to kill Loach in a way that would not arouse suspicion he'd been murdered.'

She was sounding more certain than she actually felt but was reluctant to start hedging now. 'It fits in with all we know. Presumably Ellitt as well as providing orthodox protection services also offers final solutions if the fee is right. His company could even be one of Lissack's subsidiaries.'

Fender chewed an olive with a benevolent expression. She sensed a counter attack was on the way. 'Does that altogether chime with what Bridget Boyle told you? She said Lissack seemed hardly to know Ellitt. That was also the impression I got from the Gordon woman – that he was a virtual stranger.'

'All right, it doesn't affect – '

He went on as though she had not been speaking. 'What I find totally inexplicable is why Lissack should choose a man like Ellitt, assuming him to be what you say he is, as his house guest on an occasion when he was presumably engaged in wheeling-and-dealing with an Irish Cabinet Minister.'

'Cahill would have been concerned for his security

when visiting this country. His anti-British line and sympathy for the IRA must have made him a lot of enemies. When Lissack invited him over for a private visit, he said he'd come – but what about his personal security? Lissack told him not to worry, he knew somebody who was in the protection business. He'd have him about the house the whole weekend.'

'You'll forgive me if I retain a fraction of doubt.'

'Can you do better?'

'Not at the moment.' He was frowning. 'Incidentally, what caused the maid to suppose you would be interested in Ellitt?'

She shook her head. 'I've told you only half the story. Her account of the weekend when Cahill and Ellitt were at the house came out only by the way. The reason she telephoned for a meeting was that she felt she ought to report that somebody else was making enquiries about Lissack.'

She told Fender Bridget Boyle's story of the man who had claimed to be a writer. 'At first it seemed to me that was probably all he was. But I doubt if her judgment of people is often wrong. Anyway when it led on to Lissack's weekend party and her description of Ellitt I got caught up with that to such an extent that I forgot to ask her what sort of a man the writer was, whether he gave a name and so on. I had to run after her when she left me to get a description. He hadn't offered his name.'

'Was the description useful?'

She hesitated.

He raised his eyebrows. 'What *was* it?'

'Tall, grey-haired, American accent.' She paused again.

His eyes were fixed on her face. 'What caused you to hesitate?'

She was opening herself up to ridicule. 'A rather eerie

125

coincidence. I realize it makes no sense to imagine there's more to it. But it stuck in my mind.'

'You might as well tell me.'

'This man's main interest seemed to be finding out details of Cahill's stay in the house. Bridget said something about him which echoed a remark Antrim made to me the other night. He'd met a man attached to the staff of Cleveland, the White House envoy to the Anglo-Irish talks. His name's Tom Busch and be belongs to the CIA. Busch apparently had an accident once that left him with a limp. The coincidence is that Bridget's writer also had a limp.'

She saw, or thought she saw, his lips twitch. 'I know,' she said. 'It makes no sense. What possible interest could Cleveland have in getting Busch to make enquiries about the weekend Cahill spent at Rushers Lye? It's ridiculous.'

His expression was indulgent. 'No, no, one must keep one's mind open to all possibilities.'

It was plain he didn't want to risk spoiling the evening with a more acid rejoinder.

One of Fender's intimates, the village cat known as General Tarragon, appeared on the garden wall but observing her presence withdrew. 'I'm beginning to feel guilty about Mansell,' she said. 'If I'm staying to dinner, I ought to telephone and let him know how the talk with Bridget went.'

He waved a hand dismissively. 'No need.'

'Why?'

'He's confined to bed and not taking calls.'

'I thought it was just a cold he had coming on.'

'No, it's more serious. I spoke on the telephone this morning to his wife. She said he couldn't be disturbed.'

He could be exaggerating, in order to consign Mansell to the back burner. That way he might hope to arrogate fresh intrigues in the *Curia* but the night they had spent together in the *pensione* in Trastavere.

Midway through their meal he said, 'What do you consider should be done about Antrim?'

She avoided answering. 'I'm glad that's something I don't have to decide. At least we know now there was nothing wrong with his reasons for stopping Loach's investigation.'

She wondered if he would remind her that they only had Antrim's word for that. But he let it go and said, 'We are still left with his relationship with Sylvia Keysing. It can hardly be dismissed as unimportant. Some would say he has opened himself unacceptably to the risk of blackmail.'

'I don't believe that. Nor do you.'

Fender traced a small circle with the base of his wine glass. 'You retain a certain regard for him.'

She shrugged.

'It's not, of course, a case of simple whoring – in view of what appears to be his taste for – for violent encounters.'

'The newspaper story probably exaggerated. Anyway, people who have difficulty in controlling violence in their sexual feelings sometimes find it a help to use ritual acts for what would otherwise be dangerous. I imagine he paid the girl to go through the ritual with him. Is that so very wrong?'

She saw she had embarrassed him. He was wondering about her own relationship with Antrim, about how far it had gone and whether she would call what took place between them ritual . . . But to those questions, neither he nor anyone else would learn the answers.

She adopted a lighter tone of voice. 'Anyway, you were asking what ought to be done. Perhaps you and Mansell

131

should find him a wife who'll agree to cope with his particular needs.' She smiled.

He didn't smile back: facetiousnes was plainly not welcome.

She said briskly, 'So far as I'm concerned, the most important thing is to bring Lissack and Ellitt to book for Loach's murder. I'm going to start investigating Ellitt when I get back to London. Do you agree?'

He was frowning. 'This ought not to be going on without Antrim's knowledge. Didn't you say he was on holiday in France?'

'Yes, but he could be called back. Baxter must have his address.'

He shook his head. 'I can hardly take that decision in Mansell's absence.' He seemed genuinely in doubt as to what he should do. Eventually he said, 'I agree you should make enquiries about Ellitt – but with great care.' He reached out and touched her hand. 'This has become a dangerous business.'

When they returned to the cottage he said, as he brought coffee from the kitchen, 'If the drive back to London tonight lacks appeal, I should be delighted if you would stay over.' His voice was carefully casual.

She took a cigarette from her bag, irritated that she had failed to allow for the possibility that he would say something like this. 'I really ought to go. I'd planned an early start tomorrow – I'm spending the day with my mother in Shropshire. It's her birthday.'

'Of course,' he said, 'you *must* go in that case.' He stood with his back to the inglenook, impassively drinking coffee. He offered no further comment.

She remained uncertain whether she should leave it like that. It would have been possible for her to drive direct to Shropshire from his cottage. She had half-expected he would make that suggestion. Shyness could have dictated his response; she was almost sure he was masking disappointment.

But had he simply decided to make a virtue of her going? This could be an occasion when re-asserting self-sufficiency was important to him. For years he had fought to conceal loneliness from the world, to pretend that a room empty of all except God and memories was enough. If he now wished to appear indifferent to her going, she ought perhaps to allow him that kind of victory.

Her own desires were in any case obscure to her. So much of the feeling that impelled her to sleep with him in Rome had been simple pity. But this was not the whole story. She had also felt, despite his maddening ways, a fondness, a wish to experience his tenderness, even a purely animal longing. The physical act which she had supposed would be at best a charade had mysteriously avoided absurdity. From that vast dungeon of flesh had emerged a lover.

He put down his cup. 'I almost forgot – my new acquisition.' He left the room and reappeared holding a miniature sedan chair, delicately enamelled, the frame studded with tiny stones, white and green. Through the window in the door of the chair, a man and woman could be seen, resplendent in powdered wigs. They were seated side by side in icy formality.

Smiling, she shook her head, touching the enamelled sides with the tips of her fingers.

'There is more.' He reached to turn the chair around in her grasp. 'Look through the window.'

On this side, by some trick with mirrors, a different version of the couple was presented. Here the propriety of their other selves had been abandoned. They were locked in a passionate embrace, the woman's arms drawn tightly about the man, her head thrown back against the velvet lining of the sedan.

'It's charming,' she said. But under her breath the window of the sedan door had misted, bringing an echo of something less pleasant.

Fender had seen the slight change in her expression. 'Tell me what you were thinking.'

'It was nothing to do with this. Just a memory.'

'Of what?'

'Something I read about Paris in the last century. A little girl would stand beside a parked carriage, offering her sister to passing men. When she had attracted a client she would climb inside the carriage as well. Her job was to breathe on its windows so that if the police came by they would be unable to see what was happening.'

'Ah,' he said. He wrinkled the corners of his mouth. She thought with a stab of guilt that perhaps she had spoiled his acquisition for him. She handed the sedan back to him and smiled until he responded. 'It's very beautiful.'

The grandfather clock in the corner began to chime. He glanced towards it as to a voice. 'Eleven-thirty. You mustn't leave it too late. At least the roads will be reasonably clear.' His manner had become avuncular.

Driving north a few minutes later, she felt tiredness pulling at the muscles beside her mouth. Her head had begun to ache. She half-wished she had boldly opted to stay at the cottage. A convoy of Army trucks with undipped headlights was moving towards her. She pulled into the side of the road and switched off her engine.

She played with thoughts of turning back, of what she might say when he opened the door to her.

Ludo, can I stay after all? I'll sleep with you, if you want me to. But please understand – that isn't why I came back . . .

134

Of course, that wouldn't do. There was no way of saying just the truth. Between them were too many pretences, too many evasions; and they were hers as much as his.

She tried the radio until she discovered pop from the sixties, messages from a hopeful world in place of the harsher music that was now. Under her breath, she spoke a few words of a song; it was absolutely dead. Lighting a cigarette, she drove on.

12

The ground floor of the premises in Crawshaw Street that housed Ellitt Personal Protection Services was given over to a showroom; a door at the side led to upstairs offices and, above those, a flat. The showroom was expensively fitted out, a lush affair of flock wallpaper and bleached wood, oddly chichi as a background for the merchandise displayed. It was empty when Antonia entered; but aloneness was not the sensation the room offered. Cameras gazed from the corners, lights winked omnisciently. It was a place in which no movements, no spoken thoughts, were left unshared by others. Through a half-open door at the far end she could see a girl seated at a typewriter. Beyond, a television screen flickered.

Antonia bent to examine the room's treasures, nestling on velvet pads – the cigarette case recorder, the cuff-link moulded round a microphone, the key-ring gun capable of firing needles that would paralyse. Holding the cuff-link in her palm, she heard a voice behind her saying, 'Wonderful workmanship . . .' It might have been referring to a Fabergé egg.

Wearing a dark suit and gold-chained moccasins, Ellitt lacked the country air the liquor store manager had tended to convey in his description. But the thinning straw-coloured hair and small moustache didn't leave room for doubt. He looked tough and very fit.

'What can I do for you?'

She adopted a helpless expression. 'I'm not sure. I have a problem but – ' she waved at the marvels about them the decision about what to do next. 'Had she called in a doctor?'

'Yes, he'd been shortly before I rang. He suspected viral pneumonia and was in two minds whether to summon an ambulance. However he decided against it, pumped some drugs into Mansell and said he was to have complete rest. There's no prospect of his returning to the Bureau before the middle of next week at the earliest. Your conscience can rest easy.'

She still wondered a little. But on the whole it seemed that he was telling the truth.

Fender glanced at his watch. 'Dinner I think.'

He had risen and was preparing to load the tray when she saw him straighten slowly. He was frowning again.

'What is it?'

He stared into the wisteria on the wall beside him. 'A sudden thought: Mansell's wife's mention of drugs being pumped into him . . . Have we found the corpse after all?'

She laughed. 'Mansell?'

'Cahill.'

When she made him repeat it, he went on, 'Cahill's nightmare as described to the maid echoes something I haven't told you. It seemed irrelevant at the time.'

'What?'

He made a dismissive gesture. 'I must give it more thought. It would be very half-baked if I talked about it now.'

Experience warned that, allowed off the hook, he would go on procrastinating or being enigmatic until finally ready with some *coup de théâtre*.

'I'd still rather you told me.' She gazed at him grimly. Eventually he sat down again with a sigh.

'The Gordon woman told me something in passing which I didn't recall when I was telling you and Mansell

127

about my talk with her. As I say, it didn't seem relevant at the time. Shortly after the weekend Cahill and Ellitt spent at Lissack's house, she met the girl who had been the – ' he fluttered his fingers ' – the duty playmate. In performance of her role she spent time with Ellitt in his room. She mentioned to Gordon that he was on drugs – she'd glanced in his overnight bag and had seen a hypodermic syringe. Which brings us to the nightmare Cahill spoke about to Bridget Boyle.'

He was beginning to look pleased with himself. 'Suppose it *wasn't* a nightmare at all. Suppose there *was* somebody with a hypodermic in Cahill's room. Suppose *he had actually been given an injection*.'

'By Ellitt?'

'Yes.'

'But he would have woken up while it was happening.'

'Not if a strong sleeping pill had been slipped into his drink before he went to bed.'

'But what would have been the purpose?'

'Murder. Murder that would create absolutely no suspicion that Cahill had died by other than natural means.'

She just stopped herself laughing. 'You're not serious?'

'Certainly I am.'

'Your theory is that Ellitt injected Cahill with the AIDS virus . . .?'

'Yes.'

'But the time scale rules that out. The antibodies would still – '

He interrupted her. 'You're thinking of the normal strain.'

'Shouldn't I be?'

'No, because it's not the only strain that exists now. The cultures which have been produced in vaccine research would have far more dramatic results. I noticed the other day somebody in one of the laboratories involved being quoted as saying that accidental infection with the culture he was using would reduce the gap before total breakdown of the immune system to under three months.'

'Are you saying Ellitt injected Cahill with one of these laboratory strains?'

'Yes.'

'But he would need to have access, to know how to handle the stuff and give injections – '

'Plenty of people can give injections. And these places aren't fortresses.'

As always he slid between hypothesis and bold assertion so rapidly, it was difficult to decide where best to attack his pronouncement. He was already in full flood again. 'Don't ask me yet why Lissack should want Cahill out of the way. But his business practices in Eire may be just as corrupt as elsewhere. Perhaps some event was imminent which could lead to Cahill discovering facts that would effectively ruin Lissack.'

'I can't believe that between them Lissack and Ellitt couldn't have contrived an accident for Cahill which didn't involve such an elaborate ploy.'

'Murders guaranteed to raise no suspicion whatever are less easy to arrange than you're suggesting.'

'Even so . . .'

'You're not persuaded by my theory . . .?'

She wanted to tell him it was the most implausible she'd ever heard him utter. Opening her mouth to be scathing, she paused.

'What is it?'

She shook her head silently, partly out of excitement but also because she was going to have to abandon her attack.

'Loach must also have developed your theory. It's the only reasonable explanation for the press cutting he kept

129

in his desk drawer about AIDS research. The point of the story as far as I can remember was that the director of the laboratory where it was going on was denying lax security after a report that virus culture had disappeared.' She frowned, trying to remember more. 'He said nobody would be at risk unless that person went to the length of deliberately injecting himself.'

'Ah,' he said. 'Did he indeed?'

They sat gazing at each other. 'How right you were in having faith in Loach,' Fender said softly. 'Clearly an imaginative investigator. Lissack had good reason to fear him.'

His expression became more sombre as another thought seemed to strike him. 'So might others have had, of course.' He sat silent for a moment then sighed and struggled out of his chair. 'Dinner I think.'

In the restaurant he said, 'Do you remember this place?'

'Of course – you brought me here a few days before we went to Rome to investigate the Ropner allegation. You were very domineering about what it was best to eat.' She smiled. 'Have you thought of going back? Didn't Hebden invite you? I expect by now something else is brewing in the Vatican that could bear looking into.'

They should have asked him to stay, she reflected – made him completely one of their own. It had always seemed the perfect habitat for him. In her mind's eye she saw him in cardinal's robes advancing towards her along some endless marble corridor, with meek companions in *birettas* bobbing along at his side.

He shook his head. 'I think not.' He was gazing down at the table cloth with that sudden shyness which while it could be touching was also oppressive. It came to her abruptly that his thoughts were not on the possibility of should find him a wife who'll agree to cope with his particular needs.' She smiled.

He didn't smile back: facetiousnes was plainly not welcome.

She said briskly, 'So far as I'm concerned, the most important thing is to bring Lissack and Ellitt to book for Loach's murder. I'm going to start investigating Ellitt when I get back to London. Do you agree?'

He was frowning. 'This ought not to be going on without Antrim's knowledge. Didn't you say he was on holiday in France?'

'Yes, but he could be called back. Baxter must have his address.'

He shook his head. 'I can hardly take that decision in Mansell's absence.' He seemed genuinely in doubt as to what he should do. Eventually he said, 'I agree you should make enquiries about Ellitt – but with great care.' He reached out and touched her hand. 'This has become a dangerous business.'

When they returned to the cottage he said, as he brought coffee from the kitchen, 'If the drive back to London tonight lacks appeal, I should be delighted if you would stay over.' His voice was carefully casual.

She took a cigarette from her bag, irritated that she had failed to allow for the possibility that he would say something like this. 'I really ought to go. I'd planned an early start tomorrow – I'm spending the day with my mother in Shropshire. It's her birthday.'

'Of course,' he said, 'you *must* go in that case.' He stood with his back to the inglenook, impassively drinking coffee. He offered no further comment.

She remained uncertain whether she should leave it like that. It would have been possible for her to drive direct to Shropshire from his cottage. She had half-expected he fresh intrigues in the *Curia* but the night they had spent together in the *pensione* in Trastavere.

Midway through their meal he said, 'What do you consider should be done about Antrim?'

She avoided answering. 'I'm glad that's something I don't have to decide. At least we know now there was nothing wrong with his reasons for stopping Loach's investigation.'

She wondered if he would remind her that they only had Antrim's word for that. But he let it go and said, 'We are still left with his relationship with Sylvia Keysing. It can hardly be dismissed as unimportant. Some would say he has opened himself unacceptably to the risk of blackmail.'

'I don't believe that. Nor do you.'

Fender traced a small circle with the base of his wine glass. 'You retain a certain regard for him.'

She shrugged.

'It's not, of course, a case of simple whoring – in view of what appears to be his taste for – for violent encounters.'

'The newspaper story probably exaggerated. Anyway, people who have difficulty in controlling violence in their sexual feelings sometimes find it a help to use ritual acts for what would otherwise be dangerous. I imagine he paid the girl to go through the ritual with him. Is that so very wrong?'

She saw she had embarrassed him. He was wondering about her own relationship with Antrim, about how far it had gone and whether she would call what took place between them ritual . . . But to those questions, neither he nor anyone else would learn the answers.

She adopted a lighter tone of voice. 'Anyway, you were asking what ought to be done. Perhaps you and Mansell

131

' – I don't think these would be much use. Of course I don't know what half the things are for.'

'They get more sophisticated all the time. It's an exploding industry. If you'd tell me your problem . . .'

'I suppose what I want is straightforward protection.'

'From the world? Or just one person?'

'Just one person.'

He pulled forward two brocaded chairs and stood politely behind one of them until she seated herself. 'Relax and tell me what's worrying you.'

His eyes settled on her face. There was a stillness in them, an exceptional calm. As a killer, she thought, he wouldn't find himself bothered by last minute doubts.

'This person's a man – is that right?'

'Yes, we were . . . close at one time. Now he won't accept it's finished. I think he's gone a bit mad. He's threatened to beat me up. He talked once of killing me if he caught me with anyone else.'

'Has he been violent with you yet?'

'Once. He had a key to the flat where I used to live and was waiting there when I got back one night. I told him to leave and he started hitting me. Luckily the people upstairs heard me scream.'

'Did you tell the police about it?'

She hesitated for a few moments. 'No, I didn't.'

'Why not?'

'There are reasons why I don't want to go to the police, personal reasons.'

'Is he a criminal?'

'No.'

'Have you been involved with him in anything that's against the law?'

'No.'

'You're quite sure?'

'It's nothing like that. I just don't want the police involved. It's something I want to keep private.'

'I see.' He seemed content to accept it without further probing. His tone became warmer, more intimate. 'Well, I gather you've now moved to new accommodation.'

'Yes, I took another flat.'

'He hasn't found you there yet . . .'

'I'm not sure. I saw his car following the bus I was on a few nights ago. I was on my way home. When I got off the bus there was no sign of him. But I'm sure it wasn't a coincidence. If he doesn't already know where I am, he's going to find out soon. He's very persistent.'

She was conscious while speaking that he had embarked on a swift inspection of her body. He was checking the flesh as a possible bonus over and above whatever he got her to pay for his services. His gaze settled on her legs. She crossed them to assist his calculations.

'You want a bodyguard?'

'No, I couldn't possibly afford anything like that. It's the thought of his coming to where I live that worries me most.'

'I expect we could make your new flat pretty secure. Is it in a modern block?'

'No, a Victorian house that's been split up.'

He wrinkled his nose. 'There's a common entrance I suppose.'

'Yes. The door's controlled from inside each flat. The trouble is, other people in the house often leave it slightly open.' She looked up into his face. 'I'm having nightmares of finding him at the top of the stairs one day.'

He patted her thigh lightly; he'd decided that as long as he kept her a little scared, she'd be a pushover.

'This is what I'll do. As soon as you like I'll come to your flat and make an inspection. When I've decided what ought to be fitted to make it absolutely secure, a technical chap of mine will visit and do the installation. There's probably some improvement for the common entrance we can dream up as well. After that we can decide if there's anything more needed.'

He fetched a desk diary and took down her address.

'When would you like me to come?'

'I don't suppose tonight would be possible? I'd appreciate it enormously if you could . . . Say at six-thirty? Come for a drink.'

He smiled. 'Six-thirty.' He touched her again before she left, this time on the rump, to remind her she was now going to be in good hands.

Her plan had been to return in time to change into something which, without being incendiary, would look fairly encouraging. She also needed to book the alarm call that was to be her white knight when the going got sticky. But a late conference at the Yard meant she was back bare minutes before six-thirty. She had done no more than fix the call when through the window she saw what was presumably the car Bridget Boyle had remembered, a brown Mercedes Estate, nosing into a kerb space behind her own car.

Ellitt made it plain that he liked to get business over before embarking on pleasure. He left his drink untouched while he made an examination of the locks and window catches. Afterwards he spent ten minutes in the common entrance hall. When he returned he said, 'Right, I think we might replace the spring on the door down there with something that will make it impossible for people to leave it open. The actual mechanism is pretty good. Up here I know exactly what you should have and it needn't be expensive. We can talk about that tomorrow when I've done a few sums.'

'You're marvellous,' she said. She sat down on the sofa

and patted the space beside her. 'I've stopped shaking for the first time in days.'

He tried his whisky then reached for the siphon behind her and added some more soda. His life was made up of calculations, a disciplined pursuit of ends.

'Have you done this sort of work for a long time?' she asked.

'Long enough. Actually I started out to be a doctor. Then I decided I wanted to do something more active so I joined the Army for a few years. At the time I came out there was a crop of kidnappings of wealthy people. I saw the possibilities and went into protection work on my own account.'

'It must be dangerous at times.'

'You have to know what you're doing.'

'Do you ever have to get – physical with people who are threatening your clients?'

'When necessary.' He gave her one of his still-eyed looks. 'Protection means playing it rough sometimes. It may be the only answer. People learn from getting hurt.' He turned more towards her and smiled. 'I prefer being physical in other ways actually.' He was absolutely confident of his appeal.

'I imagine you might be very good in all the ways,' she said.

He had stretched his arm along the back of the sofa. 'I was wondering if you'd care to have dinner.'

She reached for her glass but he took it from her fingers, shaking his head slowly. He began to press her back, his free hand closing on her breasts. It seemed she might have booked the white knight for a later arrival than was going to be helpful. To employ delaying tactics that wouldn't raise the risk of irritating him would demand ingenuity. As he started on her shirt buttons she wriggled from under him with a sudden movement. She kissed him on the brow as she stood up. 'Wait, I'll do it.'

He rolled back obediently enough, ready to be entertained. She had the last button unfastened and had moved to the waistband of the skirt when the alarm call came.

She crossed to the telephone and picked it up. At intervals she made appropriate noises of surpise, annoyance and, finally, grudging agreement.

Ellitt frowned as she returned to him, buttoning up.

'Problems?'

'It was the police. They're coming round in ten minutes. It's absolutely maddening.'

'But I thought you said you hadn't reported – '

'This is something else. My bag was snatched as I was coming out of the tube the other night. I gave them a statement at the local police station although I didn't get a really good look at the man who did it. Now they say they've got a man in custody who might have done it and they need to go over something in my statement straight away.'

She put her hand on his arm. 'I'm terribly sorry, I tried to put them off. I'd still like to have dinner with you sometime. Would tomorrow night be all right? Perhaps I could come to your place?'

She held her breath but he displayed nothing more than controlled irritation. They agreed she would go to his flat at seven-thirty the following evening.

As he was leaving she said, 'You look terribly fit. I suppose you wouldn't agree to do something physical about my problem – really scare him off ever trying anything on with me again?'

For a moment she feared she had gone too far. His face became expressionless for a moment. Then he relaxed, or so it appeared. He put an arm round her shoulders. 'Everything's possible. We'll talk about it.'

She dialled Fender's number with a feeling of triumph. He listened to her story with monosyllabic grunts. At the end, he said, 'You seem to have made progress.' He was being grudging, she thought. But perhaps he was worried for her.

She went on, 'There's quite a bit more about Ellitt which I discovered this morning. And I've traced the AIDS news item about vaccine research which Loach kept a copy of in his desk. Most of the story I'd remembered correctly when we talked the other day. Somebody in the laboratory had leaked the fact that culture had disappeared and reassuring noises about it were being made. What I hadn't recalled is that there'd apparently been a television programme a month before in which it was said a particularly deadly strain of the virus had been developed artificially in this laboratory and that if mutations like this were to occur in humans, death would be a certainty in a matter of weeks after initial infection.'

'Ah.' He was purring.

'You'll also be pleased by what I found on Ellitt's Service file which the MOD produced after I told them he'd been proposed for a job in the Bureau. Prior to joining up, it seems he'd been a medical student in London for no less than four years. So the operation against Cahill wouldn't have fazed him.'

'What about his Army career?'

'He was an officer in an infantry regiment, Prince Albert's Rifles, and did a tour of duty in Northern Ireland. Later he transferred to the SAS and served with them in Northern Ireland as well. Perhaps he met Lissack there – his service could have overlapped the time Lissack was taking over his Belfast company. I thought I would check tomorrow to see – '

He interrupted her. 'Did you say he served in the SAS?'

'Yes.'

She heard his breath being expelled very slowly.

'What is it?'

He came back with sudden urgency. 'Pull out of this straight away. Don't go to Ellitt's flat. If he telephones make some excuse – you're no longer interested in security equipment or anything else. Drop the whole thing.'

'*Drop it – the investigation?*'

'Yes.'

'Why?'

'Because I fear that Ellitt's role is quite different from what we thought.'

'In what way?'

'What we have been investigating is plainly not a piece of private enterprise. This venture is not for us to meddle in.'

It took her a few moments to work out what he was driving at. Before she could speak, he went on, 'The thought we might have stumbled on some government operation crossed my mind when we were talking at the cottage but I rejected it as unlikely. We can't shrug off the implications of the SAS connection. You have to remember Cahill was probably viewed by the government as the major obstacle in the way of getting Dublin to enter into a new deal.'

'You can't be serious!'

'Why not?'

'For a start the idea makes no sense in explaining what happened to Loach.'

'In the course of his investigation of Lissack, Loach obviously stumbled on something which pointed to the truth. It would then have been necessary to shut him up. It can't have been easy to take the decision they did but there was a great deal at stake.'

'And Lissack – was he a part of this?'

'I don't know. It's very possible.'

She shook her head at the wall opposite her. 'At times, Ludo, you're unspeakably cynical.'

'I'm sorry,' he said. 'Unfortunately I have to face facts as I find them.'

'*Fortunately* I can tell you that you've got them all wrong.'

He reacted with a satisfying sharpness. 'What do you mean?'

'I mean there is no possibility that Ellitt was being used by the government. He left the Army because he was cashiered – not only for misappropriating funds but engaging in operations in Northern Ireland without authority. What he got up to wasn't specified on the file – it has a secret annex consisting of the Court Martial papers which they didn't show me – but it's clear he did something pretty awful. The last thing on the file is a note saying that in no circumstances is any government agency to employ him in the future.'

'It could have been a cover – ' he hesitated, clearly on the run, ' – intended to mislead.'

'That doesn't make sense. And in any case the idea of the government deciding the achievement of a new deal with Dublin justified an assassination is preposterous. You *know* that!'

He made her go over the wording of the note again but finally gave up. He sounded deflated. When she returned to the subject of her appointment with Ellitt the next evening, he said, 'All this remains very dangerous for you.'

'Don't worry, I shall be careful.'

'What is your plan?'

'To develop our relationship. I'll have to make it up as I go along.'

He was reduced to saying grimly that he hoped she realized it wasn't just a game.

'I'll call you when it's over and tell you how I got on,' she said. 'Do you mind if I ring off now? There's no food in the flat. I want to slip out to the delicatessen before it closes.'

She had never reduced him to such abject surrender before. Exhilarated, she set out for Clifton Gardens, planning gluttony, indifferent to the prospect of extra poundage.

It was a fine evening, the sky rinsed clean, the heaviness of the past few days quite gone. From the canal came the sound of disco music, presumably a passing tourist barge. Against the railings above the canal, a tall young man in dazzling white trousers stopped studying a guide book to watch the barge. From the other side of the road a dog was adding its voice to the noise from the water. She left them to it and turned into Randolph Avenue.

Her triumphal mood sagged when she reached the delicatessen and saw a notice announcing it was closed for its annual summer holiday. Thwarted, she stood and stared across the street. Her options had reduced to a meal in the Italian restaurant next door or returning to the flat with something frozen from the grocery store.

The young man with the guide book reappeared round the corner of Randolph Avenue. He paused outside the pub opposite. He looked as irresolute as she felt. But it occurred to her that he was perhaps assessing the prospect of picking her up. She decided her choice would be the restaurant.

It was nearly full and she took the last empty table. When she ordered her *lasagne*, the waiter offered the wine list, but she waved it away, suddenly out of humour with the idea of making this a celebratory feast.

About her were tourists from the nearby bed and

breakfast hotels and what she guessed to be locals escaping for an hour from Maida Vale bed-sitters. Silent and withdrawn, the locals read their newspapers while they ate. Their apathy seemed to affect the tourists who were keeping their voices low. It was going to be deadly dreary, she told herself. But it was too late to cancel the *lasagne*.

Her back was towards the entrance so that she failed to see the newcomer until he was already beside her. With an outstretched hand he was making silently polite enquiry about the chair opposite her. He was fortyish, tall with humorous eyes. He looked civilized and unpredatory. 'It's free,' she said.

While he read the menu, she studied him. He was not English, she felt sure: possibly German or Dutch, a businessman. He wore a light-weight cashmere suit and a louder tie than she would have chosen for him; but there was nothing else to criticize.

'How's the *lasagne*?' he asked.

The accent told her she had been wrong, he was an American. Glancing at his greying hair, she heard the first alarm bell ring in her mind. Another explanation for the reappearance of the tall young man round the corner of Randolph Avenue occurred to her. If her wild guess at the true identity of Bridget Boyle's bogus journalist had been right, if, notwithstanding Bridget's refusal of help, he'd succeeded in getting the details he wanted about Cahill's stay at Rushers Lye, this *could* be Tom Busch. And if, as it seemed, he was having Ellitt and his contacts followed, that surely meant he was interested in what happened to Cahill that weekend. It was all hypothesis, of course. But she had been in the restaurant rather more than twenty minutes – time enough for the tall young man to have summoned Busch from the Embassy or any hotel in central London.

The man placed his order and picked up a copy of *Time*

146

Out he had brought with him. He was studying the theatre listings. Once he yawned. She told herself she had probably been fantasizing. Too much exposure to Fender's theories could make one paranoid. And Fender after all had hardly troubled to hide his scepticism that Bridget's journalist had been Busch.

When he put the magazine down she said, 'On holiday? Or do you live in London?' If he decided she was making a play for him, he'd just have to be disabused later.

The man smiled. 'I'm visiting.'

'On business?'

'Yes. But maybe I'll get a few days' holiday in afterwards. I certainly hope to. There's a lot I want to see.'

He told her he was in electronics, had plans for linking his corporation up with companies in the same line in England and France.

'What sort of electronics?' she asked.

The detail came in a steady flow, the language adapted but without condescension for a lay listener. The odds against him being Busch looked very long. There was one more thing left to try. 'I wonder,' she said, 'if I could bother you to pass the wine list in the rack behind you?'

As he rose he said, 'Why not share a bottle with me?'

He had to move barely five paces to reach the rack. It wasn't an ideal test. But when he turned back, she saw the momentary awkwardness of the left knee dipping as the other leg changed direction. No mistake: it was a limp.

13

Listening to Bridget Boyle's description, she had pictured Busch as unsubtle, even brash. The reality bore no relation to that. Perhaps Bridget had disliked him and coloured her account accordingly. Here he seemed the reverse of thrusting; easy, relaxed, content to make small talk. His sense of humour was dry, just a little cynical. She could imagine him at the Embassy reception for Cleveland, offering Antrim one-liners about a need for sources in touch with King Billy while his eyes scanned the room.

They had drunk half the bottle of wine before he asked his first serious question. 'Is your home round here?'

She nodded. 'Near the canal.'

'That's what they call Little Venice, is it?'

'Yes.'

'Those houses look pretty large. Do you live alone?'

'No, the house where I am is split into flats.'

'It's a nice location. I like water. If I lived in London, I think I might go for an apartment on the canal.'

She decided to start convincing him that whatever interest he had in Ellitt, she had no worthwhile contribution to make.

'They can be expensive. There are other problems too. The burglary rate is horrendous. I've just had an expert checking the security of my apartment.'

He looked sympathetic. 'You've been robbed?'

'No, but there have been so many break-ins all round me, I can't believe it won't be my turn soon. I decided to get advice from one of these companies that specialize in protection. The man who runs it came. He's been telling me what has to be done about locks and so on. I'm waiting to hear how much it will cost.'

'Some of these security people can rip you off – they're only interested in unloading their hardware. You should perhaps watch out for that.' He spun his fork amongst the coils of *tagliatelle* on his plate. 'But maybe this man's a friend.'

'No, I've never seen him before today. I passed his showroom in Pimlico and on the spur of the moment went in. I just have to hope he's being honest with me.'

It seemed to be going down well although she felt he was watching her closely. 'Does he say he's been in the game a long time? If he's done security work or under-cover stuff in some government agency in the past, that could be a recommendation.'

Even Fender would have admitted his technique was smooth. She shook her head. 'I don't know, he didn't volunteer anything about his background and I didn't think to ask him. Perhaps I should have done.'

He smiled reassuringly. 'Don't pay any attention to me. I have an over-suspicious nature. I expect it'll all work out perfectly.'

By the time they were drinking coffee, she was sure he'd decided she had nothing useful to contribute. When she rose, saying she had letters to write, the expression on his face suggested disappointment. In the face of her refusal to relent, he said, 'Maybe we could do this another evening before I leave – perhaps take in a theatre? Do you have a telephone number I might have?'

As she hesitated, he went on, 'That is, if you'd be happy to meet again. I enjoyed our talk.'

To refuse her apartment number, she told herself, would be ridiculous. In any case, since she couldn't believe his interest remained a professional one, the idea of seeing him again appealed. He was after all the most civilized male to have swum her way for a while. She took the open diary and pen he was holding and wrote. In her mind's eye, Fender was shaking his head grimly. I have a life of my own to live, she could have told him, and good men are thin on the ground; anyway, I *could* learn something that will explain why the Americans are also taking an interest in Cahill's experiences at Rushers Lye.

'Could I have your name?' she said. It seemed an interesting test to discover whether his training or a lingering suspicion of her, or both, would drive him to supply an alias. But he answered without hesitation. 'Tom Busch. If you need to contact me, just leave a message with reception at the Dorchester Hotel.'

Outside she glanced about her, curious to see if the tall young man had been told to wait in order to tail her from the restaurant. But there was no sign of him. Declining Busch's offer to drop her off in his taxi, she walked back home along Randolph Avenue.

Away from Busch, she found herself deflating fast. It had all been too agreeable, first the little game of fooling him about her reason for contacting Ellitt, then the discovery that she liked his company and he liked hers. Perhaps on the last point she had, after all, been deceived by a display of purely professional charm. On balance it seemed improbable he would contact her again and that might be as well in the circumstances. Difficult though it was to imagine the scenario, his role *could* be hostile. If it was, she didn't want to know. Discovering she had misread the signs, as she had too often before, was something she could do without. This time she meant to stay defended.

The dark blue Jaguar XJS that passed her as she man-oeuvred her own car into the kerb, twenty yards short of

Ellitt's showroom, had begun to slow down. It halted a little way ahead of her. Two men got out. Then it slid on and round a corner; from its crawling pace she judged it was in search of parking room.

Caution made her sit tight. Not that she feared that she had been followed, by the Jaguar or any other car. Driving from her flat she had spent ten minutes or more criss-crossing the streets of Maida Vale to make sure she was clean of attention from Busch or anybody else who might be interested in her movements. She had only turned south to head for Pimlico when she was absolutely confident.

The two men crossed the street to the door alongside the showroom that gave access to Ellitt's flat at the top of the building. They were casually dressed in jeans and blousons; one carried the sort of bag she associated with plumbers. But even in central London, plumbers seemed unlikely to arrive in chauffeured Jaguars. They might be two of the technical people Ellitt had talked about employing. But their method of arrival jarred with that idea as well. In any case the best course seemed to be to wait for a while.

Presumably they had rung a bell because the door opened and Ellitt appeared. In the brief glimpse she had of his face, she thought he looked displeased. But before she could see more, the men had moved inside and the door had shut.

It was seven-forty, ten minutes after the time she had been invited by Ellitt to arrive. Delaying until around eight o'clock would not seem out of the way. Whatever business he was conducting in the flat was best disposed of before she made her presence known; and she wanted to get another look at the visitors. She lit a cigarette and settled back in her seat.

Fender had asked her what her plan for the evening

was. She had answered flippantly; but in fact she had only a vague idea of how she would play things. Her objective was to get an impression of Ellitt's keys and, if possible, to take a quick look at any papers lying about. Accomplishing that without paying the price of sleeping with him could involve ingenuity no amount of pre-planning would provide. On occasions like this she preferred to rely on the inspiration that was born in crisis.

Fifteen minutes later, boredom drove her to leave her car. She strolled round the corner ahead to see whether her guess that the Jaguar was planning to park there had been sound.

It was at rest beside the entrance of a block of mansion flats. The driver's head was visible. Something about its outline made her wonder suddenly if it belonged to Busch's acolyte, the tall young man. But moving closer she saw the driver was at least ten years older and wearing spectacles.

She retreated to her own car, memorizing the registration number as she went. She had barely noted it in her diary when the driver came into sight around the corner. His manner was casual, too casual. She could have sworn he had not noticed her, checking on him. Yet here he was, making a check of his own.

He walked slowly down the street away from her, glancing into parked cars. When he turned about, if he walked twenty yards in her direction, he would certainly see her face. On impulse, she started her engine, swung the wheel and slipped into the safety of the Pimlico Road.

When finally she halted again, among the dusty greenery in Ormonde Gate, she asked the windscreen where any of this was getting her. Ellitt was her target: dark suspicions of the Jaguar driver were causing her to forget it. She was making a fool of herself. If she wasn't on hand to ring Ellitt's bell as soon as his visitors departed, he could decide she had lost interest in his company and go looking for other diversions.

As she nosed back into her old kerb space in Crawshaw Street, she was once more overtaken. This time it was an ambulance. A faint anxiety rose, then subsided, as she saw that the ambulance men were heading for the basement flat of the house next to Ellitt's premises. Two punks, strips of brilliant plumage across shaven scalps nodding in the light breeze, had been waiting beside the area railings and followed the ambulance men down the steps. Another remained smoking a cigarette in the angle of the steps, knees drawn tightly up beneath the chin.

Whatever had happened in the basement flat was no reason for more procrastination. She checked round the corner ahead and saw the Jaguar was no longer there. Returning, she rang Ellitt's bell.

The voice behind her was hardly raised enough to carry; it had spoken twice before she realized it came from the punk seated on the steps.

'What did you say?'

The punk's face was smooth and chalk-white. It was possibly but not certainly female. 'I wouldn't bother.'

'Why not?'

The punk drew hard on the cigarette, then began to struggle upright to lean against the wall behind. It proved to be a girl; she made a gesture with the cigarette and hunched her shoulders as though against cold. 'Done himself in.'

By the time the ambulance men reappeared with their burden, strands of the story were coming together. They were contributed by the girl, an Arab emerging from the house, hand-in-hand with a silent, doe-eyed boyfriend, finally by a locksmith arriving late on the scene.

It seemed that at the back of both Ellitt's premises and the house in which the punks and the Arab lived was a narrow courtyard. Into this Ellitt had fallen, smashing his skull. Nobody had seen it. That was unsurprising, since the lavatory and passage windows that overlooked the yard from the house had obscured glass in them.

The girl punk had been the first to discover what had happened. Glancing above the cistern after using the lavatory of the basement flat, she had seen the steady drip of blood through an air vent. Investigation by her companions had led to Ellitt's body sprawled against the vent in a corner of the yard. Above, on the floor of the premises that comprised Ellitt's flat, a sash window was wide open.

The puzzling question was how – assuming he had not deliberately jumped – Ellitt had come to fall. The locksmith reported taking a call half an hour earlier from someone giving Ellitt's name and address. The caller had explained that while seeing friends away from his premises, he had locked himself out of his flat on the upper floor. When the locksmith had said he could not guarantee arriving in less than an hour, the caller had become angry. He had spoken of trying to fiddle the lock himself. After some argument, it had eventually been left that the locksmith would come and would receive payment unless a cancelling call reached him before he set out.

It was the Arab, watched admiringly by his doe-eyed friend, who provided a theory of subsequent events. He knew the wide open window to be at the end of a corridor outside the door of Ellitt's apartment. He had noticed that another window, immediately alongside the first, but *inside* the flat, was ajar. Failing in his effort to fiddle the lock open, Ellitt, according to the Arab, must have opened the corridor window. Beneath it ran a narrow ledge towards the other window. Obviously Ellitt had worked his way along the ledge and begun to push the sash up. Then he had overbalanced.

'If he had waited half hour,' the Arab said, spreading his hands and shrugging, '. . . still alive.'

The occupants of a police car that had arrived soon after the ambulance were emerging from the basement flat. Antonia decided it was time to leave. As she turned towards the car, the Arab touched her arm. He was puzzled that she seemed to be unimpressed by the illumination he had offered. 'You not understand?'

She shook her head. 'Not one little bit.'

14

As she turned the corner into Blomfield Road, not quite twenty-four hours later, she saw that Fender had arrived already. Despite the return of sultry weather, he was back in a grey flannel suit; it made her hot even to look at him. He stood gazing down at the canal in roughly the same spot where she had observed Busch's acolyte. She waved.

He raised his hat gallantly and lumbered across the road. 'I suppose we owe it to Kenneth Grahame that water rats appear so much more attractive than their terrestrial brethren.'

His eyebrows lifted for her response. Whatever train of thought he happened to voice, he expected it to be picked up at once. When others faltered in their attempts to meet his requirement, his reaction could be scornful impatience.

'You've seen one?'

'Several.'

She shuddered.

'If you insist on living by the canal, you must learn to appreciate man's closest companion.'

'Never.'

'Think of Ratty.'

In her flat she embarked on an account of the previous evening's events. She had telephoned him at his cottage after getting back from Crawshaw Street but when she had begun to speculate about how Ellitt had met his end, he had cut her short. 'I think further discussion on the telephone might be unwise. This whole affair is becoming far too odd.' She could only think he had become apprehensive her telephone was tapped. But by whom?

He had gone on to say he would come up to London the next day and they could talk when she finished at the Bureau. Because she was going out to dinner, they agreed on a drink at the flat.

He heard her out, pacing up and down the room with his hands linked behind his back. He was in a magisterial mood. 'So you believe Ellitt was murdered by the two visitors . . .'

'Yes. They presumably smashed his skull before pushing him out of the corridor window. Then they opened the other window slightly to encourage the theory the Arab was offering as to how he fell. The call to the locksmith would have been put through as they were leaving.'

He was nodding.

'You agree?'

'Certainly I find it hard to believe that anyone in Ellitt's business would have called for assistance to pick one of his own locks. If he thought it was likely to defeat him, there were presumably employees he could have summoned.'

He leaned further back in his chair, grunting with satisfaction. His expression had become animated. He was like a dog presented with a bone and anticipating a busy half hour ahead.

'Do we know what view the police took?'

'No, I left as they were coming up from the basement. I imagine the Arab's theory would have appealed to them.'

'The Jaguar waiting round the corner – you've checked the licence number?'

'False: it belongs to a series that hasn't been released yet.'

'So who were these men?' He raised his eyebrows at her. 'Busch's organization?'

She shook her head.

'Are you sure? Cahill's death seems to have excited their interest. They were clearly investigating Ellitt and no doubt shared our suspicions of him. They *could* have done it.'

'I agree. But what possible interest of the United States government would be served by killing him?'

He was nodding again. He gave the impression that she had convinced him; but at times like this he was adept at concealing his real thoughts, and took pleasure in doing so.

'Lissack?'

'That makes no sense either. We believe Ellitt was working *for* him.'

'Perhaps he was becoming awkward – demanding a bigger pay-off for disposing of Loach as well as Cahill.'

'Perhaps.' But she knew he believed it as little as she did.

They sat in silence, bereft of inspiration. Eventually Fender placed the tips of his fingers together and tapped his chin. 'To go back to Busch: some thoughts came to me on the train. Let me try them on you.

'The other day I lunched with Roper-Hoare of the Northern Ireland Office. He was talking about the White House's interest in the talks between London and Dublin and about Cleveland activities. Roper-Hoare said Cleveland had been very friendly with Cahill, regarded him as the man of the future so far as Irish politics were concerned. But, what is more important, it seems Cleveland had a very close relationship with the widow.

'Here is a woman appalled at her husband's death and the cause, as given out by the hospital after the initial announcement of pneumonia. She is certain Cahill had no blood transfusions in recent years to have infected him with AIDS in that way. She has also persuaded herself Cahill didn't have any extra-marital relationships to provide the explanation. Surely the doctors have got it wrong. Something starts to nag at her mind, Cahill telling her of a curious nightmare during his weekend with Lissack in England, that a man had come into his bedroom to give him an injection. Perhaps he really *had* been given an injection – of a lethal drug the doctors have mistaken for AIDS. Was Lissack, whom she has never trusted, involved in some British Intelligence plot to get rid of her husband because his opposition was thwarting London's attempt to make a new deal with the Irish government?

'She confides in Cleveland on one of his trips to Dublin, asks him to help over investigating her suspicions. Cleveland no doubt believes it's a case of a widow avoiding a truth she can't bring herself to accept. But he wishes to appear helpful. Furthermore, if the British government *have* been up to tricks, he wants to know. He agrees that somebody on his staff will try to find out what really happened during Cahill's weekend at Rushers Lye. Enter Busch.'

One of his bravura performances, she thought – and without a single scrap of evidence to support it. She smiled sarcastically, 'So he somehow discovers Ellitt was responsible for Cahill's death, reports back to Cleveland and is told to rub out Ellitt on behalf of the grieving widow.'

Fender compressed his lips, looking put out. She was tempted to continue on the attack, remembering occasions when he had rubbished far more modest flights of fancy of her own. But if she was to be on time for dinner, she needed to shower and change.

She drained her glass with a flourish, hoping he would take the hint. 'The thought that occurred to *me* is that

Ellitt's murder was perhaps unconnected with anything that interests us. After all, he belonged to a dangerous world – operating as a killer for hire, when he wasn't running a legitimate business. Someone we've never heard of could have decided he had to be eliminated. Which thought, incidentally, makes me very uneasy about the fact I've said nothing to the police about what I saw when I was parked outside his place.'

He waved it away as an irrelevancy. 'Don't worry about that.'

'But I'm almost certainly the only person who saw his killers arrive and knows what car they were using.'

'All right. But you also checked on the licence plate and found it was false, so that would provide no lead. Furthermore, if you get in touch with the police about this, they may have some awkward questions as to why you were in the area at the time.'

'Am I *never* going to tell them?'

He was silent.

'Ludo?' she said sharply.

He gave a grunt that was impossible to interpret. He had rested his whisky on his paunch; his fingers fluttered against the side of his glass while he brooded. But he still said nothing.

She rose to her feet. 'I have to change. If you reach any conclusions, come and tell me.'

She was towelling herself when she heard his breathing outside the bathroom door, followed by a tentative knock.

'What have you decided?' she asked.

'That nothing should be said to the police for the moment. Mansell must take a decision about it when he's recovered.'

'So we're going to do nothing more in the meantime . . .'

'Not exactly. I shall be making a journey. To Dublin.'

She frowned. 'Dublin? Why Dublin?'

'I propose to talk to an old friend there.'

She put on her robe and opened the door. 'Who *is* this friend?'

'An Irishman I met in India years ago. He came out not long before Partition as a recruit to the Indian Police. In the fifties he went back to Ireland and joined the Garda. I met him again over a case in which they cooperated with the Bureau and found him very helpful. He may have retired by now of course. But he will still be knowledgeable.'

'What are you planning to ask him?'

Direct questions could make him more than usually evasive, but she hadn't time to conduct a stately dance.

'I've not altogether decided, I must think it through. But now that Ellitt is dead, I suspect we stand little chance of discovering why Lissack had Loach murdered – if he *did* – through further enquiries here. We need another angle on Lissack, some pointer to his motivation in all this that we can exploit. So far as I feel confident about anything, I continue to believe Cahill's death was accomplished while he was staying in Lissack's house. Why was it necessary? Did he in some way constitute a threat to Lissack's interests?

'It seems to me that the key may lie in Lissack's business activities in Dublin. My friend in the Garda could have something to contribute on that subject. There is also the enigma of Busch's interest in Lissack and Ellitt. I may also turn up something that makes the theory I offered you a few moments ago seem less outlandish than your expression suggested.'

It didn't strike her as a particularly promising venture. Yet past experience had taught her that his instinct for a new route when an investigation had run into the sand was usually sound. She went off to dress. 'Do you want

161

me to do anything while you're away?' she asked him over her shoulder.

'No, thank you. Although I may make one other call over there, I expect to be back very soon.'

'If Mansell returns to the office, he's bound to want to know what you've been doing – whether we've made progress over Loach's death. What am I to say?'

'You're quite safe for the time being. His wife telephoned me this morning – he'd told her to enquire if I had any news for him. He still hasn't been allowed out of bed. There's no date for his return to the Bureau. Clearly he's had a very rough time.'

'What did you tell her?'

'That there was nothing he needed to be troubled with.'

When she finally returned to the living room, she found he had been working himself up into a passion over an item in the evening paper she had brought home.

'Are you aware that there are now such things as High-fliers' *Conferences*? That you pay to *attend them*? No doubt organized for aspirants to the ranks of the nation's élite, the financial barrow boys and their kidney.' He seldom had his knife out of the City's flesh nowadays. 'I see a rude awakening ahead for all these posturing parasites.'

Over his reading glasses, he examined her appearance.

'You look very charming.'

'Thank you.'

'May I ask who it is you're dining with?'

'Someone in the Canadian Embassy, a friend of Muir's.'

There was a danger she was unleashing a further interrogation on the subject of why she had broken with Muir. She reached behind Fender for her handbag. He had placed the evening paper beside it. The headlines read: ANGLO-IRISH ACCORD IN SIGHT ONCE MORE, PLOWRIGHT SAYS, 'AGREEMENT ON ALL MAJOR ISSUES IS VERY NEAR'.

She pointed. 'You may have to admit I was right about Plowright. He's going to pull it off.'

He gave one of his non-committal grunts.

'He sounds very confident.'

'Any man who sounds confident about solving Irish problems is either a knave or a fool.'

She stood meaningfully in front of his chair while she closed the handbag. He began to struggle to his feet.

'What will you do for the rest of the evening?'

'I shall book my flight to Dublin for tomorrow and eat at my club. Then go back to Mayfield.'

'If you want the spare bed – '

'No, no, I shall not impose.' He wore his self-sacrificial expression.

They shared a cab as far as Grosvenor Square. When she was leaving him, she said, 'Tell me honestly, have you a theory that covers *all this* – Cahill and Loach *and* Ellitt?'

He shook his head in silence.

For once, she decided, he was being absolutely frank.

15

With the years Declan Heeney's hairline had retreated to form an insubstantial ginger quiff at the cranium. It gave his forehead a lumpy and forlorn appearance. Otherwise, coming towards Fender across the lounge of the hotel, he seemed largely unchanged – perhaps a little slower in movement, a little more deliberate in speech. His skin was rough, as though exposed too much to the elements. But even when Fender had first encountered him, newly recruited to the Indian Police, he had had a weathered look.

He sat reviewing the other occupants of the lounge while Fender ordered tea, then took a small tin box from his pocket and played with it between his fingers. 'So tell me – how do you find Dublin after all this time? It must be fifteen years since you visited us.'

'Over twenty in fact.'

He had worked it out before he ventured from the hotel earlier in the afternoon to take the air and look for remembered vistas. His mood had sunk into melancholy in the face of streets and landscapes rudely changed. Mirror glass and reinforced concrete had marched in and invested whole areas, like some barbarian army of occupation. Lowering over blinded Georgian terraces were curtain walls of manganese bronze. Mounds of rubble promised more of the same. It was a city put to the sword and left unburied.

He had returned at last to St Stephen's Green, to commune with the mallards on the lake. Busy with their patrols, they glided past him, indifferent to the sights beyond the greenery, even to the modern Stonehenge that had materialized in their very territory.

'You seem to have had a purge of the spectral mansions,' he said. 'Surely some of them weren't so spectral as all that?'

'Progress,' said Heeney. From the contents of the tin box, he was rolling a careful cigarette. 'Dublin has to keep up with the rest of the world. So I'm told by the politicians. Is it any worse than Birmingham or Manchester?'

'They didn't start with Dublin's advantages. You had a perfect eighteenth-century city.'

'. . . With eighteenth-century slums to match.'

Heeney lit the cigarette and blew smoke at a wall of green watered silk. 'I admit it's not the place it was when my father brought me to see the sights.'

'What do you remember best?'

He took a little while. 'The old man with the tin whistle by Halfpenny Bridge. The imitation palazzo by the Liffey that Sean O'Broin built, with the sun setting on its windows. The monkeys playing billiards on the façade of the old Kildare Street club.' Heeney exhaled more smoke, vigorously this time to dispel any notion of childish nostalgia. 'The monkeys are still there, I'm glad to say.'

'Not the palazzo?'

'That went years ago. A developer knocked it down and built the usual tinted glass box.'

Tea had arrived, scones and jam and cream, with eclairs on a two-tiered silver cake stand. Fender reached for the tea-pot. 'Let me be mother,' he said. The sight of the tea had seduced him: he felt a reluctance to address his mind to the business that had brought him here.

Heeney was gazing round the lounge again with his policeman's eye. 'I admit things have gone rather far. We're pretty good vandals. And you have to remember,

Dublin's a legacy of the British. A lot of the knocking-down has been done with an easy conscience.

'You know what a sensible fellow here said once? "Money talks everywhere but in Ireland nothing else talks." There's a fine gang of businessmen driving their Mercedes cars round Dublin these days who've made fortunes out of what you see.' Heeney maintained an amused expression. He didn't intend to show whether or not he really cared.

Fender applied jam and cream to a scone. The priest in the rumpled black suit and thick woollen socks he had noted earlier at the next table lifted his gaze from a newspaper to watch, brooding perhaps on the spectacle of gluttony. When Fender had swallowed the scone, he went back to making notes on the newspaper.

'It was about one particular businessman that I wanted to talk to you,' Fender said. 'Carl Lissack. You know who I mean?'

He thought he saw Heeney's eyes harden momentarily; but his manner remained bland. 'I know Lissack of course.'

'I understand he has substantial interests around Dublin.'

'. . . And a good deal of influence.'

'Notwithstanding the fact he's British . . .?'

'Bread spread upon the waters is a fine antidote to prejudice. In any case he's not really British of course.'

'Why do you say that?'

'He was born in Germany. You naturalized him in the fifties. Didn't you know? I believe his real name is Lissaeker.'

Fender frowned, hating to have been caught out. He had failed to explore Lissack's background before coming. Presumably the fact just revealed had figured on Loach's file. Perhaps Antonia had known about it and thought it

166

not worth mentioning. He could hardly blame her – it seemed irrelevant to their present concerns. 'He's viewed favourably then?'

'Not entirely. But we have a soft spot for Germans. There was a time when it looked as though they might help us get rid of you.' Heeney's smile was teasing.

'Do I deduce you've taken a professional interest in Lissack?'

'I have had occasion to.'

'Can you tell me why?'

Heeney hesitated. It seemed for a moment as though he might refuse. Then he said, 'Since the other persons involved are now dead, perhaps I can. You'll have read about Cahill, the Minister for Commerce who died a week or two back.'

Hope flickered in Fender, grew into a tiny flame. 'I remember the press story.'

'Before he went into politics, Cahill made a fortune as a property developer. He owed his start to Lissack who put up the money. Lissack saw there was a killing to be made in office building but he lacked the local contacts. Cahill had them. He was a Mayoman from the snipe grass, wonderfully ambitious. He did very well for Lissack and himself – they must have made millions out of their developments. In the process they knocked down a fair bit of Dublin – including Sean O'Broin's palazzo on the Liffey. There was a great fuss over it from the conservationists but of course they lost.'

'So what was the Garda interest in Lissack?'

'He and Cahill seemed to be getting some exceptionally helpful verdicts out of the Minister who dealt with planning permission deals at the time – he's dead as well now. One of the conservationists' lobby with some political muscle made allegations about the relationship of the three which I was ordered to investigate. It's a fact that the Minister built himself a nice villa somewhere in the sun. But I didn't come up with any evidence to clinch the allegations.'

'Nevertheless–Cahill and Lissack were successful partners in crime . . .?'

'Between the two of us, the answer's yes. Now tell me why you're interested in what I know about Lissack.'

'He's been the subject of a corruption enquiry. In the course of it one of the Bureau's officers was found dead in mysterious circumstances. We have to explore the possibility that Lissack was behind the death.'

'You believe it was murder . . .?'

'Yes.'

Heeney shook his head. 'If you're asking if we've come across anything to suggest Lissack uses murder in his business operations, the answer's "No". He usually gets what he wants by being generous.' He paused then gave a brief, slightly weary smile. 'I could however introduce you to someone who'd be only too pleased to go along with your darkest suspicions.'

When Fender raised his eyebrows, he said, 'Strictly between ourselves, Mrs Cahill has been unwilling to accept the implications of her husband's final illness. In view of the public image they'd cultivated for political purposes, that's not altogether surprising. She had in fact talked herself into a suspicion that he was murdered. By his old business partner, Lissack.'

An expression combining scepticism with interest seemed the suitable response. 'How does she imagine he did it?'

'Cahill apparently spoke to her of dreaming about someone with a hypodermic syringe coming into his bedroom during a weekend he spent at Lissack's house in England. She said he was never well after that weekend. She went to the Taoiseach with this story, saying she was

168

sure now it hadn't been a dream and that Cahill had spoken of another mysterious guest in the house he hadn't trusted. She maintained Lissack had arranged for Cahill to visit him to make the murder possible. She demanded an investigation. She also said that if the Taoiseach wouldn't help over this, she'd ask for help from another quarter.'

'Did he order an investigation?'

'No, apart from asking us to make sure it really was AIDS Cahill had died from. The hospital said it was beyond doubt. But it so happened the Taoiseach knew, from some very delicate coverage we'd had on Cahill at his request, that because of a particular deal Lissack had in the pipe-line over which Cahill's help was essential, he had the strongest reasons for wanting Cahill to stay alive. The Taoiseach couldn't of course tell Mrs Cahill why he was so certain she was fantasizing. He just gently pointed out it really was AIDS that killed her husband.'

'Is she still pursuing her suspicions?'

'I haven't heard she is. But I wouldn't be surprised.'

'Whom do you think she meant when she talked of getting help from another quarter if the Taoiseach turned her down?'

'At a guess, Cleveland, the American politician who's often here because of his part in the talks with London. According to reliable gossip Mrs Cahill is his mistress. And he and Cahill were friends from some time back.'

Fender celebrated the news with another cake: it was pleasant to have his guess about why Busch had taken an interest in events at Rushers Lye so amply corroborated. But that was *all* he had to celebrate. The rest of Heeney's news was a disappointment. A worm of misgiving began to wriggle in his mind. Had he also been fantasizing, along with Mrs Cahill? Perhaps Cahill's nightmare had been just that – a nightmare. Ellitt's hypodermic might have had the purpose assumed by the girl who saw it in his bag – to give injections to himself.

And yet – Ellitt had certainly been involved in something big enough to result in his own murder. And he was also the last person seen with Loach before he died.

He said, 'Of course I wouldn't dream of asking you why the Taoiseach asked you to maintain coverage on one of his Cabinet colleagues. But I suppose his sympathies with the IRA weren't wholly irrelevant.'

Heeney was shaking his head in mock reproof. He started to roll another cigarette. 'Let's just say Cahill was a tiresome fellow in a number of ways. A lot of people here were glad to see the back of him.' He produced the sly smile again. 'No doubt the British government felt the same. Bearing in mind that accident to James Tull in Ulster, perhaps we should have taken the grieving widow more seriously.'

'Tull? The Loyalist politician?'

'You have to admit it *was* timely.'

Fender stared but Heeney was shaking his head and laughing.

From behind Fender's chair a voice spoke. 'Ludo!'

Fender turned his head. Above a spotted blue bow tie, the features of Roper-Hoare looked down at him. He was carrying a black briefcase, not the heavy strapped affair Fender remembered being issued with by Her Majesty but one with shiny combination locks. In his other hand was a room key.

'What brings you to Dublin?' Roper-Hoare asked. He shot a glance of bird-like curiosity towards Heeney.

Fender rose, suppressing irritation at Roper-Hoare's arrival. 'A visit to my only surviving aunt: planned for many years but never accomplished.' He introduced Heeney simply as an old friend from Calcutta days.

Roper-Hoare showed no signs of moving off. Fender

170

subsided into his chair again. 'May we ask why *you're* here – or can we guess?'

'Bag carrier and humble adviser to my Secretary of State.'

'More talks?'

'Eight hours so far today.'

'When is the agreement to be announced? Or isn't there going to be one?'

'You may deduce the moment of truth is near from the fact that the Foreign Secretary is in our party this time. He and my Secretary of State are staying with the Ambassador. We sherpas have been allowed to pitch camp here. I've looked in to change for the evening – rather early but Plowright wants a briefing session before the working dinner tonight.'

'A clever fellow, your Mr Plowright, so the newspapers here tell me,' Heeney said. 'But can he deliver? What we want is something that really cuts the ground from under the IRA *and* can be made to stick in the North. Can your Mr Plowright deliver *that*?'

'The odds are as favourable as they've ever been. If we don't succeed this time, we never shall.'

Someone in a dinner jacket was calling to Roper-Hoare from the hotel lobby. He sighed. 'My Foreign Office colleague, changed already. What would we do without the Diplomatic Corps?' He went away.

Heeney picked up a crumpled tweed hat. 'I must find out what's going on back at the office. This aunt of yours lives in Dublin, does she?'

'Cork in fact. But she keeps a small flat in Fitzwilliam Square for her little trips to town. I'm going there to have dinner with her.' He reached out to Heeney's arm, trying to hold him back. 'I'd hoped we could talk a little more.' There was probably nothing in it to pursue; but he would

171

have liked to understand rather better the joke about James Tull.

Heeney shook his head regretfully. 'There's a mountain of files on my desk. It was nice seeing you again.' He raised an arm in farewell. 'We've kept the aspic round your aunt, you'll be glad to hear.' His smile was mysterious.

A pianist had appeared. Seating herself in a corner of the room, she launched without ceremony into a song Fender hadn't heard for more than thirty years, 'Alice Blue Gown'. On the whole it suited the room, and what went on in it, very well.

He could almost believe he had entered a time warp. In the corner a youth of aesthetic appearance read a novel propped against his cake-stand. Small children were giggling over their eclairs under the eye of a silently brooding father who had kept his hat on to drink his tea. The priest at the next table was still studying his newspaper. His pen was being employed on the horse-racing columns. All the meetings must be over by now; so presumably he was engaged on an academic exercise, betting against himself.

The world elsewhere should still be like this, Fender told himself. He could be totally, blissfully happy at this moment, were it not for the thought that his investigation was getting nowhere. Far from having found a star to steer by in Dublin, he was floundering more than ever, tossed about on a sea of contradictions, quite rudderless.

16

Hurrying down the Bureau steps, Antonia saw that clouds, isolated enough earlier to have seemed of no account, had melded to form a seamless canopy over Somerset Square. The sullen heaviness promised a storm: already coin-sized blotches were visible on the pavements. She looked for empty cabs but, as ever, there were none. Reaching the Underground station in Baker Street before the storm broke would be a gamble.

She toyed with a change of plan, a return to the bundles of files abandoned five minutes ago. But the day had already lasted too long. Moreover, at its close, there had been a disagreeable clash with Baxter, Antrim's Private Secretary. Vicarious authority had turned Baxter's head. The boyish eagerness to please was gone, replaced by condescension that was barely civil. The argument had been of small importance; but she had tasted gall when having to give way. She decided to press on.

Before she had reached the corner of the square, the rain came down with the saturating perpendicularity of summer cloudbursts. She stopped, resigned now to retreat. In the same moment her name was called from a car parked nearby.

It was a black and tan Cadillac. The head framed by the lowered window belonged to Busch. 'Hallo,' he said. 'Remember me?'

She blinked away raindrops, unprepared for this challenge, and particularly for the implications of Busch being parked within thirty yards of the Bureau.

He opened the car door. 'Wherever you're going, I wouldn't. Not without an ark. Come aboard.'

The shoulders of her dress were soaked. To refuse the offer in the circumstances would be ridiculous. She slid in beside him.

'Where would you like to be taken?' he asked. 'Little Venice?'

'I'm not going home, as it happens.'

'So you have time for a drink with me.'

She shook her head. 'Thanks but I'm due somewhere in twenty minutes' time.'

'A very quick one.'

'No.'

He lost none of his equanimity. 'All right – just point me in the direction you want to go.'

Demurring noises had no effect. She gave in, more or less gratefully. 'It's the Caxton Institute. Start by going east along the Marylebone Road. I'll tell you where to turn off.'

Busch eased the Cadillac into the traffic. She had to direct him to the Marylebone Road so his knowledge of London was clearly rudimentary. He was wearing the suit and mildly strident tie she remembered from their restaurant meeting. Now that she could study them in profile his features seemed leaner, perhaps a little more worn. He had a way of looking with amused resignation at cars and pedestrians failing to do what he expected of them.

'What happens at this Institute we're heading for?' he asked.

'Book-binding. I take lessons once a week when I get away from my office early enough.'

'That's a sort of hobby is it?'

'Yes.'

He made a small dipping movement of his head, intended to convey interest mixed with surprise.

174

The Marylebone Road was a windswept wilderness.

'So this is summer,' he said.

'We don't have summers. This is the interval between winters.'

'I imagine your Tourist Board don't feature that in their sales pitch.'

'All Tourist Boards exist to deceive.'

He glanced out at dripping trees planted in an island of cobblestones. 'I think you're a little hard on your climate.'

'I just want weather that's dependable. You never have that here. I want a real summer.'

'There was nothing wrong with the evening we met. London's more fortunate than you think. The weather's dependable in Washington at this time. But you wouldn't prefer it.'

Since it was businessman cover he'd opted for when she'd asked him what he did, she wondered if the fact that he'd instanced Washington rather than New York or Chicago or some other commercial city could be classed as a small slip. But Washington after all must have its share of businessmen. She decided it was time she probed his appearance outside the Bureau. 'Why were you parked in Somerset Square? I don't think there are any electronics companies in that area, are there?'

'I was waiting for you,' he said evenly.

His directness took her aback. He went on, 'I was about to step inside your reception hall to find out how much longer you'd be when you appeared.' He smiled. 'I think we'd find things a lot easier if we were frank, don't you?'

'Frank about what?'

'About what we're interested in, you and I. We might begin with the fact that you know very well I'm not in electronics.'

'How did you discover where I work?'

'Routine. Your explanation of why Ellitt was with you

the other evening was so convincing I almost didn't bother to check. But my suspicious nature won in the end. The Embassy's contact in the police came back with the news that you belonged to the Central Crimes Bureau. Now that was very interesting. Because I met an old professional chum the other night who told me he'd been appointed its Director. He also told me he'd gone legitimate.' He grinned. 'I said I'd believe that when *I* went legitimate.'

Busch reached for a duster and wiped condensation from the glass in front of them. 'I tried telephoning him today hoping for a little cooperation for old time's sake. But I was told he's away on holiday. So I'll just have to convince you.'

'Of what?'

He was still grinning. 'The value of the Special Relationship. Has Antrim told you about those operations we ran together in the Far East?'

'No, and there's no reason why he should have done. You have to understand he and the Bureau have nothing to do with intelligence. If you really want the facts I'll tell you what the Bureau does.'

'I know what the Bureau *exists* for. I also know that with someone like Antrim having been put in at the top, that's only half the story. You don't have to fence with me.'

He had driven his ball so far into the rough, she could almost feel sorry for him. 'You're mad,' she said.

He gave a long sigh. 'Come on, be honest, admit you know who I am and what I do and why I'm here.'

Intuition told her that if she went on blocking him completely, it would achieve nothing; also, it might stop her picking up useful information. 'All right, it's true I happen to know what you really do. But the fact I know is the result of pure chance.'

'Will you admit that when we met you'd been taking a professional interest in that guy, Ellitt, and the brief you had from Antrim had nothing to do with anti-corruption?'

'Wrong. For a start Antrim's unlikely ever to have heard of Ellitt.'

'So you were just getting advice on the security of your flat . . .'

'That was what I asked him to call about.'

The rain was not as heavy now but above the wipers the windscreen remained little better than a blur. Busch slowed to let a taxi pick up a bedraggled pair dressed in formal clothes, fugitives from some City church wedding no doubt; or perhaps it had been a Garden Party day at the Palace.

As he accelerated again, he said, 'All right, if you were just buying Ellitt's security advice, perhaps you'll explain why you were keeping watch on his place in Crawshaw Street the evening he had his curious fall.'

She felt her stomach tighten. He went on. 'I meant to bring the photograph. You're looking rather thoughtful in it. It was taken when you stepped out of your car for a minute or two. My people decided you must have wanted to check on the car in which Ellitt's visitors arrived. Unfortunately we weren't able to do the same. Did you get the licence plate details? Or didn't you need to? And why did you drive off in such a hurry?'

Now the initial shock was past, it was irritation of which she was most aware, irritation that she had failed to spot the surveillance. He seemed to read her thoughts because he went on, 'We were using a room in the hotel at the end of the street. That's why we couldn't check on the car.'

Busch offered a cigarette from a pack he had taken from his pocket. She shook her head and watched him light his own before she spoke.

177

'What exactly are you after?'

'Primarily, because it's what I've been asked to do and because my professional pride is going to suffer serious trauma if I don't succeed, I'd like to know who the hell Ellitt was working for when he carried out his contract on a politician you won't need me to name.'

When she only raised her eyebrows, he sighed and said, 'The late Minister for Commerce in the Government of Ireland, Mr Joseph Cahill. Whose death, I happen to know incidentally, has caused your Prime Minister to become very agitated.'

She could make nothing of that, and chose the safer ground. 'But he died of AIDS.'

'Which made it a very original contract. So original, I couldn't believe there was anything in the story until I was shown a cutting about some missing AIDS culture which is deadly in a matter of weeks.

'My first thought, I hope you won't mind my saying, was that Her Majesty's Government was behind it. After all, Cahill was a major obstacle in the way of a settlement with Dublin. But it seemed an extraordinarily risky operation – even Antrim in the days when we worked together would scarcely have proposed anything quite so hairy for such a relatively modest dividend. When my research on Ellitt brought out the fact that he was categorized as unusable, I realized there had to be another explanation. Which left me with Lissack. The trouble there was that although I'm sure he'd have no compunction about having somebody killed if he needed that, the word from Dublin is that there were the best of reasons why he wouldn't want Cahill dead. So who the hell *was* Ellitt working for?'

She shrugged for want of any safer response. She would have liked to ask the reasons for eliminating Lissack so firmly; but, on balance, it seemed better to hope he would just go on talking.

178

'Secondly,' he said, 'although this is not part of the requirement I'm trying to meet, I'd be fascinated to learn who those guys were who liquidated Ellitt.' He shot her a quick glance. 'I take it we're agreed, he *was* liquidated?'

She had to say something. 'I fail to see what legitimate interest the United States Government has in any of this.'

For once he looked as though his temper might be shortening; a muscle in his neck had started to throb. 'You know very well there's a major political dimension to the circumstances of Cahill's death. But your interests and mine *aren't opposed*. You have to believe that. So how about being frank?'

She shook her head. 'There's something you need to get straight. I wasn't acting on my Director's instructions when I asked Ellitt to my flat, or when I was waiting outside his place the night he died. I had a personal reason for investigating him. Not for what he might or might not have done to Cahill. But because I'm convinced he killed a colleague in the Bureau.'

Busch showed surprise. 'A colleague?'

'Someone named Loach. Who, believe it or not, was investigating pure unadulterated corruption. Which is what the Bureau, *believe it or not*, spends its time doing.'

It silenced him for a while. She guessed he was intrigued by what she had said but not inclined to accept it as the truth. Eventually he said, 'Well, whatever the reasons for your own interest in Ellitt, it would still make sense if we pooled our information.'

She had to reckon with the possibility that if she turned him down flat, he might tackle Antrim when he came back from leave. And as things stood at the moment, that would produce hideous complications.

'Let me think it over,' she said. 'Meanwhile, I can tell you the licence plate on the car that brought Ellitt's visitors was false.'

He made a gesture of resignation; she guessed he was not surprised. 'Since you say Antrim hasn't been briefing you, how did you discover who I was?'

'I suspected I was followed from my flat the night we met. Your chap shouldn't wear such tight trousers, it's bound to get him noticed. I imagine he telephoned you as soon as he saw me settled in the restaurant. The pure chance I told you about was that my Director had happened to mention meeting you at the American Embassy and that you were on Cleveland's staff.'

'How did you know what I look like?'

'I'd had your appearance described to me.'

'Quite a coincidence,' he said. He didn't believe her and she could hardly blame him.

The storm was passing over, a few streaks of blue had appeared in the sky. The Cadillac was already in Fleet Street. She pointed out the Institute for Busch. 'You're attached to Cleveland's staff for the Irish talks. Anything I told you about Ellitt would be reported back to him. How do I know it would be a good thing for the political dimension you were talking about? From the British point of view, that is.'

'Why should you think it would necessarily go to Cleveland?'

'You're on his team.'

'The Agency wouldn't want him burdened with information that wasn't strictly his concern.' His expression was dead-pan.

'But he's the President's envoy.'

'United States foreign policy is a many-splendoured thing,' Busch said. 'You mustn't pay too much attention to titles. Clout is what matters.'

He pulled into the kerb at the entrance to the Institute. 'You wouldn't prefer that drink to book-binding?'

She shook her head, smiling.

'I'm still holding you to dinner and a theatre one night.'

'I don't promise to have anything to tell you.'

'I'll take that chance.'

When she was crossing the pavement he called out, 'I almost forgot to tell you – you're the most beautiful bookbinder I know.'

She reflected going into the class that as a compliment it was heavily qualified. But it *was* a compliment.

17

Heeney's reference to aspic became explicable as Fender's taxi turned into Fitzwilliam Square. By some miracle the demolition gangs with their monstrous swinging balls had passed it by. Unbroken Georgian terraces stretched on every side; evening sunlight glittered on fanlights that, like the doors beneath them, seemed never to repeat exactly the same design as their neighbours'. The square remained a perfect, tranquil unity.

Outside the house in which Aunt Edith had her flat stood an elderly Porsche. Apart from a Rolls, it was the only marque which Fender could name without hesitation. Unlikely surmise floated into his mind. He paused to look at the Porsche. Caked mud and straw clung to the chassis; the bodywork displayed a variety of more permanent blemishes. The thought that, at eighty-three, Aunt Edith was still gripped by the passion for which she had abandoned horseflesh, chilled the blood. But inside lay the proof, the black leather gauntlets.

Five years had passed since they had met at York, for the funeral of her sister. Then there had been another car, almost equally lethal, identical to the one Antrim had salvaged from his divorce when the wealthy Juliet had finally tired of his *affaires*. Wearing those gloves, Aunt Edith had driven him away from the interment at the cemetery, scattering other mourners as they went. Later, at her sister's house, she had resumed ancient authority to tell him he was revoltingly fat.

When she answered the door in answer to his ring, her expression held that questioning, faintly severe gaze he

had once feared but learned to recognize in later years as
no more than unvarnished concentration. 'So it *is* you,
Ludovic!' she said, as though she had been allowing for
the possibility of some imposture.

The hair was now completely white but her skin seemed
if anything finer, and certainly no more lined. She wore a
tweed suit that hung a little loosely. Beneath the jacket of
the suit was a high-collared silk blouse, clearly expensive.
On clothes, like cars, she had always been a big spender.

She clicked her tongue as he manoeuvred his bulk into
the hall. 'So the quacks haven't made you get that weight
off . . .'

'I *am* lighter than when we last met,' he said meekly.

She moved past him, snorting disapproval. Her gaunt
frame mounted stairs with intimidating agility and turned
to monitor his progress.

'You look well, Aunt Edith,' he said.

'I hope so.'

'And driving still, I see. No more trouble with the
eyes?'

'Good *Heavens*!' she waved his remark away. She had
the same capacity for dismissing inconvenient testimony
from the past that in his bleaker moments he acknowledged in himself.

The apartment was dingily furnished. Even to his eyes
the curtains and carpets looked as though they had out-
lasted reasonable service. Since he guessed she now used
it only for shopping expeditions and the Horse Show, its
run-down appearance was perhaps not surprising. Keeping it on all these years was a breath-taking extravagance
maintained in part to impress the locals back in Cork.
According to family rumour it had once been a place of
assignation with a fox-hunting surgeon from one of the
hospitals. In the sitting room to which she took him he

hoped to see photographic proof of this shadowy figure but there was none.

Gin and tonic came in tumblers. She sat swirling her own and appraised him. 'When are you getting a woman to take you in hand, Ludovic? You're not fit to be left on your own. God knows, she'd have to be a saint, of course.'

'Sadly I've had no offers.'

'Have you *made* any?'

'Any woman I might choose would certainly not choose me.'

'I suppose you want a young one. At your age you can't afford to be fussy.'

He scowled, dispelling unwanted thoughts, the foolish, impossible dream. 'I don't need anyone. As the years go by, I value my privacy more and more. You must find the same.'

She gave one of her snorts. 'You were always a liar, Ludo. Clever with it of course. I told your mother when you were small that you might make a very clever crook.'

He looked down into his glass, suddenly impatient, unwilling to make the allowances he had resigned himself to before coming here. It was all going to be the same as years ago, and he was too old for it now. Why had he bothered to visit her? Why, when he had telephoned her in Cork before his trip, had she decided to make one of her shopping expeditions to Dublin so as to be here to see him? For them both, some subterranean tug had been at work, impossible to explain as affection.

'I hope you weren't expecting anything elaborate to eat,' she said. 'I never bother to cook when I'm here. But there's a little Volnay. I knew that would be to your liking.'

She rose to refill the tumblers. In the lamplight, near the drinks tray, the slender bone of her wrist had a porcelain gleam. He thought of her as possessing – with the less desirable qualities – the self-sufficiency he had spent a lifetime trying to effect. Or was she also a dissembler?

He turned to look at the view of the square through the window. 'You must be glad your corner of Dublin has escaped the developers.'

'Not for long I expect.'

'Does it bother you, the way it's all gone?'

'It's not in the Irish nature to look after things. And when there's a pot of gold to be made out of knocking them down, nobody with any influence is going to object. The politicians least of all.'

It seemed just worth trying her out on Cahill in case she had picked up some gossip that might be helpful. 'I hear the one who died the other day, Cahill, made his fortune out of knocking things down.'

'Cahill!' She registered extreme distaste. 'I suppose we should be grateful the wrath of God finally descended. He certainly left it very late. If I'd ever seen him along the street, I'd have run him down myself.'

'I suppose he had a lot of enemies.'

'His friends were what worried me. People who thought he'd make the next leader of the government. I'm sure he spent most of his time plotting against the Taoiseach. When he wasn't getting into bed with the IRA. Detestable man. If I'd been the Taoiseach I'd have found a way of having him put down.'

He smiled at the echoes. 'A small assassination?'

She sniffed. 'Unfortunately when it comes to *organized* violence we're still rather backward.'

Over supper she said, 'Cahill it was who knocked down the palazzo on the Liffey. The owner's best friend was K. P. Rafferty, a great uncle you would never have met. He was a Resident Magistrate in Cork. Unfortunately he had too great a liking for the bottle. When he was fifty the bureaucrats in Whitehall suddenly made him retire. His pension was reduced on the grounds that his service to the State had been drink-ended. A few years later somebody shot him dead, paying off a score.'

'Political?'

'No, no, a little local quarrel, nothing special.'

When he smiled she said, 'People like to blame Cromwell you know but it's always been in the bones here.' She swallowed some more of the Volnay. 'The Irish are one big, warm, murderous family.'

'You include the North of course.'

'Of course, they're part of the family. They hate to admit it but deep down they know it's true. Only the English could be so stupid as to suppose any good could come from splitting us.'

'Do you keep in touch with the Belfast cousins?'

'I was visiting them in the spring. Why?'

'I wondered if you heard any talk about the accident in which James Tull died.'

'Tull – that ranting monster! Another happy release for us all!' She looked sharply at Fender. 'What do you mean – *talk*?'

'Were there any odd circumstances? I seem to remember the newspapers reporting he'd driven his car into a river at night and drowned. Was that all there was to it?'

She smiled. Somehow she had sensed his question was not as casual as he had tried to make it sound. 'Probably not.'

'What do *you* think?'

'I've really no idea. According to the cousins, the RUC – ' she raised her eyebrows to indicate she was entering territory where endless turpitude must be assumed ' – the RUC explained the accident by saying there was a patch of oil on the road which had made the car skid.'

'You don't believe that . . .'

'Oh, I'm *sure* there would have been a patch of oil! But why did they only find Tull's body when somebody who saw the car five minutes before it must have gone off the road said there was a second person in it?'

'Who said that?'

'Some simple creature of a village girl, willing to be laughed out of it later.'

'So you think it may not have been an accident after all . . .'

'As I told you, I've really no idea.' She was playing him like a fish, and enjoying it. 'If there had been anything peculiar, you'd think those mad supporters of Tull's, helped no doubt by their many friends in the RUC, would have ferreted it out by now. And we know, of course, no British government these days would have the guts to do anything so sensible as killing him off.'

She reached behind her for a second bottle of the Volnay. She had drunk more than half the first one but as far as Fender could see was entirely unaffected. The Treasury would never have got away with drink-ended service if K. P. Rafferty had had Aunt Edith's head.

'Why are you interested in a deceased Ulster politician, Ludo?'

'Somebody mentioned the case to me this afternoon. That's all.'

She shook her head. 'I doubt if you're being frank. I always thought of you as a very devious boy. You haven't of course told me *why* you're in Dublin. Don't pretend you came simply to visit me.'

'How could you doubt that?'

'Very easily.'

He smiled. 'Surely to you I've always been an open book.'

'Written in a very peculiar language,' she said.

18

From the far side of the island, a boat appeared. It was being rowed with a brisk, stylish ease that compelled attention by contrast with the more leisurely progress of other boats on the lake. The rower was an attractive girl, minimally covered by singlet and shorts. Across the front and back of the singlet the name of a Japanese manufacturer of television sets was printed.

Antonia heard Fender snort. Unintelligible noises continued to come from his throat as the boat receded into the distance. Choler at advertising which caught him unawares, and continued to lasso his attention, she had witnessed before: it could render him speechless for minutes. Malevolent but intent, his gaze followed the girl until she was out of sight.

Noonday heat and the atmosphere of unbuttoned relaxation in the park made concentration hard. Antonia braced herself to review what Fender had reported of his conversation with Heeney.

'You don't believe he could possibly be wrong?'

'Over what?'

'In saying there were compelling reasons for Lissack not wanting Cahill dead. However close the Garda coverage was, there could still have been other factors which Heeney knew nothing about.'

Fender shook his head. 'He was very confident. As was your friend Busch, remember – although no doubt his information came from the Garda also.'

'Against that, we know Lissack had specially arranged

for Ellitt to be the only other guest that weekend at Rushers Lye. Can we really rule him out?'

'I think so.' He spoke quite flatly. She supposed she had to go along with it.

They were seated on a bench beside the Serpentine. Fender had telephoned in the late morning to announce his arrival back from Dublin. He had pressed her to join him for lunch. She had refused because a source promising news on one of her cases had agreed to a rendezvous in Knightsbridge at one-thirty. They had finally fixed on a brief meeting in Hyde Park since it was more or less on her way to Knightsbridge.

'So your trip was wasted,' she said. She was conscious of tartness in her voice; but she had never thought the visit held out much hope.

'Heeney's information on the relationship between Cahill and Lissack *was* disappointing,' he said mildly. 'Of course I was glad to see my aunt again after all these years. Still remarkably fit and full of gossip.'

Later she realized there had been a wisp of smoke. If she had worried at him, she might have discovered where it was coming from. Or she might not. That secretiveness he so much prized, the determination to keep a trump up his sleeve until the last moment, would probably have prevailed.

He mopped his forehead with a handkerchief and squinted at the sun. 'No news of Mansell returning I hope . . .' He was no longer bothering to conceal his desire to have the field to himself for as long as possible. 'Wondering how best to tackle Antrim about Sylvia Keysing is not proving an ideal recipe for recovery, I daresay.'

She sat forward, suddenly remembering. 'By the way, the morning Antrim went on holiday, Baxter sent for the file containing the account of his visit to Lissack at Rushers Lye. Later I asked when I would get it back.

Baxter said I wouldn't, Antrim had told him that from now on it was not to be released to anyone without his personal authority.'

He looked amused. 'No doubt he wishes to reduce the risk of staff jumping to wrong conclusions.'

'You're not worried . . .?'

'If you're asking me whether it encourages in me the fear that Antrim may be the person Lissack referred to in his telephone conversation with Checkley as being under his control – it doesn't.'

He flicked a leaf from his sleeve with an expression of satisfaction. 'As a matter of fact, I believe there is a way of establishing the identity of that person. Assuming my theory is correct, it will provide the explanation for the deaths of Cahill and Loach. But we shall need to stage a small provocation.'

'Against whom?'

'Lissack. He remains the key to unlock the door. We have not been paying enough attention to the *nature* of his relationship with Ellitt.'

'We've no information about it.'

'Exactly. Is that because it hardly existed? The maid, Bridget Boyle, believed Lissack didn't know Ellitt at all well. Fay Gordon confirmed that to some extent when she told me she and the other girl in the house just before Cahill arrived were instructed to play up to a story that Ellitt was an old friend of Lissack's. Was the reason for Ellitt's presence in the house that weekend that Lissack had been *asked or persuaded to invite him*?'

She shook her head. 'If you're going back to the idea of Ellitt being employed by the government, even Busch was convinced there was no chance – '

He was holding up a plump hand. 'I wasn't thinking of this as government-organized. The explanation could be much simpler. And rather astonishing.'

When she began to question him, he said firmly, 'You must bear with me, I would like to make a few more enquiries on my own before I say anything else.'

The oarswoman in the advertising singlet was making a return run. Fender narrowed his eyes as though a painful obligation required him to keep the boat in view. 'How much of the technical training you were given for your part in the Mancini investigation remains fresh in your mind?'

'Not much – why?'

'If we assume, as I think we can, that while Lissack is away during the daytime at his London office, Bridget Boyle could arrange for you to have access to the appropriate rooms for a short period, would you feel able to put a tap on the telephones at Rushers Lye and arrange to record out-going calls nearby?'

She was conscious of her jaw muscles slackening. 'You can't be serious!'

He sailed on regardless. 'Lyell presumably runs the Bureau's technical division. A few hours in his workshop would no doubt bring everything back to you. Tell him you need to be refreshed.'

'Would I also be explaining what I planned to do?'

He was oblivious to sarcasm. 'Just borrow the necessary equipment afterwards. Say you want to conduct a trial exercise or two on your own phone. You're senior enough now for him not to make difficulties. I remember you were always very forceful dealing with Lyell. I'm sure it will be all right.'

'But, I'd be acting with no authority from anywhere! I wouldn't even have Mansell's backing!'

'I'm sure he'll approve when I eventually talk to him.'

She shook her head in exasperation. 'Surely we should wait until Antrim gets back and then tell him the whole story about Loach and Ellitt and the rest?'

He was shaking his head. 'We *can't* wait. This is too urgent. And it's the only way we're going to establish with certainty who got Ellitt to murder Loach. Leave aside the other considerations – although they're not exactly minor – surely that's still important to you?'

She sat silent, her feelings a mixture of apprehension and resentment that he had backed her against a wall. But she was conscious too of a tension that was not unpleasant.

'What are your thoughts?' Fender asked after a while.

'That even supposing I decide, after a little practice, I can pull off the technical side, this could take a lot of time. Bridget would need to be briefed. She would have to watch for a suitable opportunity to let me into the house to fit the tap. That means being very close at hand so that she can get a message to me quickly. It could take ages. People in the Bureau would be wondering where I was.'

'You'll have to take leave. Or go sick.'

'A few more lies to add to the rest.'

He ignored her. 'In any case, I would rather you were unavailable when Mansell returns to work. He will be panting to learn what progress we've made. It had better be leave – a walking holiday on the Yorkshire Moors perhaps. I shall have to be equally elusive, of course, until we're ready to talk to him. But that's easier for me.'

He was at his most maddening: given the strength to shift that great carcase, she could cheerfully have pushed him into the Serpentine. Her eye caught the watch-face on his wrist. Unless she left soon, she would be late for the rendezvous in Knightsbridge.

'You haven't explained why you think Lissack is going to have a telephone conversation in the near future which will tell us what we need to know.'

'That is where our provocation comes in.'

'*You're* arranging that, are you?'

'What I envisage,' he said smoothly, 'is that once you have the tap in operation you arrange for the Boyle woman to let you know as soon as an evening seems to be coming up when Lissack will be at home but not taken up with guests. You then telephone him, identifying yourself simply as a member of the Bureau with knowledge of a recent investigation into his dealings with someone in the Defence Procurement Executive. You say that you have learned of a new development which is of great significance to him. An important Minister is now demanding prosecution. You are not prepared to say more on the telephone. You will however come to Rushers Lye and give the details if you are promised a payment of one thousand pounds in cash. You'll insist it must be that same evening – the next day could be too late for any action to stop the investigation being passed to the police.'

'So as well as carrying out an unauthorized phone tap, I'm offering to sell official information.'

'. . . Only pretending to offer.'

She stared at him. 'My God, you have a nerve, Ludo!'

He placed a hand on her knee, an unprecedented boldness. 'No, no, *you* have the nerve!'

19

The call had come through to Fender's cottage when he was almost ready to leave for the train. His overnight bag was packed, a taxi ordered, Mrs Bastin – engaged now on the weekly re-arrangement and hiding of his possessions – told that, failing his club, the telephone number of Antonia's flat in Little Venice would find him. When he picked up the receiver, he supposed it might be Antonia, following up her message of an hour earlier, to say that the arrangement to see Lissack at Rushers Lye that night had been changed. But the voice had been Antrim's.

His immediate reaction had been anxiety. Mischance, or perhaps some blundering initiative by Mansell, returned to the Bureau unexpectedly early from his sickbed, had alerted Antrim to what they had been doing behind his back – this was the only likely explanation. For a moment or two he had held his breath. But as enquiries about his health, the weather in Sussex and the state of the garden succeeded each other, it became plain that far from being on the attack, Antrim was in the role of supplicant.

'Ludo,' he had said at last, 'I wanted to consult you. Nothing to do with the Bureau, at least not directly. A personal matter.'

The door bell had started ringing, he had had to twist sideways to hammer on the kitchen wall behind which Mrs Bastin's faculties were absorbed by the floor polisher she was operating.

'I'd enormously appreciate your advice.'

Even in his early days as Fender's subordinate, when

ambition had held arrogance in check, Antrim had never deferred so handsomely. 'Unfortunately it's not something one can discuss on the telephone. I'd thought of driving down to see you this evening.'

At the open door to the High Street, Mrs Bastin had now turned, hand raised dramatically to attract his attention. Her lips moved grotesquely as though required to convey a soundless message from the furthest tombstone in the churchyard across the street. His taxi was visible behind her.

'Actually, I'm spending the night in London. Perhaps we could meet for a drink in the early evening.'

It had finally been agreed that he would go to Antrim's apartment at six o'clock. He would still have plenty of time to reach Antonia's flat before there was any chance of her telephoning with news of her encounter with Lissack.

Antrim's appearance when he opened the door of the apartment in Harley Street came as a shock. Antonia and Mansell had talked of a deterioration; but not to this extent. Not only had he lost weight, his facial muscles seemed to have slackened. Despite the tan, presumably acquired on the holiday in France, his skin had a rubbery look. That apparently indestructible self-confidence of a year or so back had crumbled.

Fender gazed at the Hockney on the wall while Antrim poured drinks. 'A new acquisition?'

'Not really. I got it supplied for the flat a couple of years ago, on the grounds I had to do official entertaining here. But perhaps it's new to you – I can't remember when you were last here.'

'You were still married to Juliet.'

Antrim made noises indicative of distress. 'As long ago as that. How sickening to have been so busy I haven't had an old friend like yourself here since then!' He was determined to be ingratiating.

'Do you see anything of Juliet?'

'No. She's married you know. An Irish horse dealer. I imagine he's getting through her money very efficiently.'

But perhaps with more circumspection, Fender thought. He wondered how much Antrim now regretted what he had carelessly thrown away in his neglect of Juliet – the house in Wiltshire, the villa in Sardinia, the game of being a country gentleman at weekends. All gone on the back of self-indulgence, the relentless pursuit of desire.

He took the whisky Antrim held out to him. 'And how are you? You look thinner.'

Antrim shook his head, not as an answer to the question, more to indicate a view that the time for preliminary civilities was over. As though at a flick of a switch his manner had become impersonal. He sat down abruptly opposite Fender. 'I have a rather trying problem. I hope you'll regard what I'm going to tell you as confidential.' The old arrogance flickered. He would never be capable of sustaining humility for long.

'Somebody, a woman I've never met before, is trying to blackmail me. It's rather bizarre. She's an old bag who, I would guess, is more than halfway to being dotty. Unfortunately she's bright enough to mean what she says and to be capable of carrying out her threat.'

So at least this wasn't going to be a confession of being in Lissack's pocket. That had to be registered as a plus. 'She wants money?'

'Yes. Not in the hand however. In the form of monthly donations of two hundred pounds, to a museum she claims to run. She says the money is to maintain it.'

'*A museum!*'

'Somewhere in Oxford apparently. She calls herself the curator.'

196

Like the first streak of dawn, he saw light.

'It's supposed to be the home of some woman who was a murderer of children in the eighteenth century. The old bat herself lives there now.'

He shook his head, marvelling. The possibility of this happening had never occurred to him. In his mind's eye, he saw again that tiny figure leading him up the stairs of the crooked house, the rabbit fur slippers, the dyed hair that was neither one colour nor another, the smudged mouth with its ambiguous smile. Iris Keysing's eerie insight into his past had chilled. But he had left her thinking that, her strange gift apart, she was of no significance.

He had underestimated her. After she had watched him away down the street, she must have decided there was something sufficiently unusual about his enquiries to justify research on her own account. How she had got to the truth one might never know. Probably she had gone through diaries kept by Sylvia, had found an indication that Alistair Cottrell was not the real name of the client in Harley Street; after she had discovered it was Antrim and what position he held, she had told herself that a man like that could surely be shaken down for enough to keep the wolf from the door of the house of Betsy Frogg.

'When did this happen?'

'She turned up here last night. At first I thought she was collecting for some sort of charitable trust. She said she'd heard what an important job I had and felt sure I would be willing to help her in her work.'

It was more than time to ask the obvious, albeit redundant, question. 'Who exactly is she?'

'The mother of a tart named Sylvia Keysing who died recently. I had a relationship with Sylvia. She'd come here when I wanted her. Once or twice I took her away for the weekend – I won't bore you with the details. The

197

mother had found out I was a client. Perhaps Sylvia had told her – I fancy she was on the game herself once – or she'd discovered some clue in a diary. Anyway she said that the story would be very interesting to a particular newspaper. Then she went back to the cost of keeping up her bloody museum. There was no direct threat – she talks in a very disconnected way – but I wasn't left in any doubt about her meaning. She left her telephone number and said in effect she'd be in touch with the newspaper if she didn't hear from me before tomorrow morning agreeing to be a subscriber to the museum.'

'She was saying she'd tell the newspaper that you had been a client of her daughter's – nothing else?'

'No, there's rather more than that. She knew the sort of things I was keen on – what I did with Sylvia. The story could be dressed up to be pretty sensational.'

'Do I need to know what sort of things?'

Antrim rose and went to stand by the fireplace. There was dampness on his forehead near the hairline. He wiped it with the blue show handkerchief he always wore. 'They're not all that unusual. The girl would let me tie her up and beat her – not in ways that would do her a lot of harm. Occasionally I'd do some other things to her which could be quite uncomfortable to someone who wasn't either keen or used to them. But this was all with her agreement – I paid her very well and anyway she had a sort of taste for it. Unfortunately the night she wrote herself off driving home she'd just left here. She was upset because I'd gone rather further than she reckoned had been the agreement. I gave her an extra fifty but it didn't do much to calm her. She was bruised and bleeding a bit. She went out into the street in a temper. I suppose it could have been a factor in her crashing the car.'

He had turned so that his back was towards Fender. 'A Sunday newspaper ran a piece about her crash in which they mentioned it had happened just after she'd left an apartment in Harley Street. The piece almost pin-pointed this block. I had an uneasy few days wondering if anybody would follow it up. But nothing happened, thank God.'

'This was the newspaper the mother mentioned . . .'

'Yes, the *Clarion*. They'd go to town on me of course, if she told them.'

'And you really think she might?'

'I doubt if she was bluffing.'

When Fender remained silent, Antrim turned back to him wearily. 'Sorry if you find this rather unappealing. But what the hell am I going to do? You're the shrewdest person I know, Ludo. Tell me how you'd handle it.' There wasn't much finesse to his buttering-up.

Fender gazed up at the Hockney, trying not to think how much he loathed Antrim, bracing himself to be dispassionate, objective.

'I take it you believe nobody saw the girl leave your flat that night?'

'Yes.'

'You're sure none of the occupants of the other flats was about at the time . . .'

'Absolutely.'

'What about earlier occasions? Do you have anybody who comes in to clean and could have known about her visits?'

'The wife of the caretaker cleans for me. She also prepares meals sometimes. But she's out of the way by the evening. Sylvia never came here before nine o'clock. There's nobody else.'

'Can you be sure the girl didn't tell others about you?'

'She knew it was important to me that she never said who I was. I rather think she would have stuck to that. But of course I've no means of knowing.'

'Did she live with anybody?'

'I don't believe so. I went to her flat only once. There was no sign of anybody then.'

'Did you ever send letters or give cheques?'

'God, no.'

Fender rubbed his eyes. 'From what you say, unless your name or the number of this flat appears in a diary of the girl's which the mother has in her possession, the newspaper are going to be in difficulty getting independent corroboration of the mother's story. Since she also gives the impression of being unbalanced, there's a good chance the newspaper's lawyer would advise against publishing. If they did run the story and you chose to sue they'd face heavy libel damages.'

Antrim's fingers were at work, against the side of the mantelpiece, as though discovering roughness in the wood. 'There's one more complication I should tell you about – a person who's aware of my connection with Sylvia. I first met her when I went to interview the financier, Carl Lissack. It was at a time when we were trying to get information about Dyerson who, if you remember, pushed off to South America to avoid a corruption case being brought against him.

'Lissack agreed to talk if I went to his house at Rushers Lye in Surrey. I drove down one evening. After we'd dealt with Dyerson, he invited me to stay to dinner. Sylvia was staying in the house – living there actually. He liked to have girls around in case any of his house guests were interested. I thought Sylvia was very attractive. Lissack told me things about her when we met on one or two subsequent occasions which made me think she'd suit me rather well. When I heard she'd moved out of the house at Rushers Lye I decided to make contact. That's how the relationship began. The complication is that I know she stayed in touch with Lissack and used to go back to his house some weekends for special parties. She would have told him I was a client.'

Fender said, watching Antrim's face, 'Lissack might have regarded himself as in a position to try blackmailing you, if it ever suited his book.'

'I suppose so.'

'But he hasn't tried . . .'

'No.' Antrim seemed to be only half-listening. 'I haven't seen anything of him for ages anyway.' He drained his glass with an abrupt movement. 'Although, to add to general bloodiness, the fact I once knew him has been a source of potential embarrassment to me in the Bureau. However, we needn't go into that, it's not relevant now.'

To press him to say more in order to hear his account of the Loach business and the shutting-down of the Lissack investigation was tempting. But it would seem odd to do so. Fender said, 'So far as the newspaper is concerned, if by some chance they got on to Lissack, I can't believe he'd want to be helpful. He'd see it as possibly opening himself up to adverse publicity.'

'So are you suggesting I do nothing – just sweat it out?'

'Not entirely. But before we get to that, I suppose you've accepted that you have to stop using prostitutes? You can't go on taking that kind of risk.'

A nerve was twitching in Antrim's cheek.

'*You do accept that?*'

Antrim said violently, 'Christ, I'm not yet fifty! Are you asking me to stop leading a normal existence?'

'Normal?'

'Don't turn it into a moral issue, Ludo, for God's sake! The things I do I pay for! Most of the women want them done to them anyway!'

'Then get one of those women to marry you.'

Antrim sat down again. He was making a considerable

effort to control himself. 'Sorry – I'm rather edgy. You're right, of course, I realize that. Your solution isn't exactly the easiest thing in the world however.' He stared into his drink. 'I *can* think of someone who would have filled the bill – someone you know actually.'

Fender felt a dryness in his mouth.

'I'm doubtful if I could persuade her to marry me now. At one time it would have been easy. She was rather cool when we last talked. Still, she must realize she's not getting any younger.'

He was thinking seriously about it. 'Would you be interested to know who it is?' He looked up, smiling a little.

Fender turned so that he would no longer have to see Antrim's face. 'It's a private matter between the two of you. I prefer not to know.'

The sound of an ambulance siren rose from the street outside then died away. Antrim said in a brisker tone, 'Well, let's leave that. You were going to tell me what I should do about the old bat's threat.'

Fender strove to make his voice matter of fact. 'Two things: telephone her and say that if her story appears in any paper, you'll go straight to the police and tell them she attempted to blackmail you into paying money to have it stopped.'

'Right.'

'Secondly, since she's obviously unpredictable, warn somebody in Whitehall there could be an embarrassing news item. If you don't do that and something appears as a bolt from the blue, you can expect no sympathy and no help.'

'Who would you talk to?'

Fender watched a fly crawl down the sleeve of his jacket. Soon it would face a choice between moving on to his wrist or along the arm of the chair. His mind went back to the evening in Twickenham when Mansell talked about whom it would be safest to tell; about the ways of the Home Secretary and the advantage of confiding in Finnessey, the Permanent-Under-Secretary.

'That's a very difficult question. I might advise you wrongly.'

'I know you wouldn't do that.'

He saw the fly hesitating. But he no longer felt doubt about his own choice.

'Since you press me, I suggest you go straight to the Home Secretary.'

'I see.' Antrim sounded taken aback.

'If there *was* a damaging story about you, he'd have to handle the parliamentary flak. On the other hand, if nothing appears, he'll appreciate your having been frank and given him advance warning.'

Antrim said hesitantly, 'You don't think it would be as well if somebody who knows better how to play him – Finnessey, the Permanent-Under-Secretary these days, for example – '

'You're the best qualified person to put your own case.'

'I suppose so.'

'But it's very much a matter for you.' Fender levered himself out of his chair. 'You could of course pay the woman what she wants.'

'Do you really think I would give in to blackmail?'

He couldn't deny him the truth over that. 'No, I would have found it hard to believe you would do such a thing.'

At the door Antrim touched his arm almost shyly. 'I'm very grateful, Ludo. We've disagreed over things in the past sometimes. But I've always felt I could turn to you in a crisis. Thank you.'

Out in Harley Street Fender paused. Disgust was beginning to take possession of him. He uttered the sounds of his revulsion to the street at large, not caring when passers-by stared.

Walking on, he came to a church and went inside, hoping that a stillness would settle upon him. He prayed. But when the time arrived for him to leave for Antonia's flat, the agitation within was just as great. Sinking into a taxi, he finally yielded to truth: it was not what he had now been obliged to accept about the nature of Antonia's relationship with Antrim that was denying him peace. Surrendering to hatred, he had played Antrim false, sought to steer him to certain downfall. The grub in his soul was fatter than he had ever imagined.

20

Lissack removed the cigar from his lips. He inspected the tip then angled it towards Antonia as though she too had a need to take note. All his gestures were studied, conceived as metaphors of power. He said, 'Why should I take you seriously when you won't even give your name?'

The hair on the back of the hand holding the cigar was a handsome black. It would run across the shoulders, she imagined, probably down the spine as well. She would have recognized him well enough from his newspaper photographs, the broad, heavy head, the features just beginning to signal a losing battle with indulgence, the gaze in which ruthlessness was blurred by a hint that his ultimate verdict on all he saw was amused contempt.

Less easy to credit was the picture conjured by Antrim's file note of the insatiable swinger prancing with playmates in an air-conditioned grotto. His clothing was deeply conventional, not even particularly well-cut. He had removed the jacket of his suit as he sat down. Revealed as supporting his trousers high above the navel were braces that seemed to be made from deck-chair canvas.

He rocked himself in the swivel chair behind the desk. 'Show me something that says you work at the Crimes Bureau.'

She took out her pass and held it in front of him, with her thumb over the number. He gazed at it and shrugged. The chair in which he had seated her was far enough away from his desk for him to take in her whole appearance. He chewed his lip and studied her.

'What work do you do in the Bureau? Secretary?

Investigation? Some sort of Personal Assistant?' He delivered his words slowly, the voice deeply pitched.

'It's a job that enables me to know what goes on in the Director's Private Office.'

'You're on his personal staff, are you?'

'Yes.'

'Are you aware that *I* know him personally?'

'Yes, I'm aware of that.'

'Describe him.'

When she raised her eyebrows he said, 'I want to hear if you really know who I am talking about.'

He cut her short before she had gone very far. 'All right, you know him. Now stop being tiresome and tell me who you are and exactly what you do. I'm not going to report you to anybody.'

She shook her head. 'No. You can either deal with me on my terms or not at all. Do you want me to leave?'

He widened his eyes theatrically as though portraying shock. Abruptly he reached forward, took her handbag and examined its contents. Handing it back he said, 'You'll have to excuse the preliminaries, life has taught me to be cautious about strangers. I'm particularly allergic to having my conversations taped. Now let's hear this story you think I'll find so interesting.'

She cleared her throat. 'There's been a development at the Ministry of Defence that's going to affect you very seriously in the near future unless you take action to stop it. This morning, Jobell, the Head of Defence Procurement, telephoned. He wanted to speak to the Director but as he wasn't available he was put through to his Private Secretary. I was able to hear the conversation. Jobell said the Bureau's case against you and one of his officials, Checkley, in connection with the Orange Tip contract, was to be reopened at once. He'd been speaking to the Secretary of State for Defence who had said it should never have been suspended. He wanted the police brought in without delay and expected to see a prosecution.'

'The Defence Secretary wanted a prosecution? Or Jobell?'

'The order was from the Defence Secretary.'

The telephone on Lissack's desk rang. Cursing, he lifted the receiver. Antonia listened while some financial transaction of impenetrable complexity was discussed.

She had become aware that the most interesting thing about Lissack was not the look in his eyes of a sardonic assassin but the voice. All hint of German origin had been erased from it; for his adopted country he had cultivated a drawling version of Home Counties speech. It was as though his linguistic studies had been an unremitting diet of early British films. The effect was strangely hypnotic.

Lissack had turned his head away. It was as if he had dismissed her existence. She let her eyes wander round the study in which they sat. On her previous visit, under the wing of Bridget Boyle, she had hardly had time to examine anything apart from the telephone wiring. Gilt and ormolu and foxy wood reigned supreme. It was a room furnished by someone with a mania for French Empire pieces; all that it lacked was a bust of the Little Emperor. But no doubt Lissack's living presence made up for that.

He finished the conversation at last and went to a drinks tray on a marble-topped commode. He poured himself a brandy. She needed a drink herself but he didn't offer one. When he came back to the desk, he remained standing.

'What use are you expecting me to make of this information?'

'My impression from another occasion is that you are able to make a lot of use of it.'

She could see she had shaken him now. 'What do you know about that?'

'Enough. But this time you could find it more difficult. Unless you move fast.'

'You say your Director wasn't available when Jobell called. Has he had the message yet?'

'No. He's due back around lunchtime tomorrow. That's when a decision will be taken.'

He went to the fireplace and stood thinking. The books displayed on the shelves beside him made no pretence of being there to be read. Arranged in symmetrical groups of ten or so, they existed to provide elegant leather-lined spaces. Inside the spaces small pictures and a variety of clocks and ornaments were displayed.

Lissack gestured with his glass. 'This bringing-in of the Defence Minister – did you understand *Jobell* decided to take the case to him? If so, why?'

'I can't say.' The story had begun to take on an eerie sort of reality for her. 'The thing that came over clearly was that the Minister was livid there'd been no action. Apparently he told Jobell that whatever had been decided in the past was no longer acceptable to him.'

He frowned as though still not entirely willing to credit her story. Then he picked up his jacket and put it on slowly. 'That's all you can tell me, is it?'

'Yes.'

'How many other people in your office know about this?'

'Only the Private Secretary.'

He nodded briskly. 'Right. I needn't keep you any longer.' He moved towards the door. For a moment she feared he was planning to drive off somewhere to deal with what she had told him, making the whole operation pointless. But it seemed he had opened the door only for her to pass through.

'About the money – ' she said.

'You'll get the money if and when I establish you've told me the truth.'

She wondered how fierce a show of indignation it would be sensible to make; but before she had decided, he went on, 'Telephone me here at about this time tomorrow evening. Assuming your information has proved useful to me, you'll be told where you can collect a package. It'll be in London, not here. Please don't visit me here again.'

'I have to have the money before the weekend.'

'You'll get it.'

He was studying her again as they crossed the hall.

'I gather you're not being appreciated enough in the Bureau.'

'Appreciated?'

'Salary-wise.'

'I just need a supplement rather urgently at the moment.'

He placed an arm along her shoulders. 'Perhaps we can come up with some ideas for more supplements. Would you be interested?'

'I might.'

'Good.' His fingers lightly explored the flesh of her upper arm, brushed her rump as they slid away. He had judged that, broadly speaking, a suger-daddy approach was what was needed. Plainly she looked younger than she felt.

From the steps in front of the house he gazed about the empty gravelled circle. 'Where did you leave your car?'

'By the stables. I didn't want to advertise my presence.'

He took her hand and patted it. 'You're a bright girl. I'd like to see more of you.'

'I shall telephone tomorrow,' she said, 'about my money.'

He was still on the steps and watching as she turned the

209

corner of the stables. He would be able to read her registration plate as she drove away but it didn't matter now. She had to believe he was hooked.

Stopping in the lay-by she had reconnoitred earlier, near the entrance gates to the house, she killed her engine and reached for the recorder. The relief that had swept over her as she left Lissack was giving way once more to tension. So far she had been relying on coolness and a little courage. They were resources she had known from the ploy to trap Mancini years ago she could summon up when the pressure was on. Now she was at the mercy of Sod.

No matter that the half-day in Lyell's workshop had gone well, that tapping the line at Rushers Lye had proved more straightforward than she had foreseen, that the microphone and recorder had worked like a dream when tested. Sod, patron devil of technical devices, always bided his time.

Nothing was happening on the line from the house. She went back five minutes on the tape, a generous allowance for the time that had elapsed since leaving Lissack: still nothing. Another quarter of an hour went by in silence. Sod grinned over her shoulder.

She smoked a cigarette, reflected on the pointlessness of all effort, hated Fender for the whole idea. Then an outgoing call lifted her heart for a brief while. The ringing tone lasted for over a minute but there was no answer from the other end. When the receiver was replaced she lit another cigarette.

The call was repeated at ten minute intervals. She could picture Lissack cursing behind his desk or prowling the study, brandy glass in hand. It was getting late. The disagreeable thought occurred that a moment must come when he would abandon his efforts for the night. She could accept the discomfort of staying in the lay-by until morning in the hope that Lissack would be more successful then. But, suppose he wasn't? He might decide to leave for his London office and try again from there. In which event the work of the last few days would have been a total waste of time. Staring grimly into the night, she felt her spirits sag to zero.

When hope had almost vanished, a call was answered. The voice was male, curt and neutral. 'Who's that?'

'Lissack.'

There was the briefest of hesitations. 'Yes?'

'I've been trying to reach you for some time.'

'It's been a very busy evening. As you may have heard.'

'Are you alone?'

'Yes, but is this urgent? I'd prefer we dealt with any business in the usual – '

'Some news has reached me which I find extremely disturbing. I'm told that instructions have been given for a certain investigation to be reopened. The police are likely to be brought in.'

'Impossible.'

'I should like to think so. But I'm told there's now a strong wish to go for a prosecution.'

'Where did you get this information?'

'From someone in the office which carried out the original enquiry. Do you follow me?'

'Yes.'

'This person decided I would be prepared to pay something for advance warning of what was in the wind.'

'Who is asking for action?'

'Apparently the head of the Department that granted the contract has discussed the case with his Minister. A message has been left, to be given to the Director of the orginal office when he gets in tomorrow – late morning I'm told.'

Lissack paused, evidently waiting for a response. Getting none, he said, 'I hope you agree with me something must be done to put a stop to this once and for all.'

The voice at the other end sounded suddenly furious. 'This is some stupid mistake. I made it plain that all proceedings were to stop. That was clearly understood.'

'Did this particular Minister know that?'

'I found he hadn't heard of the case when we had a brief conversation. I said that if it was ever referred to him I wanted him to have a word with me before issuing any instructions.'

'He doesn't appear to have remembered that.'

'Are you sure your informant's sound?'

'I've no reason to think otherwise.'

There was a pause before the voice said, wearily this time, 'Well, leave it to me. You don't have to worry.'

'You'll stop it?'

'It will be stopped.'

Lissack said with careful emphasis, 'Good. Because I don't think the fact that friend Ellitt is no longer of this world would make the press any less interested in his attentions to Cahill during that weekend you asked me to set up.'

There was another longer silence. Then the voice said, 'Your worries will be taken care of. I shall speak to the people concerned first thing tomorrow. I think we should not continue this conversation. Goodnight.' The line went dead.

She played it back. It came over as clearly as the first time. Leaning back in her seat, she laughed into the night. Sod had failed to strike after all.

From the telephone box at the other end of the lay-by she called her flat. Fender's voice announced her number. He sounded expectant but quieter than usual.

'Success,' she said.

She heard a faint sigh of relief. 'And the identity of the other party . . . ?'

'I can't tell at present. But the dialling on the tape will give us the number. I'll check first thing tomorrow. Unless you recognize the voice when you hear it.'

'You didn't find it familiar yourself?'

'No.'

'Are you sure?' He seemed shaken.

She hesitated. 'Once or twice I thought I might have heard it before. But that's all. Are you saying I *should* know it?'

'. . . Unless my conclusions have been totally false. Which is always possible of course.' Once more he was sounding unlike himself.

'Tell me.'

'I'd rather not. Listen and think about it again on your way back to London.'

'Are you all right, Ludo?'

'Perfectly.' He disconnected before she could speak again.

Back in the car about to switch on her lights, she was conscious of another car slowing down. It stopped about twenty yards further on, close to the phone box. Moments later a second car appeared and parked behind the first. Both switched off their lights. In the gloom she dimly saw someone get out of the first and speak to the driver behind. They went to the phone box. So far as she could judge they were oblivious of her presence.

There was no point in hanging about. She started her engine and pulled out of the lay-by. Her headlights briefly caught the rearmost car and she saw two or three faces illuminated for a second. Then she was past and heading for London.

North of Guildford she switched on the radio to catch the midnight news. The signing of a new Anglo-Irish agreement by the two Prime Ministers was the lead item. Cross-border pursuit of terrorists by both police forces had been agreed, along with the inclusion of a Garda element in a new anti-terrorist intelligence machine being established in Belfast. The Ulster Defence Regiment was to be replaced by a body under police command. In return, Dublin had agreed to arrange a referendum for changes to the language of the Irish constitution to allay fears in the North on unification. A massive programme of economic cooperation was planned. The White House had sent a message of warm congratulations. In a brief interview, Plowright said he believed this was a truly historic event, making the possibility of lasting peace in the North a reality at last.

Reaching for the recorder, she played the tape again, chiding herself for being dull-witted. Fender had been right. Of course she had known the voice.

214

21

Entering her flat she found Fender slumped in an arm-chair in semi-darkness. The sole illumination came from the smallest of the table lamps. She snapped on the overhead light and saw his head jerk as he stirred out of a doze; he half-shouted some word. Although the smell of his pipe tobacco hung in the room, there was no sign of a glass. That he should have lasted all these hours without recourse to her whisky was something outside her experience. The subdued way he had spoken on the telephone came back to her.

He levered himself upright, then hovered, offering to relieve her of coat and overnight bag. She reached inside the bag and handed him the recorder. He took it silently. Studying his face, she decided that he didn't look unwell, merely morose. Possibly he was sinking into one of his troughs of melancholy when all responses were despairing or bitter, or both. She felt resentment that, returned victorious from an expedition into which he had virtually dragooned her, she was being received like this. He could surely have made more of an effort at welcome. Apart from which, for him to have such a mood at this time was inexplicable.

'Is there something wrong?' she asked.

'No, no. I've had rather a trying afternoon, that's all.' His tone was stilted.

She looked at the clock: not quite one A.M. 'I'll make some coffee.'

He was gesturing shyly. 'I decided that perhaps . . .'

She turned. On the table behind were plates, cutlery

and glasses, sandwiches and a bottle of Vouvray. He had been rummaging at the back of one of the drawers of a side table where she kept linen and had discovered place mats she had hoped were lost for good.

He said, 'I found a delicatessen open on my way here. I hope you like turkey.'

She told herself she had been mean-minded. 'I'll go and change. Listen to the tape.'

When she returned he was back in the armchair, the recorder beside him. He looked marginally more cheerful.

'You've listened?'

'Three times. Congratulations, the whole thing seems to have worked perfectly. Was there a moment when you feared it might not come off?'

'The only really bad part was waiting while he tried to raise a reply to his calls.'

He refused a sandwich, claiming, remarkably, that he wasn't hungry. She poured the wine and sat down opposite him. 'Did you know George the Fifth insisted on turkey sandwiches beside his bed every night?'

'Especially in Bognor Regis,' he said. He smiled at last and she was aware that her presence was slowly lifting his mood.

'How long have you been sure it was Plowright?' she asked.

'I made some enquiries earlier today which convinced me it couldn't be anybody else. So you did recognize his voice in the end . . .'

'The television programme we saw came back to me. It was after I heard the agreement with Dublin had been signed that I remembered. I don't quite know why but I was very shaken. I suppose I admired him, more than most politicians. He seemed so determined to do something worthwhile.'

'No doubt he was. His judgment of acceptable means happened to be slightly flawed.'

'But it wasn't only *his* judgment, was it? We were wildly wrong, thinking it couldn't be a government operation because of Ellitt!' She shook her head. 'All the same, I still don't understand how they could employ him when they'd decided he was totally unreliable.'

'But they didn't. Plowright did.'

She paused with a sandwich halfway to her mouth. 'What do you mean – *they* didn't?'

'I mean that the murder of Cahill didn't take place as a result of a government decision. I believe the government as such knew nothing about it. Plowright was acting throughout *by himself*. He had reached the conclusion that there'd never be a worthwhile deal with Dublin while Cahill was in the Cabinet there to block it. So he decided he should be removed. He knew the government would never sanction the operation. If it was to be done, it was down to him. Plowright *solus* – unaided – except by Ellitt acting as his personal agent – massaging history to take the course he believed was right. Fascinating!'

He put his head back against the chair, half-closing his eyes. 'But I'm sure the story goes back before the Cahill business. While I was waiting for you to return, Plekhanov came into my mind. Do you remember Plekhanov?'

So they were to have foreplay and there was no way of knowing how long it would last. She steeled herself to patience. 'No.'

'He was the determinist who invented historical materialism. Individuals according to Plekhanov couldn't bring about fundamental changes. Fitting people like Napoleon into his thesis of course proved a problem. Plowright would have worried him too.'

It seemed it was a night for Napoleons. 'I'm quite tired, Ludo. Tell me when it all began.'

'Very soon after Plowright became Secretary of State for Northern Ireland. He came to the conclusion that with certain obstacles removed, there was a chance he could turn his tour into a personal truimph. He would go for another negotiation with Dublin, and this time for a deal that could bring real changes in the North.

'There were two favourable factors which had been in existence before he arrived but which his predecessor hadn't been able to capitalize on. A President in the White House with ancestors on both sides of the Border and a quirky inclination to get involved in finding a solution; and a Taoiseach in Dublin who was sympathetic and strong enough to deliver a radical deal.

'The obstacles, as always in Ireland, were politicians exploiting the old hatreds to sustain their power and influence. In the North the ones who really mattered were Wedderburn and James Tull. None of the other Loyalists, for all their talk, had the muscle to lead an effective rebellion against another deal with Dublin. But in the South, there was the growing influence of Cahill who saw himself as the man to topple the Taoiseach by taking the line of no more concessions to the British and certainly no tampering with the Irish constitution.

'Then Wedderburn fell ill with throat cancer and became a spent force. And Plowright decided, no doubt after taking a lot of soundings, that *the North at least would be manageable if he could be rid of one man: Tull.*'

'. . . Who drove his car into a river at the beginning of the year and drowned – is that right?'

'Certainly he drowned.'

'You're saying it wasn't an accident . . .'

'I'm saying that the accident was arranged.'

'At Plowright's instigation?'

'Yes.'

'How can you be sure of that?'

218

He shrugged. 'I can't demonstrate certainty. Even to offer you evidence of likelihood would amongst other things involve extracting some frank answers to certain questions from the Royal Ulster Constabulary. But while I was in Dublin I heard an interesting story. A few minutes before the car left the road and sank in the river, someone saw it. At the time, according to this person, it contained two men. Only one body was found inside the car – Tull's.'

'Did this person tell the police?'

'They seem to have decided she was mistaken.'

'Perhaps she was.'

'I don't believe so. I think the police decided that pursuing a line of enquiry on that assumption might lead them to stumble on something they would rather not know. It was a very welcome death to them in many ways, provided Tull's erstwhile supporters continued to believe it was accidental. And there was a convenient patch of oil on the road.'

'You believe Ellitt was in the car . . .?'

'It will never be possible to prove it, but, yes, I do. I can also tell you how Plowright came to use Ellitt as his agent.' Fender steepled his hands on his chest, looking smug.

'Earlier today, in search of a little more background information on Plowright, I got in touch with his constituency agent. He was proud to fill me in with details of his Member's activities before entering politics. Go back to the file for Ellitt you saw at the Ministry of Defence. Which was his regiment during his first tour of duty with the Army in Ulster?'

'Prince Albert's Rifles, I think.'

'You will be interested to hear that a captain in the regiment serving in Ulster at that time was Plowright.' He paused for it to sink in. 'I suggest we are entitled to

219

assume that as fellow-officers Plowright and Ellitt knew each other very well. We can also guess they kept in touch in later years after they had both left the Army. When Plowright came to his momentous decision that one or two players should be removed from the political scene in Ireland by private enterprise, as it were, he had no need to look far for an instrument. An old friend had demonstrated he had just the right qualities and motivation in the operation that had led to his leaving the Army in disgrace.

'Disposing of Cahill was of course the more difficult proposition. In Northern Ireland, Ellitt was operating in a country he knew well. He could have got into a relationship with Tull by offering, as a former SAS officer, to talk about what he recalled the security people had known about Tull's involvement with Loyalist paramilitary organizations.

'But operating in Southern Ireland would have been altogether more dangerous. And Plowright's requirement in the case of Cahill was much more ambitious. He was not only to be removed from the scene by a method that would rule out suspicion of foul play. His end was if possible to carry an odium that would leave the political group he had built up round him with a nasty image problem. How they lighted on the AIDS solution we may never know. Perhaps Plowright saw the television programme on the research laboratory and had the idea of using the culture that had been developed there. Ellitt's medical background was obviously going to be an advantage. However Cahill needed to be lured into circumstances where he could be first drugged and then injected with the drug without his knowledge. Which is where Lissack came in.'

'So he was a party to the whole thing?'

'No, I don't believe he was. Plowright's intention was

220

to use Lissack as an unconscious agent for getting Cahill to England in circumstances where Ellitt could do his stuff. Plowright would already have known Lissack as a major employer of labour in Northern Ireland. And I believe there was more to the relationship than that. It was obviously to Plowright's house that Antrim was summoned that night he was told the Lissack investigation had to be dropped. No doubt Plowright explained the requirement as arising because he was getting valuable intelligence from Lissack. I'm sure he *was* – Roper-Hoare told me Plowright had a private source on Dublin intentions. Lissack with his contacts and influence there was well-placed to be the source. So there was a convenient story to feed to Antrim.

'In supplying information Lissack no doubt saw himself getting into a position where he could ask for a *quid pro quo* one day – more subsidies from the NIO for his business interests in the North perhaps. And when Plowright pressed him to get Cahill over to his house for a weekend and have Ellitt to stay at the same time, he would have been happy to oblige. I've no idea what line Plowright gave him about Ellitt's status and purpose. Perhaps he said he was an intelligence official whose role was to study Cahill at close quarters and report back to Plowright on the prospect of inducing him to modify his opposition to the new deal.

'If I'm right, Lissack had no idea that he was providing the facilities for an assassination. Unfortunately for Plowright however, Ellitt was neither as careful in his general conduct nor as efficient over the actual operation as he ought to have been – Cahill should have been drugged so effectively he couldn't have regained consciousness for even the second or two he subsequently supposed had been a nightmare. When after Cahill tells his account of the nightmare at breakfast, Lissack hears from the girl

221

who went to Ellitt's room that she believes he's on drugs because there's a hypodermic in his overnight bag, he may at first think it's no more than a faintly amusing coincidence. But Cahill goes back to Dublin, begins to be ill almost at once and dies. Lissack reflects how convenient that death is proving to the government. The more he broods on it, the odder Plowright's request to him to set up the weekend at which Cahill and Ellitt can meet, appears. He decides there is only one logical explanation. And if he's right, he has Plowright – in fact, *the whole government* – in the palm of his hand.'

She rubbed her eyes. Fatigue was catching up with her and she was not in the best shape to find the holes in his case. But one she could think of straight off.

'None of this explains Ellitt's own murder. Or are you suggesting that Plowright became nervous he'd talk and found another ex-Army friend to eliminate *him*?'

Fender looked pained. 'Ellitt's death calls for rather more thought than I've had time to give it.' His expression implied that she was being unreasonable.

She sighed and rose. 'I'm going to make coffee. When I come back, I hope you'll tell me how you intend to nail Plowright. There's no way you can prove Tull's death was arranged on his instructions. And establishing a direct connection between Lissack's words on the tape and Cahill's killing will take some doing.'

He gazed at her sombrely. Some marauding mosquito had identified him as a juicy target and attacked an eyelid so that he appeared on the point of winking. 'Did you know you've been bitten?' she asked.

He got up to examine himself in a mirror, made noises of extreme irritation mixed with disgust. To analyse the fine balance in him between vanity and self-loathing was a challenge she had never felt she had the time to tackle.

When she returned with the coffee, she found he had

been bathing the eyelid but to no noticeable effect. 'Have you decided what to do?'

'I shall go to the Prime Minister. If he expresses disbelief after hearing the tape, I shall tell him he need only allow me to confront Plowright with Lissack, when I will guarantee to get the whole story.'

She frowned. 'Aren't you intending to tell *anybody* first what you're doing?'

'We can't wait for Mansell to return to the office and I see little to be said for making a journey to Twickenham in order to fill him in. This is far too urgent.'

He was adopting his imperial manner, looking forward personally to blowing a hole in the Cabinet and watching the fall-out.

'I wasn't thinking of Mansell – what about Antrim? The Prime Minister would find it extraordinary that nothing had been said to *him*.'

'I think not.' His voice was curt; mention of Antrim's name had revived the stilted manner with which he had greeted her.

'But *he* should be the person who goes to No. 10. Loach worked for him, *I* work for him – so does Mansell for that matter! The investigation that uncovered what Plowright has done was a Bureau affair. You can't make it *your* personal business.'

'There would be no advantage in bringing Antrim in. I have good reasons for saying that. You must leave the decision on this to me.' She noticed the fingers of a hand working irritably against his chair.

Well, rot you, Ludo, she thought: if that's the way it's to be, I'm not staying to keep you company. She put down her cup. 'Right, there doesn't seem any more to be said. I assume you've worked out a way of handling this so that I don't lose my job. I certainly hope so. I'm going

223

to get some sleep while there's still time. The bed's made up in the spare room when you're ready.'

He shook his head. 'I shall be perfectly comfortable here. I should like to think for a while.' He looked guilty, but obstinate.

If he was hoping she would now stay and try to wheedle him out of his mood, he was doomed to disappointment. She left him with the coffee. The eyelid, she was glad to see, was getting worse.

She slept badly. Some of the time she was back in Lissack's study, conscious of his basilisk eye upon her, as she made a hopeless mess of her cover story. At other moments, it seemed she had insisted on accompanying Fender to No. 10. Finishing a magisterial account of Plowright's infamy, he told her to supply the climax by switching on the recorder. There was total silence. It became borne in on her that, through some error, she had wiped the tape.

When she rose, she discovered Fender was already washed and shaved. He looked remarkably unrumpled, considering the fact that he had apparently stayed in the armchair all night. Even the eyelid had resumed its normal proportions. From the window he was watching a dustcart devour the discard of the terrace. When she voiced mild annoyance because she had overflowing bags of rubbish in the kitchen, it was as much as she could do to restrain him from lumbering down the stairs in pursuit of the truck. It was clear he was trying to make amends for the last minutes before she went to bed. But he remained tense.

While she was in the kitchen, fixing toast and coffee, he called out, 'If I may, I shall make a telephone call.' She noticed he shut the door between them. He came into the room later, looking frustrated. Apparently there'd been no reply.

In the next quarter of an hour he tried again twice, still without success. He volunteered nothing about his purpose; but she sensed it was to do with whatever had so disconcerted him the previous day.

There was an incoming call shortly before eight o'clock. When she lifted the receiver, a voice said, 'I hope I didn't get you out of bed.' It was Busch.

She felt a mixture of pleasure and caution. 'How are you? Should I be congratulating you on settling The Troubles over the water?'

'Don't be chauvinistic,' he said equably. 'Listen – I'm calling now because I'll be tied up most of the morning. There are problems about the dinner we were going to have. During the night a message came in from Washington to the effect that I should fly back today. I've been booked out on a flight this afternoon. I wondered if you could possibly make lunch with me? I didn't want to leave without seeing you again.'

When she hesitated, he went on, 'In case you're wondering, I'm not planning to ask questions about the subject we discussed the other evening. I've guessed all the answers anyway – at least as many as I need to.'

She could justify accepting his invitation on the basis that she felt a vague duty to probe what answers he'd arrived at. Hopefully they weren't the right ones. But why should there have to be a justification? She wanted to see him again, anyway. They agreed to meet at Langans.

Back in the kitchen, Fender had switched on the radio for the eight o'clock news bulletin. 'That was Busch – ' she began, but he held up a hand to silence her. She listened.

'. . . burglary last night at the country home of the City

225

financier, Carl Lissack, in which Mr Lissack was shot and killed. The shooting apparently occurred when Mr Lissack disturbed the intruders who had tied up the domestic staff after breaking in. A number of valuables were taken, including what is believed to be one of the finest collections of Cézanne's paintings.'

Her reaction, after an initial unwillingness to believe it, was a bitter feeling that Fate had cheated her personally. Surely Lissack could have been left alive long enough for someone to interrogate him! She looked at Fender in despair. He was shaking his head slowly from side to side, his eyes cast down as though to fathom some subtlety in the pattern of the counter top.

'What will you do now?'

'*Do!*'

'With Lissack dead, you can't suggest staging a confrontation between him and Plowright if the Prime Minister wants more evidence.'

He shrugged.

'Suppose he flatly refuses to accept the tape means what we know it means?'

'Then I shall have failed.' He took a piece of toast and buttered a corner. 'But I don't intend to fail.'

She suspected he was putting on a show to hide his own despondency.

On the radio, two political commentators were talking about the implications of the new agreement with Dublin for Plowright's career. They agreed he had become a contender for the Party leadership. Confidence, one said, was his great strength, confidence that any problem will yield if you tackle it determined to succeed. And his approach to everything was quite exceptionally thorough.

She switched off the radio. 'Thorough is the word,' she said.

When Fender raised his eyebrows, she went on, 'With

Lissack dead, there's nobody left alive of those he saw as a threat to his security – first, Loach dies, then Ellitt, finally Lissack. Perfect.'

'Don't you think you're being a little precipitate in linking Lissack's death so firmly with the others? After all the house must have been a prime target for thieves. A mad collector of stolen paintings may have said to the right sort of criminal – A million dollars if you'll get me Lissack's Cézannes.'

'You don't believe that any more than I do.'

He was studying her face. 'You have a particular reason for speaking like this . . .'

She poured herself more coffee. It was pleasant to be able, on occasion, to pay him back in his own coin, keeping him in suspense. 'After I left Lissack, I stopped in a lay-by I'd already located as close enough to the house to pick up his calls. When he'd had his conversation with Plowright, I telephoned you from a box at the other end of the lay-by. I was about to drive off again when two cars stopped. The drivers exchanged a few words then went to the phone box. It crossed my mind at the time it looked rather like a rendezvous.

'A few moments ago I remembered something interesting about one of the cars. At the time my mind was full of the tape – trying to recall where I'd heard the voice on it before. But the other thing must have registered, during the second the car was in my headlights.'

She might have known he'd steal her thunder. 'You're going to tell me it was a dark blue Jaguar,' he said.

22

'Tell me how you are,' Pagett had said as soon as Fender had seated himself. The enquiry would have seemed unremarkable, left at that.

As Pagett moved to his own seat behind the desk, Fender looked about him, recalling the first time he had entered this handsome room. Pagett had been Secretary to the Cabinet and Civil Service Head for less than a week when Fender had arrived, to convey the uncomfortable news that the handsome house in Lugano owned by the Treasury Solicitor had been acquired at a bargain price from a front company of Mancini's.

'No more trouble with the heart since your retirement?'
'None.'
'You have regular check-ups I suppose.'
'Not especially.'
'What did the quacks have to say about it last time?'
'It seemed to be behaving.'

A punctilious courtesy, Fender had reminded himself, always softened the edge of Pagett's relentless application to whatever was the work in hand. And of course their dealings went back a long way. Yet there had been something curious in such solicitude.

Pagett had extracted one of the day's sixty from the silver casket on the desk between them. 'Not knowing how you'd been caused me a little hesitation over calling you.'

Uneasily, Fender had watched Pagett crumple his match, drop it with a neat flourish in the ashtray. From the moment of leaving Antonia's, the day had been going wrong. Even before that, there had been the frustration of getting no reply to his calls to Antrim's flat. As he shaved, he had at last acknowledged there would be no accommodation with his conscience until he had unsaid his advice that Antrim should go to the Home Secretary. He would substitute Mansell's prescription, a talk with Finnessey. At least survival would then remain a possibility for him. Not that he wished him to survive, only that he himself should not have encompassed his execution. But each time he tried Antrim's number, there had been no answer.

In the Edgware Road his taxi had broken down. He had had to take a bus where his bulk as he stood in the aisle had produced shaming incidents and once a total blockage. Reaching his club at nine-forty-five, he had attempted once more to contact Antrim, this time at the Bureau. Baxter, his Private Secretary, had announced that he had already gone out again to visit the Home Office. It seemed Antrim had been working on files before even the industrious Baxter had put in an appearance; so the failure of the earlier calls to raise him was explained. But that was no comfort. Gone was the last chance to escape guilt by saving Antrim's skin.

His mood was grim when he made his call to the Prime Minister's office and found himself put through to a youngish woman with a spiky manner. Getting beyond her to someone more congenial proved impossible. Mention of past service and rank in the Bureau had left her unmoved. With difficulty he extracted the information that the Prime Minister was away inspecting a new factory on Merseyside until the late afternoon. The Principal Private Secretary was absent at some meeting in Whitehall and others of the breed were all alleged to be unavailable.

'Does the Prime Minister know you *personally*?' she had asked frigidly. He had admitted he didn't but countered with Pagett's name as that of someone who could confirm his bona fides. She had remained unimpressed. Gritting his teeth he had been driven to agree to telephone again at noon when the Principal Private Secretary was expected back in his hutch.

Afterwards he had paced the hall of the club, looking for someone or something to lash with his tongue. Complaint at the continuing absence of the *Tablet* from the periodicals in the reading room provided no relief. At last he had taken himself onto the streets again, a battleship, full of menace, ready to sink without warning lesser craft that failed to scurry from his path.

There he had found only cause for more irritation. Gawping tourists surged like tidal flotsam. A brown perspex box, identical with the monstrosities in Dublin, was being Lego-ed up on a building site off St James's Square. In Jermyn Street windows, shirts of exceptional vulgarity were on display, intended for high-flying, market-oriented, Mammon-programmed creatures of an alien world.

He had returned to the club, telling himself he would brook no nonsense this time from the spiky creature at No. 10. But there had been activity while he was out. A call had come through from the Cabinet Office, he was requested to ring back urgently. Somebody, perhaps the very creature he had spoken to, had presumably decided it would be as well to consult Pagett about his earlier approach.

When he rang, he found himself talking to a pleasant youth. 'Your housekeeper suggested I might catch you at your club. Sir Norman Pagett was wondering if you could possibly step round . . . ? Would it be helpful if I sent a car . . .?' After the earlier encounter, the youth's tone was a balm.

The reference to contact with Mrs Bastin had been

surprising since he had made clear to No. 10 that he was in his club. But all seemed plain otherwise: Pagett had undertaken to find out what he had on his mind. A momentary reluctance to be diverted from his original plan soon faded. Pagett would have to be brought into the Plowright business at some stage; it would be no bad thing for him to get the story now. Time would be saved by their seeing the Prime Minister together. Accepting the offer of the car, he had arrived at the Cabinet Office shortly before lunch and been shown in to Pagett with barely a pause to recover his breath in the outer office where the Private Secretaries sat.

'Ludo,' Pagett had gone on to say, 'there's been a rather tiresome development.'

He had stilled his hand as it reached inside his bag to bring out the recorder.

'It affects your old office and may cause you some distress.'

'I see.' And of course it was now becoming clear: this meeting had nothing to do with his earlier call to No. 10 of which Pagett presumably knew nothing. An accident of timing had led him to draw a wrong conclusion. He was about to be told of Antrim's visit to the Home Secretary and its inevitable outcome. But once more Pagett was saying something he had not expected.

'Antrim has attracted some unfortunate attention. A few weeks back, Bedford, the newspaper mogul, who numbers the *Clarion* among his clutch of tabloids, spoke to the Home Secretary. He said that one of the *Clarion*'s reporters had acquired information about a senior official which he, Bedford, felt duty-bound to pass on rather than use.' Pagett's eyebrows twitched briefly. 'It seems that some call girl crashed her car and killed herself after leaving an apartment in Harley Street. The *Clarion* has a

231

source in the hospital to which the girl was taken. Apparently the body bore marks to show that she had been involved in sado-masochistic activity of an extreme kind shortly before her death. The reporter following this up learned from a friend of the girl's he contacted in a drinking club that her client in Harley Street was a senior civil servant in the Home Office.

'Bedford said he was warning the Home Secretary so that he could do any necessary stable-cleaning without the accompaniment of publicity. Apart from a brief report confined solely to the girl, the *Clarion* would be dropping the story. A noble act; but not unadjacent, I fancy, to thoughts of possibly expediting his knighthood.'

'A knighthood! For *Bedford*!?'

Pagett tapped away ash and smiled thinly. 'The Prime Minister has found his newspapers very supportive recently. Some recognition of the fact has been mooted on both sides. Anyway, the Home Secretary spoke to Finnessey, his Permanent Head, whom I don't think you've met, and exhaustive enquiries were made. The reassuring news that emerged was that no civil servant in the Home Office, senior or junior, had an address in Harley Street. However, relief was short-lived. Yesterday Bedford honoured the Home Secretary with a further call. A woman claiming to be the call girl's mother had turned up at the *Clarion*'s office the previous afternoon asking for the reporter under whose name the original story had been printed. He wasn't in and another reporter interviewed her.

'The woman said her daughter's client had been a very important government official who'd been in the habit of using a false name. She had now discovered his true identity and wanted to know how much the *Clarion* would pay for that. The reporter fenced, hoping his colleague would soon be back and could take over. However, the woman, who seems to be an odd fish, got up and walked out. The reporter decided it would be as well to follow her. From the *Clarion* office she went to an apartment in the block in Harley Street from which the girl was seen hurrying on the night she crashed her car. Subsequent enquiry by *Clarion* bloodhounds established that the apartment is occupied by Antrim. Presumably the "Home Office civil servant" angle originated in something the call girl had misunderstood and told her friend about his work.

'You can guess what happened after Bedford's call. The Home Secretary told Finnessey that if the story was accurate, he wanted Antrim out. Accordingly Finnessey asked Antrim to see him first thing this morning. It seems that Antrim admitted it was all true, said he had been on the point of telling the Home Secretary that he was ready to resign should there be a really damaging item in the press. Finnessey unhappily had to tell him that wouldn't do for the Home Secretary, things had gone too far.'

'Is Bedford going to publish the story?'

'No, he's undertaken that nothing will appear.'

Fender shook his head. Relief at the lifting away of guilt was replaced by a feeling that he must in some way atone. 'Then surely Antrim doesn't *have* to go! If the mother can be persuaded to shut up – '

'That would not be a solution. The Home Secretary does not view sado-masochism as a suitable leisure pursuit for officials. He shares the country's concern about our general moral condition.' He gave one of his brief eyebrow twitches, then reached for another cigarette. 'But, to be fair, would *you* keep Antrim if you were Home Secretary, Ludo?'

'He will be difficult to replace.'

'I agree. But he has to go all the same. Actually it may turn out quite well for him. The Chairman of Lloyds is looking for somebody senior with experience in anti-corruption. Antrim might be rather suitable for that world, don't you feel?'

Pagett took a turn about the room, swinging his spectacles in a circle as he went, a neat, unhurried figure, content to be master of the shadows while Ministers preened in the sun's fickle rays. 'Before they parted, Finnessey talked to Antrim about the succession. There is no one in Whitehall at present Finnessey or I would regard as suitable. Antrim offered a suggestion that is more than acceptable however. It is that you should come back yourself for a while – assuming your health would allow it.'

'*Antrim suggested that?*'

'Yes.'

He made no attempt to conceal his astonishment. Pagett was saying, 'I realize you may view this with mixed feelings. Retirement no doubt has its attractions. Moreover, I imagine you wouldn't want to commute from where you're living. But perhaps you could take a small flat in town for weekdays.'

Mutely he spread his hands, shaking his head. He needed time to recover, time to come to terms with the irony that Antrim had thought of him like this.

He said, 'I'm flattered of course . . .'

'But . . .?'

'There are a great many considerations. Including whether I really could stomach working for politicians again.' He was conscious he was talking to delay the moment when he must give his answer. 'A world where expediency always wins, where knighthoods for people like Bedford are not even seen as sick jokes. Do I want to come back to that?'

'Politicians are what the system makes them. The life either brutalizes or trivializes. Never to feel free to be totally honest must deform anyone. And of course, in government, they never have time to think. Officials exist to save the country from the consequences. But I don't need to remind you of that.'

'Officials exist to be blamed for Ministers' shortcomings.'

'Blame only really stings if it's warranted.'

'I never felt that.'

Pagett shrugged. 'It's still an honourable calling. Unfashionable in the eyes of the young of course. But they are going through a grossly materialistic phase. They will learn to despise themselves soon enough.' He paused beside the window and looked out. 'Despite everything, the challenge here is more worthwhile than most things in this country. Don't tell me it's quite lost its savour for you.'

He returned to his desk and looked at a note without appearing to read it; but that was all part of his gift.

'I should say, incidentally, that if you took the appointment, it could carry rather wider responsibilities than before. We have some changes in mind. The Prime Minister is particularly keen to take away from the intelligence and security people cases having little to do with their real concerns but which they undertake in default of appropriate resources elsewhere. To make way for the extra burden you would be freed of the less delicate corruption investigations which can go to the police. You might also have oversight of the new fraud investigation body for the City's more inventive entrepreneurs. You'll find yourself reporting direct to the Prime Minister, not the Home Secretary.' He was making Fender's decision appear like a foregone conclusion.

A memory came back to Fender from an airless Oxford street. Iris Keysing was standing in the doorway of that crooked house and saying, 'A man is going to offer you something . . . I don't know whether you'll accept . . .'

So she'd been right, that not-quite-mad creature in the ridiculous slippers guarding the shade of Betsy Frogg.

Behind him the door had opened. The youth who had received him appeared and gave a piece of paper to Pagett. He said, 'The draft from No. 10 – they'd be glad if you'd look at it urgently.'

Pagett seemed merely to glance before looking up again.

'Am I expected to comment?'

'I understand so.'

He brooded. 'Say . . . I find it entirely clear. Nothing more.'

He put the piece of paper face downwards on his desk and turned back to Fender. 'Perhaps you'd let me have your decision pretty soon – tomorrow morning at the latest. We don't want the Home Secretary developing ideas of his own on Antrim's successor.'

It seemed at last the moment to raise the subject of Plowright. Fender took out the recorder and placed it on the desk.

'Before I do decide, there's something I would like to discuss. I was on the point of going to the Prime Minister about it when your Private Secretary telephoned me.'

Pagett was staring blankly at the recorder.

'I'm going to play you a short tape. I'd prefer you didn't ask me how it came into my possession.'

When Plowright's voice spoke, Pagett lifted his head slowly to gaze above Fender's head. He could have been concentrating on an intricate piece of music.

At the end, Fender said, 'My guess is that I don't need to identify either of those voices to you, although one will have been more familiar than the other. Am I right?'

Pagett's nod was almost imperceptible.

'And would I also be right in thinking I don't have to

236

tell you what Lissack was referring to at the end of the conversation?'

Pagett lit another cigarette. 'Who, apart from yourself, knows the contents of this tape?'

'One other person. She's an official – discreet and responsible, you'll be glad to hear. But with certain feelings which I share.'

'Amounting to what?'

'That Plowright must be stopped from playing God, and never given the opportunity again.' He paused, reflecting. 'In her case, she will be expecting rather more than that.'

'In what way?'

'She will expect that he's not allowed to escape the normal punishment of a murderer.'

Pagett sighed. His spectacles lay on the papers in front of him. He picked them up and examined the lenses as though they might have a contribution to make. He said conversationally, 'Do you know, I always rather admired Plowright. He had the clearest vision of what he wanted of all the Cabinet. And he seemed almost capable of *willing* success. When we were gossiping one day, I happened to quote a line of Cavafy to him. He said he admired only one poem of Cavafy's and mentioned the title. I didn't bother to look it up until after I learned certain things recently.'

He took a book from a drawer in his desk and opened it at a page where there was a marker. 'Listen.

> To certain men when there comes a day
> > They must say the great Yes or the great No.
> > Whoever he is will straightway show,
> Who has Yes within him ready to say;
>
> And on he goes and honour ensues him.
> > He never repents who has once denied;
> > He would say No again, if he were tried.
> Yet that proper No all his life subdues him.'

He shut the book again. 'I find that quite revealing.'

Fender said, 'How long have you known?'

'Not very long. And perhaps not everything. If I knew everything I should know how and why you came to be in possession of that tape. Are you going to tell me?'

'It would be better if I didn't.'

Pagett stared at him for a while without speaking. 'I have to trust you, Ludo. But of course, I do.'

'Thank you.'

'You were interested to know if something was being done.' He picked up the sheet of paper the Private Secretary had brought in and handed it across the desk.

The heading read 'Resignation of Secretary of State for Northern Ireland.' Fender looked up. 'Plowright's resigned?'

'Not quite. But he will have done by this evening. The Prime Minister still has to talk to his proposed successor and that can't happen until the late afternoon.'

He read on. It was a statement to accompany an exchange of letters between the Prime Minister and Plowright which were not attached. It explained that Plowright had been suffering from a serious illness for several months. Against medical advice he had remained in office because of the overriding importance of bringing negotiations with the Irish government to a satisfactory conclusion. Now that the new agreement had been signed by the two Prime Ministers he was relinquishing his appointment to undergo urgent treatment and to allow his successor to bring undiminished energies to consolidating the new era of hope which he believed had arrived for Northern Ireland. Because recovery from his illness would require prolonged convalescence, he had decided it would not be fair to his constituents to be without a Member of Parliament for many months and he was accordingly resigning his seat also.

'So that is what is being done,' Fender said.

'Yes.'

'Will more be said about the nature of the illness?'

'I doubt it.'

'And the treatment . . .?'

'Abroad.'

'In some secrecy, I imagine . . .'

'I daresay.'

'You don't suppose the condition might be terminal?'

'Not to my knowledge,' Pagett said. He consulted the lenses of the spectacles again for a while before looking up. 'But in these days, who can tell?'

23

At Langan's, Busch had reserved an upstairs table, away from the *glitterati*. Unless he had been taking advice in the Embassy, it seemed he knew his London better than he had made out.

He greeted Antonia with a wave, a small package in his hand. She noted a different tie, an apricot silk affair that went some way to redeem his earlier choice. Over drinks he asked her advice on buying a present for a secretary at the Embassy who had done some special work for him. His hallmark, as host, was a subtle balance of attentiveness and amused relaxation. He succeeded in conveying the impression that he was floating free in time. She had expected to sense a mind being folded up and packed away, the final distancing rites of the traveller on the point of departure. But if that was happening, he concealed it very well.

For her, time held no comparable compulsions. She drank a dry martini very slowly and decided to match his nonchalance. The afternoon's In tray could be faced in the same spirit if she took the mood back with her in no more than a gentle haze of alcohol. But in any case she would not be feeling much like work before the call from Fender came through: he had promised to telephone her as soon as his visit to No. 10 was over.

The small package proved to be a parting gift, an eighteenth-century manual in French on the making of books.

'How are the classes?' he asked. The expression in his

eyes was momentarily earnest. She realized it was important to him that she liked his present.

'They've ended for the summer break. I've decided to do another course in the autumn.'

She ran her fingers over the spine of the book, caressed the pages, decided not to dwell on how must it must have cost.

'It's beautiful.' There was no reason to deny the truth this late in their acquaintance. 'I shall treasure it.'

He leaned back. For the first time since they had met she felt she had seen him vulnerable.

When they had ordered lunch, she said, 'Is Washington going to be pleased about the new agreement with Dublin?'

'No doubt about it.'

'Did Cleveland play a big part in getting it signed?'

'He thinks he did.'

'What do *you* say?'

'Insofar as both governments knew it was the only way of getting him out of their hair and the money rolling in, the answer's "yes".' He grinned. 'Cleveland will have three minutes of glory on the White House lawn, if the television people can be persuaded to take enough interest. Then – back to the ranch, waiting for the President to call again with something juicier. Which won't happen.'

'Why not?'

'The President sent him on this mission because he'd been agitating for something to do. Also to keep him out of mischief. From the latter point of view he didn't perform with complete success. As the President will certainly have heard.'

She supposed this must be a reference to the closeness of the relationship with Mrs Cahill; and, perhaps, with Cahill himself at an earlier stage.

'You don't like him.'

Busch cast a disenchanted eye over a mural on the other side of the room. 'I'm allergic to being asked to investigate things that should be left alone. The sort of politician I admire has a feeling about what it's best *not* to know. Cleveland doesn't.'

'You won't be working for him any more . . .?'

'As from ten o'clock this morning, thank God, no.'

He told her a dryly amusing story of the farewells at the Embassy, of Cleveland wanting to be sure he would be first back in Washington.

'What about *you*?' she asked. 'What are you going back to?'

'Langley. For a short time anyway – I'm expecting a posting in the fall.'

She shook her head. 'I meant – do you have a family in Washington, a home?'

'No family. I used to be married but we divorced three years ago. There weren't any children. My parents have gone to live in Honolulu.'

For some reason he had chosen to deliver more information than she had sought. He was silent, watching her choose her *hors d'oeuvre*, but she sensed the question that was coming once the trolley had moved away.

'You've been married . . .?'

It was more of a statement than a question – he knew the answer. Presumably this was something that had come out when he had checked on her through the Embassy. She nodded.

'Divorced?'

'No, he died in a plane crash.'

'Are you planning to marry again?'

'I'm not sure.'

'You're not sure you want to . . .?'

'Rather like that.'

He persisted. 'I wondered if you'd decided that fighting

242

your way to the top of a man's world is what turns you on.'

'Do I look that aggressive?'

'I just wondered.'

She felt driven to a further statement. 'Sometimes I think it would be pleasant to be married again. Sometimes I think it may be as well to stay as I am. One discovers things about oneself . . .' Spearing asparagus, she thought: this is burbling, he'll be tempted into more questions. 'Let's talk about something else.'

'Why not?' he said cooperatively, picking up his glass. 'What about this unassuming little wine? A shy charm, would you say? A good match for the weather?' He gave a nod towards the drizzle down in Stratton Street. 'Or the sad end of Mr Lissack last night – we could talk about that. An imaginative arrangement, I thought.' His tone remained unchanged, gently bantering.

She fenced. 'Imaginative?'

'Perhaps that's too much of a compliment – the method *was* a little hackneyed. Efficient anyway. A pity about the pictures though. Cézannes! I thought that was going a bit far, there must have been plenty of other stuff, although perhaps not as portable. My suggestion on behalf of Western civilization would be that in about a year's time, they should be found unharmed in some disused mine shaft. Or better still, an Irish bog. That would be the poetic answer, don't you think?'

To discover exactly what he was driving at, she had to keep him talking.

'Is this what you were claiming on the telephone you'd worked out?'

'I admit to having had a little help.' Busch waited for someone who had paused by their table to move out of earshot. 'Did I tell you the other day that, as well as *your*

243

photograph, my people got a shot of the driver of the car that brought Ellitt's visitors that evening?'

'You *know* you didn't tell me.'

He produced an unapologetic grin. 'Must have slipped my mind. I decided to have them look at the print back in Washington. Apparently they discovered a perfect match in the index of saints and sinners: Victor Waverley Fadd, last identified three years back when he was serving under commercial cover in the British Embassy in Vienna but known still to be in government employment. I found that *fascinating*.'

The skin on the back of her neck began to creep.

'I also found it baffling – at least to begin with. Then I realized it could provide an explanation of the curious report I'd had about your Prime Minister being agitated on account of Cahill's death. If that had been an operation for which his authority had never been sought or given, he could have decided when he heard about it later that *such a dangerous situation had been produced, Ellitt and anybody else who'd been involved had to be taken out*. When Lissack's death was announced on the radio this morning I was sure I was right. My guess is that he wasn't made conscious of the operation at the outset, but, unfortunately for his well-being, discovered later what Ellitt was up to.

'What I still don't know – and presumably you're not going to be sporting enough to tell me – is who was behind the whole thing. Or will you?'

'You said you wouldn't be asking any questions.'

He sighed. 'It's got to be a politician. No official in this country would go out on a limb to quite that extent. A politician who furthermore knew Ellitt pretty well and wasn't worried by his past record. If I'd had a little longer here, I might have discovered if my best bet was right. As it is, I suppose I'll just have to watch the newspapers for a government reshuffle. That could be the trickiest part for the Prime Minister of course. It's one thing to eliminate a couple of dancers. Shooting the pianist might bring the house down.'

She adopted a look of weary disbelief. 'I suppose you've passed your fantasies on to Cleveland?'

'No, I decided not to burden him. He might have blurted out the story in the wrong place.'

'During pillow-talk with Mrs Cahill perhaps?'

'Ah!' Busch said. He raised a hand dramatically. 'A breakthrough! You've admitted to knowing something! And it happens to be one of the items I didn't think you knew!!'

'But you've told your own people . . .'

'Yes.'

'What will they do?'

'*Do?*'

'Will they put it in a report? Will the President be told?'

'Not unless somebody has a brainstorm. No American interest could possibly be served by any of this surfacing. What the US government wants more than anything else is for the Irish problem to go away. It's inconvenient domestically, it's a nuisance in relations with London. As long as you've got terrorism in Northern Ireland, we're going to have British Ministers flying into Washington, looking injured and wanting to know why we don't do more to stop arms and money being sent to the IRA. At best it's boring, trying to fend them off, at worst it can lead to the President having to do things he doesn't much like because they cost votes. Nobody would thank us for spreading around the story of how Cahill happened to die of AIDS from having a hypodermic stuck in him by your late security consultant. Far less if we said who we believed had employed Ellitt.'

He could be misleading her. Intelligence agencies

existed to provide intelligence, not hug it to their bosoms. But she had a feeling he was telling the truth.

'Anyway,' Busch said, 'I didn't ask you to lunch to talk about all that. I wanted to arrange our next meeting.'

'Since you're just off to Washington that doesn't sound too realistic a possibility.'

'On the contrary, it's entirely realistic. Let's go for mid-October.'

'What about the posting you said you were expecting?'

'Didn't I tell you?' he said. 'It's London.'

She frowned. 'Are you being serious?'

'Of course.'

She found herself unable for the moment to decide how she viewed the news. 'So I'm slated as a professional target even before you arrive?'

'Could you expect anything else?'

When she didn't smile, he said, 'I can see it's going to be a long haul. When we meet I'm always attempting to get to know you better and you are always either playing possum or skittering off in the opposite direction. I told them at Langley that a posting was my one hope of cracking you.'

Reaching across the table to touch her hand he waited until she looked fully at him. 'What I'm trying to say without sounding heavy is that, notwithstanding those glacial looks you shoot out from time to time, I want to see more of you – and my motives are entirely *un*professional. I'm asking you to tell me you're not unalterably unopposed. I hope that doesn't ruin the lunch.'

She looked down at his hand. Removing it from her own she placed it on the table a few inches away. She had to admit he had made her feel quite good.

'Unalterably isn't a word I use much.'

He digested the sentence with due solemnity. 'I'm glad.'

When she said nothing more, he went on, 'What's October like here?'

'It *can* be fine.' She had sounded more forthcoming than she had intended but it didn't really matter. She looked down at the mushroom field of umbrellas outside. 'I think of it as a good month to start afresh.'

Back in the office, allergic to the idea of tackling any but the most straightforward files, she waited for Fender's promised call. When five o'clock arrived and there was still no sign of it, she telephoned his club and learned that although he had appeared there for lunch, he had gone out again.

He was still kicking his heels in some ante-room at No. 10, she supposed. She rather pitied any Private Secretaries or other minions there who happened to be in range since his temper by now would be spectacular. She gave him another quarter of an hour then abandoned work in disgust and took the tube back to Little Venice.

Fender arrived unheralded at her flat, minutes after she had put her key in the door. Puffing and blowing from his ascent of the stairs, he explained that when he had called her office extension a little while before, and obtained no reply, he had assumed she was already on her way home. He had therefore come straight there by taxi.

She gazed at him in surprise. Assumptions of that sort were not his style. Wasted journeys infuriated him as much as the failure of people to keep appointments precisely on time. He looked tense and bedraggled, even a little off-balance. It seemed probable that the interview with the Prime Minister hadn't gone well.

She took the dripping homburg from his hand and sat him down with a Scotch. 'They kept you waiting at No. 10 I suppose.'

He shook his head. 'I didn't go.'

She frowned. 'Where were you then this afternoon?'

'When the sun shone briefly I went for a walk in St James's Park. Unfortunately the rain came on again rather heavily.'

Clearly he had not made for shelter fast enough. Evidence of the regulation crease in his trousers, meagre at the best of times, had vanished leaving a crumpled bin-liner effect; moisture had blackened the ancient suede shoes.

'Why the Park?'

'I had something to think over.' His eyes slid away from her. 'An unexpected proposal.'

She could see he was disposed to be evasive. 'Someone wants to marry you . . .'

He remained expressionless. 'Even more unexpected than that.'

'Why didn't you go to No. 10?'

'I saw Pagett at the Cabinet Office instead. We went over the ground. There was no need to talk to the Prime Minister in the circumstances. Arrangements to take care of Plowright are in hand. You've seen the evening paper, I suppose?'

When she shook her head, he lumbered off into the hall and came back with a moist copy of the *Evening Standard*. The main headline on the front page read: AFTER ULSTER TRIUMPH PLOWRIGHT RESIGNS TO FIGHT ILLNESS.

She glanced quickly through the story beneath. 'The line that his resignation's on health grounds – that isn't all that's going to happen?'

'How do you mean – all?'

'He isn't simply being allowed to resign and fade away, surely . . .?'

'It's possible.'

'*I don't believe it!*'

He sank wearily back into his chair. 'Considering what's at stake, what could you expect?'

She stared. 'What would *I* expect? Nothing unreasonable – just that he's made to answer for what he did! I want him treated like any other murderer. I can't pretend my heart bleeds over Cahill. Or Tull – assuming you're right and he *was* murdered as well. But what about Loach? He wasn't a politician, feeding fear and hate for his own ends! He was an ordinary official who saw something wrong going on and tried to stop it! Or have you forgotten?'

She had stung him. 'I have not forgotten. Nor have I any doubt that Plowright was behind Loach's murder. But we could never hope to prove it. For that matter, now that neither Ellitt or Lissack can be interrogated, no prosecution would ever succeed in establishing his role in arranging Cahill's death. Where would the evidence come from?'

'The tape . . .?'

'By itself? Alone, it's useless. In any case, you know it wouldn't be admissible. But, suppose adequate admissible evidence *did* exist – have you considered the consequences of allowing the story of what Plowright did to come out? The agreement with Dublin would be blown to bits in a great explosion of indignation. Cahill and Tull would acquire the status of martyrs, one for each community, the worst suspicions of British skulduggery would be confirmed. Even if the government managed eventually to calm people down north of the Border, the chance of any Dublin Cabinet ever agreeing to consider amending the Southern Constitution and implementing effective cross-border security during the rest of this century would be nil. The best hope of undermining terrorism in Northern Ireland would have gone. Do you want to see all that thrown away?'

He was willing a response from her. When she made no

reply, he said, 'Whatever one thinks about the means Plowright employed, at least the end he was pursuing was good. One can't dismiss his achievement either. He may have changed the course of history in Ireland – or at least created the conditions in which change becomes a real possibility.'

'So you're happy for him to get away scot-free with murder . . .?'

'He'll never hold office again.'

She laughed derisively. 'Is even *that* ruled out? In a year or two, this Prime Minister will have gone. There'll be a new one who won't know these facts because they'll have been held so tightly. Plowright, by then recovered from his mysterious illness, will step forward, modestly willing to resume his political career on behalf of a grateful public.'

She moved to the window and gazed down into the sodden clumps of shrubbery in front of the house. Even washed by the rain, they amounted to a poor affair, the leaves coarse and greasy with the filth of passing traffic, as unwholesome as the way the whole business was turning out to be.

'In any case,' she went on, 'aren't you making too much of Plowright's achievement? Plekhanov wouldn't go along with the idea of his changing the course of history. He'd say that individuals *can't* bring about fundamental changes, they only help to nudge things along in the direction they're already going.'

She looked round. He was examining her over the rim of his glass. 'I had the impression you were unfamiliar with Plekhanov.'

'I was. But I looked him up this morning.'

His expression suggested that she had given him pleasure which was the last thing she had intended. He said slyly, 'So you're saying it wouldn't really make much difference to the course of events if Plowright were exposed.'

'Probably not in the long run.'

'Ah,' he said, 'the good old long run.'

She would have liked a stick to beat him with but Plekhanov didn't offer anything reliable in that line. She went back to her chair and looked at the newspaper story again. 'Presumably what's being done represents a decision by the Prime Minister. Are other Ministers in on the story?'

'No. Nothing of what Plowright was up to has been revealed to the rest of the Cabinet, the risk of a leakage would be too great. The Prime Minister handled the whole thing personally.'

'It would be nice to think he'll arrange a Cahill solution for Plowright. Isn't he supposed to be fond of black humour?'

He put on an appearance of being faintly shocked. She said, 'After all, it's pretty inconsistent not to do more about Plowright. He grasped the nettle with Ellitt and Lissack and had *them* removed from the scene.'

She watched his eyes flicker.

'*Didn't* he?'

He visibly played for time as he reached out to put his glass on the table beside him.

She shook her head. 'Come on, Ludo, if you hadn't worked it out before, you'll certainly have got the facts from Pagett. The tape wasn't news to him, was it?'

'No.'

'So how did the PM discover what Plowright had been doing?'

He sighed. 'I *was* going to tell you.'

She ground her teeth. 'Tell me now.'

'It seems that a week or two back the Secretary to the Irish Cabinet came to see Pagett secretly. He'd been sent by the Taoiseach with Mrs Cahill's story of something sinister having happened to Cahill during his visit to Lissack. He explained the Taoiseach had taken the line with her that she must be mistaken – as we know, he had information of his own which convinced him that Lissack himself would not have wanted to harm Cahill. But he still felt that he should look into the story a little. He was asking for a personal assurance from the Prime Minister that there had been no British Intelligence Service plot to get rid of Cahill.'

'How could he be sure he was going to get a truthful reply?'

'They happen to have a very good private relationship. And politicians at that level don't like to risk being caught out in personal lying when asked direct questions. Anyway, Pagett was authorized to pass on the Prime Minister's assurance there had been no plot by any British agency to harm Cahill.

'However the PM must have felt some pricking in his thumbs because he told Pagett a day or so later that he wanted to satisfy himself that nothing had happened in Lissack's house which, while unconnected with the government, could blow up in his face when the new deal with Dublin was about to be signed. He also remarked that he'd remembered being briefly introduced to Lissack by Plowright at some function and wondered what the relationship amounted to. Pagett was told to conduct a very secret investigation into the facts surrounding Cahill's visit and to include Plowright in it. He didn't tell me the details of how it was done. Probably it went over some of the same ground that we did.' He smiled grimly. 'Perhaps Bridget Boyle found herself earning extra pocket money, passing on the same information as she supplied to Loach and yourself.'

'I don't believe she would have deceived us like that.'

'Whether she did or not, the investigation produced results very quickly. In particular it discovered that Cahill's fellow guest in Lissack's house was an old acquaintance of Plowright's and that a cheque for £20,000 from Plowright was passed through Ellitt's business account two days after the vital weekend. It seems an earlier cheque for £15,000 was also identified. Pagett and his investigators had been at a loss to decide what this related to. I was able to point out it had been drawn during the week Tull had his fatal accident.'

'They'd not suspected Plowright of having a hand in that?'

'Apparently not.' Fender made a movement of the lips, indicative of resignation at the intellectual shortcomings of other mortals. 'It was only when it had been established that while Ellitt was serving in the SAS, he'd conducted an operation in which a Catholic couple, who under duress had sheltered an IRA man, had died in suspicious circumstances, that Pagett felt obliged to conclude Ellitt had repeated the performance with Cahill and that it had been at Plowright's behest.

'He reported back to the PM who was beside himself with a mixture of anger and anxiety that some or all of this would become known in Dublin and convince the Taoiseach he'd been played false. Pagett said he had no direct knowledge of subsequent events. The PM told him to leave the matter in his hands so that he could conduct what he called a "tidying-up". Pagett learned of Ellitt's death through seeing the inquest report in a newspaper. And, like us, he heard what happened to Lissack listening to the radio news. He guessed then that with the Dublin agreement in the bag, the PM would move against Plowright. In fact Plowright had already been summoned to No. 10 at seven-thirty this morning.'

She shook her head slowly. 'What a sickening, bloody mess.'

He was watching her with an anxious look. 'How did *you* know that it was on the PM's orders that Ellitt and Lissack were removed from the scene? Or were you guessing?'

'I wasn't guessing. Busch gave me lunch today. His people had identified the driver of the Jaguar which brought Ellitt's killers.' She told him the details.

His expression became more agitated. 'I ought to warn Pagett about this without delay.'

She restrained him as he was rising. 'Busch says his people won't be telling anybody else. They would see it as serving no useful purpose. The pragmatic view: everybody feels like being pragmatic except me.'

He appeared uncertain whether or not to be persuaded but eventually subsided. 'There is nothing wrong with pragmatism. Responsible choice in politics often involves countenancing evil for the greater good.'

'Letting Plowright escape still sticks in my throat.'

She listened grimly to the hissing sound of tyres on the road outside. She might as well stop talking about it, he would never fully understand how she felt. It was not that he had lost the capacity to be outraged. But his years as an official, here and in India, had presumably made surrender to expediency the most natural thing in the world for him.

'What was the proposal you had today?' she asked.

This time round he seemed eager to be forthcoming, relieved perhaps that she was abandoning the subject of Plowright. 'Pagett put it to me that I should come back for a year or two.'

'Back?'

'To take over as Director.'

She stared at him, startled.

'Antrim's resigned. The Home Secretary was apparently tipped off by Bedford, who owns the *Clarion*, about his relationship with Sylvia Keysing. He insisted he had to go.'

She nodded slowly, trying to sort out the implications. 'This is why you went for a walk in the Park . . .'

'Yes.'

'What did you decide?'

'Nothing so far.'

Surely, she thought, he's either pretending or deceiving himself. He could never turn down an offer like that.

'I can't believe you're really in any doubt.'

She would have liked to ask at what point in his conversation with Pagett the offer had been made. *Before* he revealed how much he knew about the Plowright saga? Or afterwards? But she shrank from revealing she could now be as cynical as he was.

'You should take it of course,' she said.

'I face the question whether it would be right. Whether I'm really . . . fit.'

She supposed he must be thinking about his health. 'See your doctor.'

He shook his head. 'Yesterday, I behaved more dishonourably than I would have thought possible. I allowed hatred to dominate what I did. Perhaps I'm losing balance, self-control. If so, I'm hardly fitted for the task.'

'Can you tell me what it was about?'

'I'd rather not. But you must accept it happened and has a relevance.'

She tried without success to imagine what he had done. 'You're exaggerating. You always do.'

'Not this time.'

It was still difficult to take his reluctance seriously, to see it as more than a piece of moral affectation.

'Has what you did harmed anyone?'

255

'Fortuitously, no.'

'Then forget it. You should accept.'

He shrugged and looked away. She knew the effect of her words would be marginal at most; he would have to work this out for himself.

One thing was certain. If he did accept, there would be no more conversations like this. Unless she left the Bureau, their intimacy would be at an end. If she was to be answerable to him as her employer, there was no alternative to a distancing, so far as she was concerned.

'If you do accept,' she said, 'when would you take over?'

'Probably October. I'd need the next month or two free in order to re-arrange commitments I've made. Also to find a flat in town where I can stay during the week.'

He was gazing at the surface of the table beside him. 'Things would change between us, I would find that a . . . great loss.' He looked up. 'It *would* be quite different, wouldn't it?'

He was wanting her to deny it while knowing she couldn't. In Rome, when she had slept with him that first time, he had whispered against her shoulder, 'If I could be given one wish now, it would be that, when you turned, you would find me quite different.'

'It *would* be different,' she said.

Wanting to soften her response, she found other words coming back, words she had used herself with Busch. She fetched more drinks to cheer him up. Holding out his glass, she said, 'I always think October's a good month to start afresh.'